1/7/05   03

Death in April

Center Point
Large Print

**This Large Print Book carries the
Seal of Approval of N.A.V.H.**

ॐ श्री गणेशाय नमः

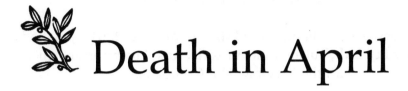 Death in April

Andrew M. Greeley

Center Point Publishing
Thorndike, Maine · USA

Compass Press
British Commonwealth

Library of Congress Cataloging-in-Publication Data

Greeley, Andrew M., 1928-
    Death in April / Andrew M. Greeley.
      p. cm.
    ISBN 1-58547-058-9 (lib. bdg. : alk. paper)
      1. Large type books. I. Title.

PS3557.R358 D4 2001
813'.54--dc21

                                                            00-060363

Australian Cataloguing in Publication Data

Greeley, Andrew M. (Andrew Moran), 1928- Death in April / Andrew M. Greeley
    (Compass Press large print book series) ISBN 1740303776 (hbk.)
      1. Large print books.
      2. Love stories.
    I. Title
    813.54

For Kevin and Sheila Starr

May this flame bring life to these waters.

—from the blessing of Easter water as the lighted candle is plunged into it

There is a lake in every man's heart, and he listens to its monotonous whispers year after year, ever more attentive.

—George Moore

PROLOGUE

The January night was chill and foggy. A bareheaded man walked alone on the Rive Droit in the XVI Arrondissement. He was tall and slender. Above the turned-up collar of his discreetly tailored cashmere coat, his kinky red hair was touched with flecks of white. He paused to watch the river, barely visible beneath him in the mists. A click of heels on the walk behind him seemed to go unnoticed.

The woman was blond and lithe, walking nervously as though aware it was too late to be unescorted on the bank of the Seine, perhaps escaping from an unpleasant tryst.

The man turned around just as she walked by him. As though he recognized her, he opened his mouth to say something, then paused in embarrassment. *"Pardon, Madame,"* he murmured in the tone of a man who has made an awkward mistake.

For a moment she was frightened; then in the gloom she saw, by the dim illumination of the streetlight, soft sad blue eyes. She had nothing to fear from him. She hesitated, considering whether to begin a conversation, then thought better of it. *"Bon soir, Monsieur,"* she said with a trace of regret as the sound of the clicking heels began again.

"Bon soir, Madame," he said into the night and then looked back at the waters of the Seine.

7

If the woman had come back, she would have noticed that the sad eyes were now vacant, seeing not the Seine but another body of water many miles and many years away.

 1

Jim O'Neill awakened from his dream, soaking with sweat even though it was late February in Paris. He cringed beneath the electric blanket, afraid that the dream was real and that his luxurious apartment on the Right Bank was a part of it.

Shivering, he grabbed for his robe and jumped out of bed. No more sleep tonight. He pulled aside a drape. Four stories below the Seine swirled by in the fog. Now that he was awake he should try to sit at his typewriter, even though nothing had come for days. "Prize-winning Reporter and Novelist Loses Touch." Still writing headlines.

He turned on the shower and waited patiently for the hot water. Even in the best Paris apartments it took a long time, especially at night. He thought of his daughter. Clare—I only have you now, but I've failed you like I've failed all the others.

The hot water of the shower stung him. He'd have a drink after he got out, or maybe two. He didn't want to end up an alcoholic like his father. Tonight he would drink just the same.

After Biafra he'd given up his romance with danger. The thrills were greater than ever, but now Clare was something more than a tiny infant; she was a bright-eyed redhead child. The correspondent-turned-story-teller needed money to pay for his daughter's education. He now made more money than he ever thought possible. Much to his surprise he did not miss the danger. Most of the time he was glad to be free of the terrible reactions that came after the battle lust had died—impotence, physical and mental, exhaustion, horror, despair. Such reactions were what drove the dogs of war to self-destruction. They needed the thrill to live, and the letdown afterward killed them one way or another. He was lucky to escape before the addiction was incurable. It wasn't as hard to give up as alcohol, but the lure of the IRA was powerful every time he read about it in the papers. Most of his friends in Ulster were dead, but the movement was still strong.

He pushed the thought out of his mind and concentrated on the pulsing tingle of the shower spray.

The romance he'd sought in his youth turned out to be ugly and brutal, rather than splendid. He no longer wanted to go back to kill dragons; lots of innocents got killed along with them.

Enough of the shower. He hugged his thick robe around himself and padded into the parlor. Only 2:45—a long time left in the night. He turned on a single pale light at his reading chair and carefully poured a full tumbler of Jameson's.

He tried to remember the dream. Biafra? The young woman whom he married there, a university-trained

Ibo who had been bayoneted to death with their unborn child? He never spoke of her; it was a closed chapter, and buried just as deeply as she was. Or was it Zena, the actress who was his first wife? How could he have a terrifying dream about her? His mother? The dream he'd had about her before she died kept returning, even if it had been ten years. He swallowed a large gulp of the Jameson's and freed his imagination.

The dream was about Lynnie. She was wounded and drowning in the lake. Dragged under by a storm. Crimson on the black waters. At the last minute she dragged him into the waves with her. The water turned to fire.

He shivered and drained the whiskey.

His dreams worried him. He had dreamed of his father's death at Dien Bien Phu. Then there was the battered cable in Hong Kong when the Vietminh had finally released him. In Enugu, drunk with the pleasure of his black bride, he'd dreamed of his mother and brother Jerry. After he returned to Capetown from Biafra, there came another cable, this time from his lawyer. Jerry, his wife, their two children, and his mother all killed in a fire at his home in Connecticut. The news of his family's destruction left him unmoved. He had already mourned in his dreams. Besides, he'd lost another family.

He had a single, vivid dream about Steve Slattery, his old friend turned enemy. Later, he bumped into Meg Halley at Heathrow, now a beautiful senior stewardess for Pan Am. She told him about Steve's death just before she got on her plane, not wanting to be with him while he tried to sort that one out.

He looked at his glass. Empty already. He stumbled over to the bar, poured another tumbler, and brought the bottle back with him. It was all so long ago. None of them seemed real anymore, not even Mary, the Ibo nurse whom he'd married thinking that they both would soon be dead. Only Clare was real.

Now Lynnie. He had not thought of her in years. He rubbed his hands over his eyes.

He tried a couple of times to write about growing up in the neighborhood. Do what Jimmy Farrell did. It never worked. A lot of tragedy all right, but bland, trivial tragedy. Farrell could handle that theme; he couldn't. An autobiographical novel about a bland and trivial tragic hero. Ugh. Studs Lonigan as prize-winning expatriate, reporter, and novelist, going to seed in Paris.

He poured himself his third drink, noting regretfully that the bottle was almost empty.

"So the woman represents death for you?" Monique traced a pattern on the tablecloth with her fork. "Well, *mon chéri,* that is not *so* unusual."

It was a most discreet little restaurant on the rue Danou, just around the corner from the Opéra, with its thick, noise-deadening carpet and tapestries, waiters walking on tiptoes, heavy linen tablecloths, and whispering patrons—either handsome lovers planning their afternoon tryst or businessmen hinting at transactions involving millions of francs. The same couples were in the same dark booths each time he

11

and Monique came here. Does everyone in Paris commit adultery in the afternoon?

He was tired of noontime psychoanalysis, even if she was one of the best therapists in France. He almost told her that he was a friend, not a patient. That would bring tears. "The woman," he said wearily, "is doubtless fat and frumpy and forty; having been spoiled by chic Parisians like you, Monique, I'd find her a bore."

A quick smile accepted and dismissed the compliment. "Forty she certainly is," her gamine face stern again, her intense black eyes absorbing him, "and if she is fat and frumpy, then you are free to accept your own aging and death. You can relinquish the illusions of youth and begin writing again. You cling to those illusions like a little boy. You are no longer a boy, Geemie, you must accept that."

Monique loved him. She and her husband were the only close friends he had in Paris. With her small stature and understated figure she was radiantly sexual in her black knit dress. How could patients put up with such sexual emanations in a therapist?

He sipped his white wine and tried to sound casual. "I am not a psychiatrist, Monique, only a storyteller. I don't see the connection between a temporary writing block and the neighborhood I grew up in." She had wheedled him into admitting that there had been a girl. Their weekly lunches would become even more like therapy sessions.

A knowing smile spread across her pixie face. "That one must be *formidable*. The rest of us do not compare well with her; she is the *femme paradigmatique*. Is she

12

not the pattern against which you, even now, find me less than perfect?"

"Don't be silly, Monique," he exploded. "She was just a girl, nothing special about her at all; every boy has a girl when he's growing up." Right now he wanted a woman. He would get Monique more tipsy than usual, take her back to his apartment, peel off her clothes, and teach her to pry into his life.

"Just so, and why did you leave this 'nothing special' girl and the community of your family, never to return?" Her voice was soothing; her face innocent. The professional reassurance of the practiced therapist.

He drained the wine glass and poured both of them more. "Sometimes I think you're the lawyer in the family and not Etienne. You'd make a superb *juge d'instruction*, relentlessly hunting down criminals."

"You do not have to talk about this at all," she said, her eyes cast down, a piece of pastry delicately raised to her lips. "I'm just a foolish woman prying where I have no right to."

He put down the glass of white wine, wondering again where the directors of the restaurant got their chablis. "All right, Monique. I'll give it to you straight, though I don't like it and neither will you. I was a very unimpressive young man. Lots of self-pity and resentment. A sad sack, as we used to say." His stomach muscles were tight at the memory; he needed something stronger than the chablis. "I had an unhappy family life and blamed the rest of the community for the misery inside me. I ran away, allegedly so I could become a great writer but really to get away from my mother. The neighborhood was a bland, dull place not worth hating, but I hated it because I needed to hate something. Hell, it hardly knew I existed. Probably still doesn't, as far as that goes. My family are all dead. There's no one to go back to, and no reason to go back. All very typical and very trivial."

He signaled the waiter for another bottle of chablis and let Monique take his hand.

"My poor dear one," she said softly, "you do have such remarkable self-knowledge. Writers must, I suppose. You are too harsh on yourself. And the woman?" She watched him expectantly.

He managed to laugh. "You want it all don't you? All right, Mother confessor. She wanted me to become part of her family, father's law firm and all. Nice girl. Pretty. Nothing special. I thought it would be trading one form of slavery for another." There was now the beginning of an absurd dull ache in his chest. He tightened his grip on Monique's submissive hand. "Maybe I was wrong. Or maybe I did the right thing for the wrong reason. Anyway, it's all ancient history now."

There were tears in her eyes; she did not pull back her hand. "I am so concerned about you, Geemie. Just this morning at breakfast my husband tells me that he has never seen you so depressed. Even Etienne, who thinks psychoanalysis is little better than witchcraft—and he may be right—" a quick flash of teeth, "says that you are now in your crisis of the middle years. For you he says it will be very bad."

There was no reason for the DuLacs to adopt him, to make him almost as much a member of the family

14

as Jean Claude and Marie, their nearly teenage children. Much less was there reason for Monique to love him. He moved a finger across her palm. No resistance. She loved to flirt. Maybe she wondered why he'd never propositioned her; her embrace when he'd come to the table would have been an invitation from anyone else. "A lonely American expatriate running out of time and talent and dying in Paris. Sounds like a plot for a novel, only about three dozen people have done it already. I'm a caricature, Monique." He laughed at his own absurdity.

Monique brushed a stray hair back from her forehead, a gesture he seemed to remember—whose? "I suppose she is married and has children?" she asked, much as though she were a teacher catechizing an impertinent student.

"Who? Oh, my paradigm woman. The last I heard she had four—or was it five—children. I don't keep in touch, Monique. My parents have been dead a long time. . . ."

Another bit of pastry to her impeccable lips. She was eyeing him closely, paying no attention to the light pressure of his fingers on her hand. "She is happy with her husband?" Monique asked a little too casually.

"No, I don't think . . . well, I heard that it wasn't all that happy." He paused. There was no need to tell Monique the truth, yet he could not resist. "Actually, he was killed three or four years ago."

Her eyes widened. "So? And you have wondered ever since whether you should try to recapture your youth by pursuing her again?"

15

"I haven't wondered about that for five minutes. There was nothing much ever there. She was a very uninteresting woman." The words were flowing easily now. "You would find her dull, Monique."

Monique seemed skeptical. Absently she extended her wine glass in his direction. She drank too much at their lunches. Pinned to his desk, pleading for mercy, she would be utterly delicious. "I will say it all, *mon chéri*, in very direct and non-client fashion." She gulped half of the wine in the glass. "Etienne and I love you and are worried about you. So is your poor Clare. You are not writing; you are unhappy; you are preoccupied with your days as a young man. You should go home to exorcise these demons, accept growing old peacefully, and then do your best writing." Her face glowed with affection.

He took her other hand and held them both tightly. "I don't deserve you and Etienne, but I'm grateful for you just the same," his voice choked. "My story is a tragic one, I guess. Dull, but tragic. You two bring some light into it."

Their eyes locked for a moment, electricity leaping back and forth. He released her hands. "I'm glad you're talking to Clare. I'm worried about her. Poor kid, she's just at the age where she's looking for an identity. There's not much to offer. A mother she never sees—an aging starlet on her sixth husband. And a father who is not much good with a lovely seventeen-year-old daughter."

A father who is so perverse, he did not add, that in addition to half seducing you, has an imagination

16

which fills up with incestuous desires whenever he is with the gorgeous little redhead.

Her body tense, she leaned across the table. "You see, *mon chéri*, does it not all fit together? Clare wished to go to the college in America—St. Mary's of Notre Dame, where your contemporaries went—curious tautology, no? She wants to solve your problem for you; she cannot do that, of course. . . ." Her voice trailed off. "Oh, no, I have a patient; no more wine!"

He filled the glass just the same. "You think it will harm Clare?" he asked uneasily. He and that lovely, mysterious stranger fought an angry argument in the café near the Cathedral at Fiesole. She won her battle for permission to go to college in America and then pushed him hard on his own childhood.

Despite his protests Monique continued to drink the wine as though it were Evian water. "About that one," she arched her diminutive shoulders, "you need not worry; she is twice as tough as you and I put together. Yet is it not strange, Geemie, that you have not married? I mean, other men make unfortunate first marriages. You were young, a prize-winning correspondent; she was a beautiful movie actress. An affair of the heart—or of the endocrines, more likely. It is over quickly . . . perhaps not quickly enough, knowing your stubbornness. A poor child whom her mother neglects. Sixteen years of brief, passionate liaisons and long interludes of celibacy. I cannot see . . ."

He kissed her hand fervently, making her blush. "Very Irish pattern, Monique. Repression followed by orgy. Right woman never came along. Or was married

17

to someone else."

She blushed again.

"Now don't go trying to find me a wife. We've been through that before."

He rose from the table, and she followed unsteadily, quite tipsy by now.

"Though I am an incorrigible matchmaker, Geemie, I know when I am defeated. I have offered you some of the most suitable women in Paris." Weaving ever so slightly, she led him toward the cloak-room of the now nearly empty café. "And you find them not interesting . . . that is why I know that *she* is formidable."

They *had* been fascinating women all right: smart, sexy, sophisticated. He had slept with some of them, mostly at their initiative; they were also very good in bed. Comparing them to Lynnie? Lynnie of the light gold hair and the burning violet eyes that could turn into polar ice. "It's you they don't compare with," he laughed, assisting with her smart fur-lined coat.

"You are a wicked man, Geemie O'Neill." She leaned up and kissed his cheek affectionately. "I do not know why mama Monique puts up with you."

He put an arm around her and held her in her tiptoe position. With his free hand he moved her mouth up against his and kissed her lips authoritatively. Undressing her would be pure delight. He released her.

"You are a *very* wicked man." She was flustered but not displeased, not even anxious to see that no one was watching.

He tilted back her tiny chin. "Which is precisely why

18

mama Monique puts up with me. Now get back to your patients, before I get so entranced that I spend the whole afternoon mooning over you instead of over *that* one." He swatted her snug derrière with sufficient force that she'd remember it for a few minutes and propelled her down the street toward the Opéra.

Monique giggled. "You are completely and irredeemably evil." She squeezed his arm, smiled adoringly, and then cut into the crowd of pedestrians like a sleek Citroën sliding into traffic on the autoroute.

It would be another afternoon of fantasies, choking, stifling, enervating daydreams. Bed partners are easy to find; friends are rare. Monique could be only one or the other.

Monique didn't go to her office behind the Opéra, but to the underground. She never scheduled patients on the days of her luncheons with Jim O'Neill. The peace of their home just off the Avenue Foch was the only place to recover from those emotionally exhausting episodes. This one had been worse than usual. Her head was already aching from the wine; she dozed in the train, almost missing her stop.

"You are in dangerous waters, Monique," she told herself as she wearily let herself into the house, oblivious to the biting February wind. "You love that one too much. . . ."

She pulled off her dress and draped it over a chair, mechanically registering disapproval at the slight, black-laced figure which flitted by the mirror. "You drink too much with him to calm your nerves, and

19

then because of the drink you flirt, and because of the flirting you become more aroused than you should be." The thick satin bedspread was reassuring against her skin. No, it would not do to be alone with him, except in a public place. Women are his problem. He hates us and fears us, but also charms us and flatters us. Death and women—he flirts with both, risks himself with both, and then runs. They are the same for him, poor man. To be possessed by a woman is to die. Classic syndrome. The last of the knights of the Round Table, a red-haired Lancelot forever seeking his grail, his sacred vessel. His kisses are magnificent. Such broad shoulders, and despite all he drinks he does not get fat. I am like Clare; I will not be happy until he is. Sad blue eyes—why does he affect us that way? Men too. Etienne says that men who meet him at his club are charmed. He could have a wide circle of important and interesting friends; instead he chooses to be lonely, convinced that he is a great suffering tragic hero. We were close to the truth today. I should be careful; I am not his therapist. I love him so.

The barge crews on the Seine were listless. O'Neill counted five near-collisions in the narrow passage of the river outside his apartment, each the result of careless boatmanship. *You drive your boats like I write.*

Finishing the last book was like slogging through mud. He had driven himself by sheer brute force. There was no inspiration in the story, just sophisticated professional cunning. He felt none of the pride a completed book usually produced. He was a writing machine, grinding out material to meet deadlines. The sport had gone out of it; he was like a tired middle-aged linebacker, hanging in there for the money and still better than most of the competition, but hurt, battered, fed up with being pushed around, uncertain about next season, and so tired.

How am I ever going to do another book? he wondered. I'm three weeks late on a film treatment. I've got two more contracts and a film script. Am I washed up? I've got enough to live off, but what will I do with my time—drink?

It had been cold walking from the underground station to his apartment, colder than the winters in Chicago. No, that could not be; it only seemed colder. Maybe the weather just seems colder when you get old. He buttoned up the Aran Isles sweater. Monique would have kept him warm for an hour or two, or the pretty girl on the underground, a university student. In his old age he was fantasizing about every attractive woman he saw, building up the repression before the orgy came. He was a character out of a Sean O'Faolain short story.

He left his oak desk and walked to the window. The Seine did not freeze in the winter; it was not nearly as cold here as the Middle West. The Seine—muddy, dirty waters, filled with corruption.

He returned to worrying about the next book. He would have to start at the beginning of March and the screenplay two weeks after that; Los Angeles in April. He was so tired of writing to meet the voracious demands of publishers, editors, agents, tax lawyers.

There was enough money to send Clare to college. The stock market would pick up again. He didn't spend much money. An impecunious writer in Paris—*that* was one of the romantic fantasies he *didn't* have as a boy.

Staring glumly at the waters of the Seine, he had a vivid sensation of a lost opportunity. What was it? He had made the right decision. He'd wanted to be a writer; he'd become one. Now his writing seemed to be slipping away from him like another lost opportunity.

He went to the refrigerator and poured himself a glass of iced tea, a concession to his daughter's warning that he would get fat after his fortieth birthday. The sedentary life in Paris forced you to watch your calories. Iced tea in the wintertime—still an American.

He resumed his post overlooking the river. Castle on the Seine.

His adjustment to the settled life was easy. Getting too old to be the minstrel soldier-of-fortune anyhow. He worked steadily and effectively, socialized only with the DuLacs and their friends, viewed every invitation to leave the XVIth Arrondissement as a personal affront to his comfort and convenience. It was his neighborhood, and the DuLacs' house just off Avenue Foch, with its large garden and big shade trees, was in the same parish. Why had they adopted him, become his closest friends? They were both famous enough, did not need to patronize an American novelist. They had created an *ambiance* (her word, though she wouldn't have used it of their friendship) which kept him from loneliness. They even insisted on

22

speaking English in his presence because "you have much opportunity to practice French, *mon chéri,* but we so little practice English." He dined with them every week, talked to one or the other on the phone every day or two, shared vacations with them, celebrated holidays at their house. Monique even cooked turkey for him and Clare on Thanksgiving—"a barbaric bird, *chérie,*" she had told his daughter as they vainly struggled to stuff it. Marie and Jean Claude called him "Oncle Jacques" and laughed excessively at his jokes. Why did they bother?

He drank the tea very slowly, not wanting to go back to the icebox. A wealthy, aging expatriate leading a dull and lonely life on the banks of the Seine, dreaming of the past and fearing the future. To grow old and die alone in Paris. His pilgrimage had traveled down the wrong fork.

The telephone exploded on his desk.

"Daddy, I hope I didn't wake you! Were you busy?"

"I haven't fallen into the siesta habit yet, honey." Why was Clare calling? Something wrong?

"You sound, *funny,* Daddy. Is there someone with you?"

"You have a dirty imagination, Clare. I was involved in a scene from the film I'm doing."

"Oh," relief in her voice. "I hope I'm not bothering you. Anyway, it was such a lovely day in Rome, I just had to call my poor old daddy and tell him that I miss him."

Clare's beauty oppressed him. Even her voice tore open the cover on his stored-up fantasies. "No, it's a

23

good thing you called. You know what it's like when I'm writing. Would've forgotten about supper. . . ."

And at *your* age." She was amused by the fortieth-birthday trauma and wouldn't let him forget his funk at the party in Florence after their fight up in Fiesole. "A man must have his supper. Coming to Rome at Easter?"

"Wouldn't miss it. Oh hell," he looked at his desk calendar. "I don't finish up in Los Angeles till the morning after Easter. Is that too late to come to Rome?"

"Whenever you come to Rome, it's not too late." She wanted him back in the church, this strange new church so different from the one of his youth. "All the girls here want to see you again. They think," she snickered, "that the famous writer is so *cute.*"

Part teenager, part woman; one moment poking fun, another moment worrying about him.

"Tell them to lose lots of weight during Lent because there'll be a pasta binge when I breeze in from L.A."

"Breeze in from L.A.," she snickered again. "My daddy is such a big deal." After he hung up, he sat wearily in his overstuffed chair, his "deep-thinking chair," Terry, who had been his secretary and then his mistress, had called it. Poor Terry. He wished she were back to cut through the gloom of the day, to bring some warmth to the cold room. Elegant room, Empire furniture, all authentic. Rich writer with a period office overlooking the Seine. And lustful thoughts about his daughter. Toward the end of the affair with

Terry sex had become difficult for him. No wonder the wide receiver took over. Impotency before you're forty, hints of things to come. There was nothing wrong with Terry—she was as pathetically appealing as ever—just no desire. Now it was back. Indiscriminate desire—friends, daughter, strangers on the underground.

The hand that replaced the phone was trembling. Clare was going to college. He was an old man. Why had he told Monique about Lynnie Conroy? Maybe she'd already remarried. Why wouldn't she? A shame to waste her life mourning for that goof.

He buried his head in his hands. I probably talked about her because she's on my mind a lot these days. I had the dream again. Last night? Or maybe the night before. She seems to want help. They all did and they died anyway. Now Monique knows about her. Damn French bitch won't let up. Wants to fix me up with a woman, so I won't be a threat to her.

He thought of Carla, the most delectable of Monique's offerings. A doll-like little blond with a perfect figure. Chic, elegant, fastidious. A lawyer in Etienne's firm. Why not?

He reached for the phone to call her, pushed it away as a foolish temptation, and bent over his typewriter. He typed furiously for a few minutes. I have no intention of calling Carla, he told himself.

She was delighted to hear his voice. No, of course not, *chéri*, I don't mind such a late invitation. A poor woman advocate has no choice. Merry laughter. She would probably cancel another date.

At supper, while Carla babbled happily, he wondered what happened to his lust. He summoned up his most violent fantasies. Women need to learn that love is a savage animal reaction, not just clever conversation over expensive wine. Desire returned, at first feebly, then with imperious insistence.

She was frightened by his grim silence when they got into the lift in her fashionable apartment building. She had reason to be. He brutally stripped her to her pantyhose in the lift and carried her down the corridor over his head, like a trophy won in battle, a limp and terrified trophy.

Inside her apartment he was a competent and tender lover. He knew the right buttons to push with Carla and pushed them skillfully. She huddled in his arms afterward, an exhausted and happy slave seeking protection from her master.

"You are a strange lover, Geemie," she said dreamily. "You ignore a woman, then terrify her, then torment her with pleasure so that she thinks she will go mad, then you become delicate and sweet."

"I didn't hurt you, I hope?" he asked anxiously.

She kissed his chest. "Of course not. You never hurt a woman. I am not complaining, *chéri*. I love it."

Tomorrow he would be able to write again.

A bird chirped at his window. Damn fool. Why does everyone have to celebrate spring, even the goddamn birds? He pecked at his typewriter. Spring came too quickly in France. Late March ought to be cold and blustery like it is in Chicago. He was revising the last section of his first chapter, a tedious task which fortunately didn't require imagination, only professional competence.

Outside, Paris was sunny and lovely, the trees beginning to bloom. To be young and in Paris in springtime—only he wasn't young, and after last night's dinner with Carla he'd concluded that it wasn't only his recalcitrant typewriter that needed repairing. She was clearly willing to go home with him or let him come to her apartment again. The desire that had hounded him for weeks vanished like snow in the springtime sun. He did his best with fantasies of violent gyrations with this splendid doll-like creature. Nothing worked. He gently kissed her goodnight and then hailed a taxi for a lonely ride back to the Avenue Président Kennedy.

There had been a time when the opportunity for violent conquest would have sent him into a frenzy. "Master Overwhelms Slave." He'd typed another headline. Angrily he pulled the page out of the typewriter and tossed it away. Passionate conquest, forcing her to release her own passions, to enjoy being conquered—it was all over now. He sighed, putting another sheet into the machine.

Why the violent passions with women? Probably something to do with his mother. If Monique were a character in his story, what would she say about it? The typewriter keys began to move as if by their own power.

"*Mon chéri*, it is obvious, no? You must earn your women in conflict, prove that you are a man by

27

defeating some fierce and dangerous enemy. Then you must conquer them to prove it a second time. Through the years you have doubtless become rather good at giving them, how shall I say it, erotic excitement. Finally you have them in your power and they do not want a knight in armor, but a man they can love back. You become terrified and flee them. Is that not the paradigm? Some, of course, are strong enough to survive their interlude with you; others, poor things, are destroyed. Was it not so even with the unfortunate Zena? Admittedly she was too much for you. Still, did she not want help, and were you not the heroic war correspondent? So far none of them have been brave enough to run after you and drag you back."

The character had gotten out of hand, as characters often do. He forced his hands away from the machine. He was sweating and shivering at the same time. That's what she'd say, all right. Only how do I know it already?

He took the sheet out of the typewriter, crumpled it, and threw it into the wastebasket. Words never said and hence untrue. . . .

He rummaged through the wastebasket and pulled out the crumpled page. With some variations it was a description of his women. One exception, though. He had won no battles for Lynnie and had never made love to her. If she was the paradigm woman, how did that fit?

Was she one of the poor things who had been destroyed?

He began to type again. Lynnie destroyed? Not on your life.

 2

The two stood in the darkness by the side of the lake like two angry prehistoric animals pawing the earth before a charge.

"You're going to be a drunken bum just like your father," she snarled at him.

"And you're already a candidate for one of your father's whorehouses," he fired back.

"You're a rotten shanty Irish coward!" she screamed. "You wouldn't know what to do in a whorehouse, even if your mother let you inside one."

He imagined her glowing violet eyes turning ice cold. "You're a dirty dago atheist; you can't buy me like your father bought your mother!"

The tall, athletic body near him tightened with fury. "You'd be in the bargain basement!" she snapped back.

"Let's stop, Lynnie," he pleaded, all taste for battle gone. So it had been with them since they were three-year-olds. Their families were still friends then; people marveled at the cute little red and blond heads bent over piles of toys. They played on the beach through humid summer afternoons and then ended each day with a bitter argument over a wrecked sand castle. Later, they were rivals in the spelling bees in school and for class honors. They made up a day or two after their fights—or they had until Lynnie acquired her lithe woman's body, and fear mixed with affection and anger in his reaction to her.

"I don't want to stop, you miserable bastard. How dare you spy on me!" She was standing close to him now, her perfume erasing the dank, fishy smell of the lake at the end of a hot August day, her exquisite breasts a few inches from his chest.

"I wasn't spying," he said apologetically. "Just walking along the beach." He had seen the young man stride off the pier angrily and guessed what was happening.

"In a drunken stupor like your father. He couldn't hold a job unless my father protected him!" she shouted.

Beer in his brain, loyalty to his father, and affection for her drove him to action. He dove at her, locked one arm around her knees, the other under her arms, lifted her off the pier, and threw her into the black waters of the lake. She barely had time to land a solid kick against his ribs as she went. No screams, only a dull splash.

Then silence.

Not a sign of her in the water. Had she hit her head on the bottom? "Lynnie?" he anxiously asked the waters.

More silence.

"Lynnie?" He was now afraid.

A drenching splash from the other side of the pier. "Goddamn shanty Irish brute," she choked and dove under the water again.

He went over to the side from which he'd been

splashed. She wasn't there. He turned around, but not in time to escape the splash from behind him. Clever bitch.

She climbed out of the water and onto the pier, strong arms pulling her body up in one quick movement. Hesitantly he offered a hand, which she grudgingly accepted. "Big redhead basketball star is brave enough to push women around. Rape will be the next thing." In the dim glow of the stars and lights on the nearby public beach he saw short blond hair pasted against her head and her delicately lovely oval face— Italian madonna features and Irish warrior hair. Her dripping white blouse and shorts clung to her body. Almost as though she were naked, he thought, as his chest wrenched with desire.

"Might not be a bad idea," he muttered appreciatively.

"Savage," she sniffed, pushing him away and trying to be angry again. "Just because you're a little bit stronger than I am, you think you can boss me around."

"I worry about you, Lynnie," he pleaded.

"You may be bigger, but I'm still faster," she boasted. "On my feet, that is . . ." She was pushing the hair out of her face and grinning her elfin smile, which began in pathos and ended in mischief.

"That's a silly thing to argue about, Lynn." He was trying his best to be reasonable. "We're too old to fight about who is the quicker runner." He deftly avoided the word "fast."

"Who says so? Anyway, Mr. Smart James

McCormac O'Neill, the last time we raced I won; and you wouldn't play anymore."

"That was before—"

"Before I got breasts and you became a drunk? Anyway, I can still beat you, especially after you've been knocking off six packs every night. I'll beat you to our pier."

A soaking wet wraith, she sped off down the shadowy beach. It was a half-mile to her house, along the public beach, through the fringes of the state park, down a stretch of highway, and then back to the private beaches. He was hopelessly out of shape, and there were four bottles of beer in his rebellious stomach.

He ran after her, knowing he could catch her, not at all sure he could last the distance. Lynnie didn't drink or smoke and water-skied and swam every day. He watched her enviously as she glided along the water, wishing that his family could afford something better than a shack a block and a half from the lake for only two weeks.

He caught up with her on the highway, his lungs aching, his leg muscles cramped, his breath coming in short compulsive gasps, his chest hurting from her kick.

"See what the beer does to you," she laughed. "You won't make it."

He didn't have the wind to reply. He was sure now he would beat her.

He almost did. A beach chair carelessly left in front of one of the big houses tripped him and sent him sprawling into the sand at the edge of the lake. He cursed the rich Irish silently as wavelets lapped at his head. She thundered by, like a cavalry troop in a movie.

Painfully he forced himself to his feet and trudged toward the Conroy pier where their big old Higgins boat stolidly resisted the movement of the lake. Lynnie stood at the edge of the pier, outlined against the night sky, her hands on her hips in triumph, like a mother who has caught her child at the cookie jar.

He was as drenched by sweat as she was from her dunking. "I tripped," he mumbled, hunching his shoulders to ward off another torrent of abuse.

Instead she put her arms around him and kissed his lips, enthusiastically, then passionately. He responded with equal passion, squeezing her solid buttocks with his hands, forcing his tongue against hers, crushing her breasts against his chest.

"I love you, Jimmy," she gasped when she was able to free her lips for a moment.

He replied by recapturing her lips and over-whelming her passion with his own. She surrendered to him, relaxing submissively in his arms. So they were sinning. He would tell it to the young priest in confession. He went right on kissing her, her face, her throat, her chest above the buttons of her blouse.

When his lips touched her throat she sighed with deep and automatic pleasure. He returned to her throat, then again to her lips. The image of the last time they kissed flashed through his mind. The summer before he started sixth grade. He had fled to the hill behind the lake, no longer a magic mountain inhabited by ghosts and demons and creatures from outer space, but a brush-covered mound where he could escape from his mother's taunts. This time it was the taunts of Steve Slattery about his father's latest drinking binge. Lynnie came to drag him back down the hill, pretending that she was a white goddess, a jungle queen and guide for lost hunters. She stole a kiss from him then, rocking him to the depths of his soul.

"A little different from the last time," he said into her wet hair.

She giggled contentedly. "I didn't need that pious fraud Slattery for an excuse this time. Is it better or worse?"

"Nicer and scarier," he replied, one of his hands deserting a buttock and caressing her wet hair. "I wish I could stay here, holding you for all eternity."

"You would-be novelists sure are good at compliments," she said peacefully.

A light went on in the second floor of the Conroy house. O'Neill realized who he was, who she was, and what they were doing. Quickly he released her.

She reluctantly removed her head from his chest. "For an amateur, you really can kiss, Jim O'Neill. Too bad you get afraid so quickly." Before he could respond, she patted his cheek and said, "I do love you, and I know you love me even if the words get caught in your mouth." She turned and trotted up the manicured gravel path to her house.

He walked back to the highway and down the side road to the battered cottage his family was renting, his emotions a jumble of joy, guilt, and fear. He couldn't afford to love Lynnie Conroy. What would his mother say if she knew? What if Mrs. Conroy saw them and called his mother?

He fled from his worries into a world of fantasy and romance. He would travel the world, fight evil in exciting, obscure places, come back a prize-winning writer and soldier-of-fortune. Lynnie would be terribly impressed. It would be too late for her. Too late for all of them.

The pain in his ribs was worse. Her kicks were wicked.

 3

Clare scanned her father's face anxiously, as though he were some Old Testament despot. Poor dear, he felt so guilty about not being a good father.

She must approach it very carefully. She poured another half glass of sauterne for him. He beamed. Like to have a pretty and gracious daughter, don't you? She thought of her fast pitches on the school softball field. What the hell, throw it, O'Neill.

"Why didn't you marry again, Daddy?" she said, hoping it sounded like a light and innocent question.

He choked on the sauterne, then managed a weak grin. Oh, those sad eyes. No wonder everyone in school thinks you're cute.

"You're getting to sound like Monique. She didn't put you up to it, did she?"

"Don't push me, Daddy," she warned him, feeling her face hot with anger. Oh damn, I mustn't get mad. Bad temper on both sides of the family. "I'm not a little girl you can brush off that way." Her fingers tightened around her dessert spoon.

He looked properly sheepish. "Gotta get my defense in order before I can answer a question like that. You don't have anyone in mind, do you? A nice fortyish teacher at school maybe?" He managed another weak grin.

She shook her head stonily.

"Okay, you've got a right to know. Guess I'm surprised you never asked before. I . . ." He nervously played with the wine glass, put it down; his head sank against crossed fingers like it so often did when he was thinking. "Well, it didn't work out very well with, with your mother, as you know. I guess I'm gun-shy. Or maybe not the marrying kind. That doesn't mean I won't, though." He tried to brighten into a smiling man of the world.

The waiter came to fill their tea cups. Paris rushed by on the Champs-Elysées, totally unconcerned with the father and daughter in the sidewalk café, except for an occasional glance, which Clare dutifully noted, of admiration for the two flaming redheads.

She let him off the hook. "Dear good father, sir," she said, neatly dispatching the last bite of Mont Blanc, "I will level with you."

"Please do." He almost spilled his wine.

She took a deep breath. This wasn't the way it was supposed to be going. She smiled and then jumped off the cliff. "You are the sweetest—oh damn it, Daddy, you're making me cry. Anyway, you are, and I'm worried about you. Like, I mean, you shouldn't be lonely and sad all the time. And, well, you know, I'm half in love with you, like every teenage daughter is with a good father, and I don't want to have to worry about you when I'm away in school next year, and I just wish you'd find someone nice to take care of you . . . so, oh hell, now I am really blubbering."

He offered her a clean handkerchief. Old-fashioned man, still carried them. She hadn't planned to cry. Okay, I'll pitch him the big one.

"Clare, I think you know what I'm going to say now, but I'll say it anyhow." Very much the mature, self-possessed old Daddy except that he had forgotten to add sugar and milk before stirring his tea. "Both of us are going to have to let go of the responsibility we feel for each other. You're no longer a kid; you're a young woman. I'm going to worry more about you, but I can't make your decisions." He plunged on, certain that he was setting the right tone. "Just as I have to leave you free, you have to leave me free. You've got to permit parents to mess up their lives if they are ever going to mature."

You're just pleased as punch with yourself. Okay, here it comes.

"Well, I just want you to know that when you finally bring her around, I'm going to hate her. fight her, and make life miserable for her." She sipped her own tea with as much nighttime Parisian poise as one could muster at seventeen.

"Her?" Terror on his face. Oh, my God, I didn't mean to hit home that hard.

"And I'll do my damndest to stay angry at her," she went on remorselessly, "and with all my effort it may actually last three or four days before I identify with her and learn to like her; and then, father dear, you will really have had it." She finished her tea. The poor man looks like someone put a knife in his heart.

"Who is this 'her'?" His lips were pressed tight in anger, his face white.

"The woman you've been carrying the torch for. Your childhood sweetheart. You still love her, don't you, Daddy? Or think you do? Why don't you go home and find her? Is she married? Somehow I think she isn't, or you wouldn't still have her on your mind." Strike three, O'Neill. You're out.

If he had raged at her, if he had accused her of conspiring with Monique, if he had laughed at her, she would have believed him. Instead he merely said, "I would be in real trouble if there were such a woman, and if she made alliance with you, my redhead waif." His eyes were far away now. "I wish there was such a person, Clare. I would certainly go home to her, if only to watch you fight." He was grinning again, confident that he'd found the right line. "But unfortunately you've been reading too many of my stories. There is no one to go home to and no home either, for that matter. I'm just a retired soldier-of-fortune, living my declining years in Paris and rejoicing in my

38

daughter's loveliness. Now let's pay the bill and go for a walk in the park. I've got a long flight ahead of me tomorrow."

Clare wasn't fooled. With sinking heart she feared she'd never meet this woman. She did so want to fight with her. *If my daddy won't come after you, why don't you come after him?* She thought momentarily of trying to find her in the States and saying just that.

As they walked toward the Arc she felt sorry for her father. *Poor sweet man. Oh, Daddy dear, whatever am I going to do about you? How can I get you to go home?*

 4

The summer they graduated from high school, they had their fight early: it was a bitter quarrel at her prom. He had refused to take her, going instead with his next-door neighbor Meg Halley, "a decent and proper girl," his mother said. A week later, driving down Austin, Lynnie saw him waiting at a bus stop on his way home from work. He was operating an elevator in an office building and taking night school courses. She was going to St. Mary's at Notre Dame in the fall.

She stopped the white Studebaker convertible, then backed it up to where he stood, trying to pretend he didn't see her. She was trim and crisp in a sleeveless summer dress which matched her eyes, at first bleak

39

and arctic with the despair that often haunted them, then they melted.

"O'Neill," she said, "why don't we end the fight? Then I can finally teach you to water ski on weekends." She brushed the hair out of her eyes, a sign of both vulnerability and determination.

He stared at her grimly. "Damn it, Conroy, why do you always get the advantage by ending our arguments?"

She extended her hand in one of her flippant fragile gestures, "Sicilian cunning." The grin made a quick trip from sadness to laughter.

He got into the car. She was, it turned out later, a very good water-ski instructor. She didn't laugh at his falls nor praise his accomplishments. All quite clinical and objective. Damn her.

Haze turned the sky gray. The waters of the lake were mirror smooth. The sun was a huge rose dipping beneath the dark clouds poised in the western sky. Lights glowed in the houses on shore. The boat drifted slowly toward the rushes. Tentatively he put an arm around her. The water-ski scar over her eye was fading slowly, a white pencil line just above the eyebrows, of which she was both self-conscious and kind of proud.

"You're getting very brave, Jimmy." Her hair was cut short for the summer, and in the twilight her face was hauntingly lovely. With a blue towel around her shoulders, the white two-piece swimming suit hinted effectively at the wonders it did not reveal.

"The young priest says it's all right to neck with a girl, as long as you know when to stop." He tightened his grip.

"Are you sure you know when to stop?" She laid her head on his arm.

Absently he watched the red outboard near him. A rented boat—young couple with two kids.

"I'll never find out if I don't try." The priest's answer when he asked the same question. She laughed and put her arm around him. "I'm glad the young priest understands how the human race keeps going. What does he say about kissing? I bet he thinks it's all right if you don't enjoy it."

The man, an ex-G.I. in college, he imagined, was having a hard time getting the red outboard started. Lynnie smelled of suntan oil and sweat. "Well, he said that there were *worse* things in the world than kissing."

She laughed again, bent over him, pressing her breasts against his bare chest, and kissed him affectionately. He disentangled himself from her embrace, turned over the ignition key, and at slow speed inched the old Higgins away from the bed of rushes. The poor guy still couldn't get the motor started. Gasoline smell . . . probably flooded his engine.

When he turned back to Lynnie, she was brushing her hair. Even in the fading light her body movements melted him into tender lust. Terribly sinful. Also unbearably sweet. He wanted to do it again.

He turned off the ignition. "I think you're one of the most beautiful sights I've ever seen," he said breathlessly.

She stopped brushing her hair and pulled the towel around her shoulders. "You embarrass me. I like to hear it, though. Tell me more."

He took her hand. "I don't know what to say, Lynnie. . . . I like being with you . . . . His words trailed off. Not very good for someone who was going to be a writer.

"I guess I could say the same things about you." She was huddled under the towel now, as if there were a chill in the air. "I've always liked being with you."

Great love dialogue, he thought. The ex-soldier was now trying to pour fuel on the engine itself. Be careful, fella, that's dangerous with those old things.

Suddenly confident of his maleness, he took her firmly in his arms, drew her close, smiled down at her pert, upturned face, and kissed her solidly, vigorously, competently. He kissed her neck. She breathed a small moan of contentment; his lips moved to her throat, feeling the pulse of life coursing up to her head; another deep sigh of pleasure. He pulled back, decided to do it again, and then heard the first explosion.

The stern of the outboard was already on fire. The man and one of the children were overboard; the woman and the baby were in the bow, screaming. Twelve gallons of gasoline were in the boat some-where. When the fire got to that—Lynnie climbed over him, turned on the ignition, and they raced toward the flaming craft.

When they were ten yards away, Lynnie braked into reverse and put the boat in neutral. "Hold it here," she ordered, and dove over the side. He watched Lynnie swim with sure strokes to the burning craft, pull the baby from the hands of its horrified mother, and then drag the woman out of the boat into the water. In a daze he took the child from Lynnie's arms. He somehow managed to help her get the young parents into the Higgins. Lynnie dove deeply under the surface and came up with a choking, sputtering toddler.

He was paralyzed by pleasure—unspeakable joy at the danger of exploding gasoline, a joy beyond the excitement of kissing Lynnie. He waited expectantly for the dirty orange ball of fire. Then he thought of the fire consuming Lynnie, broke out of his trance, dragged the two of them into the Higgins, and at full speed roared away from the burning craft. It exploded, a belch of black-and-red fire illuminating the summer night. Lynnie looked gorgeous—wet hair, smudged face, and bare shoulders, and a baby held tightly in her arms.

Later they were sitting on the edge of the Conroys' new pier in the moonlight, protectively holding each other, the sweet smell of blossoming rosebushes adding to their happy peace.

"You should've told them your name," he said accusingly.

"They were all right—a few burns and a lot of scare. They didn't need to know my name."

"You're a heroine."

She pulled away from him, surprised. "Don't be dumb, Jimmy. I don't want you to say things like that. Don't tell anybody about tonight. Understand?"

"Yes, Ma'am," he said dutifully. She rearranged herself in his arms.

"I wonder what the woman must think, Lynn. She'll go through life remembering that her husband left her and the baby. You saved them, he didn't."

"Look, Jimmy. She's not going to think that. She loves him. Besides, no one should be judged by such things. It's all instinct." She dismissed his moodiness with an imperious wave of her hand.

"Some people have good ones. Like you. Others don't. Like me."

She pulled back again, this time angry. "Will you stop being so idiotic? If we're going to neck on my father's pier, tell me how beautiful I am. Don't talk like a character in some story you're going to write someday."

He took her back into his arms and forced her down on the pier. "Keep your mouth shut," he said harshly. "I'm going to kiss you, not fight you."

"If I believed in God," she sighed happily, "I'd say that's what He made women for—don't fight them, kiss them. Then when they get too hot, throw them in the water." She chuckled joyously, at ease with her body and her passion.

"Maybe that, too," he said, his fingers digging into her belly as he held her motionless on the pier.

Admiration for her courage and lust for her body swept away his fears and his guilt, like a strong spring wind melts the last traces of dirty snow. Reckless with his own power, he tugged her T-shirt off, roughly pulling it up her unresisting arms and over her head. His fingers, trembling yet cruel, tore at the hooks of her halter. She lay back on the pier, unresisting. His anger slipped away into the night. He touched her and kissed her with tender reverence. "Much nicer than

44

fighting. . . ."

He leaned away from her so that he could admire her body, as an art lover might examine sculpture. "You're like a silver goddess in the moonlight," he said in awe.

"Great metaphor, Jim." She pushed back her hair and took his hand in hers. "I don't quite get it, but I like being a silver goddess."

A torrent of words swirled around inside of him, fought for his throat, pushed toward his lips: words of admiration, love, commitment. He struggled against them.

She took his other hand and drew him close. One eyebrow lifted in the clinical objectivity of the water-ski instructor. "Making up your mind whether I'm life or death?" she asked lightly. He hesitated; she released one of his hands and began to caress the back of his neck, gently guiding his face toward her chest. He heard his mother's voice. "She's a slut! Everyone knows she's free with her favors!" Who else but a slut would let him fondle her like this?

In the silence he heard the chirp of a cricket and the hum of a distant motor on the lake. A light wind brushed against his face. He still hesitated. She took her hand away from his neck. He stood up on the pier, looking down at her.

She sat up, hastily covering herself with her T-shirt, the other hand supporting her body against the hard wood of the pier. "We do have more fun in the dark by this lake, don't we, Jimmy?" she said bitterly. "What is it this time? Still the stuff about you're poor and I'm rich? The war has been over for years, and there isn't going to be another depression. Your mother is the only one who doesn't know it. Even a pious simp like Steve Slattery whom they didn't want in the seminary can make money. You could catch up with us in ten years if you're worried about that." She spoke softly, almost as though he had beaten her into submission. She bent over her shirt, looking battered and pathetically lovely, her shoulders and back the same color as the moon. "Why don't you crawl back to Pat Flaherty's and let me try to put my modesty back together? Just go away and leave me alone."

He left, walking carefully around the big old house and out to the highway, hoping the judge and his wife were asleep. Only when he reached the safety of the road, its asphalt soft in the summer heat, did he realize how hard his heart was beating and how wet the palms of his hands were.

He would confess his sin to the young priest. Bless me, father, I took immoral liberties with a girl on one occasion. . . . No, just kissing and touching. Immoral liberties, was that what they'd done? It seemed too beautiful to be described that way.

It was his mother's voice he heard in the back of his head. The same words she'd used the morning after they lost the city championship. The rest of the team was cold. Everyone would remember the last free throw he missed and forget the twenty-seven points he'd made before. With the missed shot went a tie, an overtime, in which the others might finally catch fire, and a chance for an athletic scholarship to Notre

Dame. Lynnie and he were angry at each other at the time; he couldn't quite remember the reason though it was only a few months ago. She drove him home from the game anyway, the March winds stinging less than his self-hatred.

The trouble with his mother started at the breakfast table. She insisted that part of her martyrdom was to get up early in the morning to make a hot breakfast for her husband and sons—even though they never, according to her, appreciated what she was doing for them. His father was on the wagon again. He was quiet and withdrawn, his silver hair neatly combed, his sunken blue eyes haunted, his old suit carefully covered with a napkin. The man only became expansive and resisted his wife when he was on the bottle. The rest of the time he lived in silent and battered dignity.

"Too bad about last night," he said as Jim came to the breakfast table, burying himself again in his newspaper and coffee. His mother was not going to let him get off that easily.

"Well, you let the family down again," she said in her martyr's voice, "with your education depending on it. You never show any consideration for the rest of us. I don't see how you could have lost the game."

He knew from long experience that it was foolish to argue. His mother had never said a word about basketball before, except to complain about the time it took when he could be home helping with the work. There was a lot of that to be done around the house. Keeping a neat, respectable-looking home was one of the last vestiges of self-respect that Laura O'Neill felt was still hers, but her husband and sons were unwilling to give her any assistance. If all their free time were spent on the house, it still would not look the way his mother wanted it to.

"Who brought you home last night?" his mother continued. "I heard a car door slam outside." She was busy at the sink washing dishes.

"Lynnie Conroy," he said sullenly.

"Everyone knows she's a tramp," his mother said shrilly. "So now you're going to get Judge Conroy's daughter in trouble, that's what you're going to do. We may not have the money he has but at least we're respectable, which is more than can be said of the judge's dago wife and slut of a daughter."

"She's not a slut!" he shouted.

"Look at him, raising his voice to his own mother and defending a slut he parked with before he came home."

He slammed down his cereal spoon, grabbed his coat and books, and dashed out of the house, slowing down only halfway to the bus stop. He didn't want to be early for school today.

His mother had been beautiful once with flaming red hair and a lovely figure. She married a promising lawyer-politician ten years older than herself and looked forward to a life of ease and success. He was deemed quite a catch—a future alderman and ward committeeman at least, if not something even higher. While her family was not as prominent as his (he was the son of a banker), they were hard-working and respectable. Her father was an assistant chief clerk in

48

one of Sears' accounting departments.

Soon after they were married she discovered that, despite his personality, intelligence, and political connections, her husband was an incurable alcoholic. After that there was nothing but a downhill slide— trivial city hall jobs given him in return for favors his father had done for senior members of the Organization. Her gaiety and charm were quickly lost, her beauty faded, her hair dulled. Still, she was not old— no more than her middle-forties; her face was round and soft; she was thought to be gentle and benign by her neighbors. She treated her husband with contempt; he could only reply with anger and occasional violence when he was drunk and meek submissiveness when he was sober.

She complained about her husband and elder son to every woman in the parish who would listen to her; they banded together against both. Jim was the worthless son of a worthless father. His high grades, his column in the *Clarion*, his basketball accomplishments were irrelevant as far as his neighbors were concerned. He was a "dreamer" like his father.

His Jesuit teachers did not like him. He read too much and asked too many difficult questions. His classmates sensed he was a potential Victim for their jokes. Eager to prove that they were part of the crowd, they could score points with the rougher members of the class by making fun of his literary ambitions. His reputation from the neighborhood doggedly trailed him into high school—an undependable, unmasculine dreamer.

The scholastics left him alone after he emerged as the

playmaker and floor leader of the basketball team, especially when the ragtag band of misfits which made up that year's team seemed to jell around him and swept through an unbeaten season. He would have to face the anger toward his success that had been building up. He lifted his chin off his fist, squared his shoulders. He could take it. Someday he would get even.

As he climbed warily onto the old red bus he thought of Lynnie's golden hair.

What would she be like when she was his mother's age? At forty-five, she probably would be a broken and bitter old hag. He pictured himself returning to the neighborhood a famous writer with a beautiful woman on his arm and not even recognizing the shell which Lynnie would have become.

It was a pleasant fantasy; he reveled in it. Then he felt guilty. No reason why he should hate her and sentence her.

The bus stopped. He got off to transfer to the trolley which would take him the last miles to school. He would be early after all. This meant there would be lots of people saying "nice game" or "too bad" or "close one," but most taunting him behind his back; cheap cracks from the students, hurt silence from the older priests. He thought of staying on the streetcar and riding by the school. He would leave the neighborhood and the city. He would travel the world from adventure to adventure and then return in triumph.

He breathed deeply as soon as he got to the street. God, how could they stand it—a dead man in a casket. They were acting like it was a party. He drank in the crisp, October air, rubbed the sweat off his face with trembling fingers, and leaned against the wall of the funeral parlor. His mother dragged him to hundreds of wakes as a little boy, grimly ordering him to get used to death. He had come to State Senator Connor's on his own, figuring he could leave more quickly. The dead man was bad enough; the excited babble of happy conversation drove him to nausea. The smell of burning leaves in the air—death was there, too. He was almost sick again.

Death fascinated him. He was afraid of it, drawn to it, and then scared away by it. Though he remembered little of the incident at his grandmother's house when he was only nine, the feeling of terrified delight was still vivid. He may have been a coward as his mother insisted but he was a delighted coward.

"It's in your blood." She said it a thousand times. "You're a coward, just like your father."

If it was in his blood, it wasn't his fault. Still, somehow, it was. He didn't know if his mother's version of the story was true. She told it often, even though her mother had been dead and buried for many years. The purpose of the story was always the same: to ridicule him for his cowardice—as though his childish reaction to the dead woman's body had somehow caused her death.

"Not a word for three days. Can you imagine that? The little coward didn't say anything for three days, and the poor woman lying there in her living room— spotlessly clean it was—as cold as death. My Jerry

51

wouldn't do a thing like that, but then he's got good blood. No, I had to go over there that afternoon and find her. He still wouldn't talk about it. If he had told us, we might have been able to do something. No, he had to come home quiet as a sphinx. The poor woman, she deserved more from her oldest grandson." Her face, lined and haggard, turned hard every time she spoke of him.

Their friends heard the story many times. When his mother began to repeat it they settled back, their faces polite masks. They knew they would have to listen. Once she was into it, she could not stop until every carefully memorized detail was recited—what the doctors said; what the firemen said; who came to the funeral parlor; what the priest, the damn fool, had said at the cemetery.

His father occasionally tried to protect him, citing the doctor's testimony that the poor woman had already been dead for days. His mother's face would twist in fury. "A lot you know about it," she said contemptuously, her green eyes flashing hatred. "You weren't any help, either."

His father would flush and withdraw into the shabby dignity of his silence. He wondered whether his mother had always hated him. Was his grandmother's death just an excuse for her to show it?

Lynnie was inside Conley's Funeral Home. He had seen her slender, black-covered back. She was talking to the young priest. What could bring the two of them together? He walked down toward Lotto's Drug Store. Closed after nine o'clock. He sagged against the window. She must have come back from South Bend for the wake. She didn't have Steve Slattery with her.

The click of heels on the sidewalk. Tailored black suit, nylons, bobbed hair—not eighteen but an elegant twenty-five.

"Hi, stranger, what are you doing here? I know, you're a male Anna Christie."

"The trouble with girls is that they go straight from eleven to twenty-five."

She blushed, as she always did when complimented. "Too much swimsuit and shorts at the lake, I guess. I can really do the woman-of-the-world thing well when I try."

"Why were you talking to the young priest?" he asked suspiciously, as they began to walk down Division Street.

"Why not? I wanted to find out what he thought about petting. I knew you'd never tell me. Well, he said he didn't see how engaged people could prepare for marriage any other way. It would never be a sin for me, he thought, because there are special rules for people with Italian blood."

It sounded like something the young priest might say. "Now all you need is someone else who's got Italian blood," he said.

"Worse luck for me in this neighborhood. Say, what do you think about that show in there? What's that terrible stench? Formaldehyde? Am I glad I won't smell it when they pump it into me. Poor old cousin Leo. I just had to come, but mama doesn't like Irish wakes. Are all wakes like that? You could have lots of fun collecting pictures of those solemn faces." Her expression

53

changed from distaste to horror to amusement as quickly as the flickering of a movie projector.

"It depends, Lynnie. They're mostly cold-sober tonight. Come around tomorrow and there'll be a much better performance." He took her hand.

"Gosh, lots of attention tonight." Her voice was suddenly thoughtful, her hand submissive. "They're laughing at death, aren't they?"

"I guess so. I don't think death is all that funny. I guess I'm not Irish enough. Your folks get bands to come and do a lot of wailing." They were on a side street edged with little rectangles of lawn, staircases of light beaming through venetian blinds in the windows above them. Quiet, dignified, respectable. "I think my mother enjoys wakes. But what does death mean to someone who doesn't believe in God?"

"It's going to happen to me someday, Jimmy, whether I like it or not. If I'm right, well, it'll be like a long sleep. That's okay. If I'm wrong, God and I will have a big laugh over it. If there is a God, he's the kind who laughs. Either way, I win."

"In the meantime, how do you live?" Something in his night-school theology class might have given him the answer to her fallacy, but he couldn't remember what it was.

"As best I can. If there is a God, that's all he wants, despite what you and the sisters say."

"Death is the most important moment of your life." Some retreat master had said that. But had he ever kissed a girl like Lynnie? Ever felt life pulsing through such a slender neck? Ever touched such a

54

swelling breast?

"I don't believe it, Jimmy. It's only the last moment of life."

They were in front of her house, an elaborate Dutch colonial with mums still blooming in the front garden.

She solved his problem by kissing him lightly on the forehead. "Thanks for the protection and the conversation, Jimmy." A hard blue frost in her eyes, a frost which seemed to mist over the usual vital mobility of her eyes.

"I'll always love you, Lynnie," he told the darkened house. Then, ignoring the insistence of his American literature homework, he turned down the street toward Pat Flaherty's. Tomorrow would be another monotonous day, riding up and down the elevator. Tomorrow night an old Jesuit, retired from the Patna Missions, would warn his English class that reading Evelyn Waugh and Graham Greene was a sin.

Lynnie drove him away. The loneliness of their long separation after the yacht club dance was too much for her. One more spectacular attempt to save him. She enlisted her mother in the plot, brought enormous pressure on the judge, and then laid in wait for him after night school at Lewis Towers to give him the good news. She had solved his education problems. Bemused, he agreed to the conversation with her father and found that he was already one of the family. At dinner afterwards Lynnie beamed with pleasure.

During the dinner, with the Waterford crystal on the Irish linen tablecloth in the oak-paneled dining room of the Conroy house, he realized that Lynnie was trying to capture him, pin him down like her mother had been captured during Prohibition. He would be a new stuffed animal for the Conroy family.

Mrs. Conroy was twenty years younger than her husband, an outcast in the neighborhood because she was Italian and a bootlegger's sister. People said she married him to keep her brother out of jail.

The judge was pontificating about the decline of ambition. "I suppose it was the war—everything came apart then. People wanted to enjoy life before they went off to fight. The first war didn't do that enough; your father and I were in the army in that one, you know . . . weren't lucky like people your age who just missed the second one."

"I suppose the Depression changed things too, sir." He didn't want to point out that his father had been in a trench in France while Marty Conroy occupied a desk at Fort Sheridan.

"The Depression has been overrated. Sure, it was hard—I don't have to tell you that—but if a person put his mind to it, he could succeed during those years by hard work. Nowadays, money seems to be coming easy to a lot of folks who started earning big during the War. They think they're great wonders. They just happened to be lucky enough to come along at the right time."

As his father once said in a rare moment of unkindness, "Marty Conroy was one of the worst lawyers who ever cheated his way through the old Bar exams." His courtroom was assigned only unimportant cases, mostly, his father had said, "poor niggers who were

56

guilty as sin and going to jail anyway." If he was immensely respected in the neighborhood, the reason was his political power, not his judicial reputation. In fact, the papers endorsed his opponents every election with nasty comments about his earlier days as a precinct captain for "the Bath" and "the Hink."

His cheating was now on such a scale and with such respectable allies that no one would say it was dishonest. In his days as a soldier in the old First Ward, he took, as his father put it, "everything in sight." State representative for "the Hink," mediator during the battles between Johnny Powers and Phil D'Andrea, Marty Conroy never got in the way of guns and never took any chances. Though Big Bill Thompson was allegedly his political opponent, as a city council-member during Prohibition he never offended the mayor and took money from bootleggers of both parties.

"He was one of the young heroes in the final days of the First Ward Ball," his father said, sinking deeper into an alcoholic stupor. "Fit right in with the pimps and bums. Clara Everleigh said he was the most promising crook she'd ever seen.

"Some boodlers showed class," his father continued. "They only took quality graft. Others earned their money; they took a lot of chances. Fair number of them went up in explosions. Marty Conroy never took any chances. That was about all he didn't take."

He had been lucky a couple of times. When Bob Sweitzer, the county clerk, was indicted, rumors spread that Alderman Conroy was involved. Nothing came of it, his father said, because the alderman paid through the nose. "He made it up quickly—got most of it back before Anton Cermak was shot. There wasn't any money to be made on booze after Roosevelt got in, but there was always gambling and the wire services. It wasn't long before he was a big-time fixer—really, it was just amazing how many defense plants got built on land he owned. There weren't many people who made more off the war than he did."

The dinner finally ended. The judge did most of the talking, proud of the new "partner" he had added to the family enterprises. Lynnie watched and listened, often brushing strands of hair away from her face and glowing with happiness. She loved the old pirate. Nothing wrong with that; girls should love their fathers. Her mother had said almost nothing, her large brown eyes vacant, her face expressionless.

"That's what I'll be like in twenty years," he told himself bitterly as he walked across the parish to the bungalow his family lived in. Why had Lynnie done it? Had she understood none of his dreams about a life of excitement and adventure, about great novels emerging from the thrill of defying danger and death? She said he was a romantic, someone who thought that Walter Scott and Robert Louis Stevenson described the way life really was.

His good-bye to Lynnie in the Conroy's Italian Renaissance parlor was quiet. No tears, no temper tantrums, no recriminations.

"If it were just you, Lynnie, I'd be a fool to go to New York and work as a copy boy. I've got to try to write."

His eyes were glued on the thick blue carpet. He had dreamed so often of leaving the neighborhood. He couldn't quite believe he was really going to do it.

"You couldn't write and be a lawyer? A lot of them don't seem to work very hard," she said sadly, knowing that the argument was already lost. Her eyes were locked once more in the tundra cold.

"Not here. Here I'm the son of a drunk." He took refuge in his carefully treasured bitterness. His mother had told him the night before that if he left, he would never be welcome in their house again.

"So I'm the daughter of a crook. Maybe we belong together." Her anger flared quickly, then died. "I won't argue with you. It seemed too good to be true, anyhow." She kept rubbing her fingers against the side of the antique chair where she was sitting.

"Will you explain to your father?"

"Sure. Funny thing. A few days ago he would have been relieved; now I think he'll be disappointed." A small grin. "He was beginning to like you. Will you ever come back, Jim? All your family and friends are here." She brushed her hair away. Silver and gold.

"All is not very many."

"You're wrong about that, Jimmy, but I guess it doesn't matter. We will never see each other again—that's what you're saying, isn't it?"

"You're being melodramatic, Lynn. Who knows what the future will bring?"

"Write a book about me someday?" She tried to smile.

"Great tragic heroine?" He tried to make it a joke.

59

"If it's all the same with you, I'd just as soon be a comic heroine. Suits my character better."

"You're a remarkable person, Lynn. I don't think I'll ever forget you," he said, feeling pompous and dumb.

"Just too bad I came along at the wrong time and place, huh?" Her smile faded.

"I'd better leave before the two of us are in tears." Awkwardly he extended a hand. "Good-bye, Lynn. I'm glad to have known you."

Her violet eyes flashed. She took his hand firmly. "So long, Jim."

He got out of the house as quickly as he could.

 5

Edward "Butch" O'Hare, the son of a mobster who turned FBI stool pigeon and was executed by the mob, had himself been killed early in the Pacific war, thereby winning a second Congressional Medal of Honor. O'Neill looked at the plaque. Mayor Daley, they told him, always called it "O'Hara Airport."

It was the first time he'd been in the city—counting the airport as a part of the city—since he'd left by overnight rail coach twenty years before. He always avoided it when he traveled to do personal appearances. Childish resentments, he told himself as he wandered into the ticket counter area.

They wanted him on the *Merv Griffin Show* the

night before. So he changed his flight plans—an early morning departure from LAX with a stop in Chicago, then on to New York for the afternoon flight to Rome. Easter Wednesday if not Easter Monday with his daughter. Easter . . . what did it mean? Life surviving death . . . how had he ever believed it?

He had a bad moment when he saw the lake on their final approach. It was only a few miles across the Wisconsin line, just a couple of jet minutes from O'Hare. It was both unmistakable in its oblong shape and ridiculously small.

In the lower level of the airport there were baggage carousels, rent-a-car stands, and masses of pushing people. The Hertz stand drew him like a magnet. No, he was not going to rent a car and drive through Chicago. He did not want to see the city again. Sears Tower, Hancock, Standard Oil—three of the five tallest buildings in the world. He had to get to Rome to see Clare. She loved the city when she was "home" last year. Tell her about Chicago. Robotlike he moved toward the Hertz counter. It was like approaching a woman, like phoning Carla. You did not want to do it, you knew you were not going to do it, and then at the last moment. . . .

Camelot, he thought, was a collection of mud huts, Tara a wooden stockade, Timbuktu mostly a stench in the desert. The magic citadel of his childhood was a sorry flop when viewed through cynical eyes which had seen four decades. Was this all?

He walked slowly down its main street. The stores

61

were small, even commonplace, in the clear, clean April sunlight. Why was he here? "It is your bizarre sense of fairness, *mon chéri*," Monique would exclaim if he ever told her. "You would not be playing the game fairly if there were not the possibility that she would be at the lake the same day. After all, she might own the same home as her father and she might be there; on the other hand, it is not likely that you would encounter her. . . ."

Not likely. He was relieved and yet disappointed. If she were fat and ugly, he would also be relieved and disappointed. The old dream would be wiped away; he could accept his inevitable death as Monique said he must. What if she weren't fat and ugly? What if she were a mature version of the dazzling girl who once— He stirred uneasily.

He would not see her today; and she would not be dazzling even if he did.

The town was now a respectable suburban development, the main street no longer the honky-tonk of old "Sin Lake." The dance hall was a lending library, a supermarket plaza replaced the ancient buildings where the bars had been, the Knights of Columbus "country club" was a subdivision, its gabled old castle building destroyed. No sign of the railroad station either, though there were some rusty tracks in the tall grass behind the McDonald's where O'Neill somewhat sheepishly ate lunch. Perhaps the village never was picturesque; now it was a dull combination of lower-middle-class resort, tidy market center, and incipient dormitory suburb, quintessentially Middle-

Western America. The children ambling down the street, probably on their way back to school; the slender young matrons in their inevitable station wagons (wholesomely sexy in spring shorts and T-shirts); and an occasional pot-bellied real estate dealer coming out on the sidewalk to lower his office awning against the slanting afternoon sun rays—they were indistinguishable from those to be found in any other American town trying to shake its past and angle for a better future.

At first there was nothing familiar after he left the expressway; then the red-brick Slovak Lutheran church loomed up on its solitary hilltop crossroads—the gateway to the land of his youth. It was a sentimental journey with no point to it. How could lightning strike at a resort village which had succumbed to McDonald's? He should get back to O'Hare—no point in taking any chances on a traffic jam and missing the flight. He pulled out his calendar. The dinner at the DuLacs' was a week from Thursday. His mind floated off in aimless reverie, the content of which he couldn't remember when a crying baby stirred him out of it. He finished his hamburger and watched the baby and its pretty mother. You're getting old when young mothers arouse your romantic feelings.

She was a neatly proportioned suburban matron, about thirty. What were these American suburban women like with their jogging and diets and detailed sex manuals? What would it be like to be married to one? Los Angeles had been a nightmare of women. They pursued authors with much more overt desire

63

than they used to in that strange city, or maybe he had been too unsophisticated to notice it before. The current crop of starlets made Zena seem modest and retiring. They were predators. Women always are; in Los Angeles they just let it show.

His fantasy undressed the pretty matron. Nice serviceable young body. Not spectacular but useful. She looked around nervously as though she knew someone was lusting for her, the mysterious radar that women seem to have. She glanced at him with mild interest and then looked away, apparently dismissing him as the possible source of psychic waves.

He paid his bill and left the restaurant, the girl's body still vivid in his imagination. Lassitude began to creep through his veins. Desire for the young mother ebbed to a pleasant memory. There was no hurry. An April hot spell, a lovely day. He would soak up the sun, get a room at the O'Hare Hilton at night, and catch the afternoon flight to Paris direct from Chicago tomorrow.

The village had built a lake-front park and boat landing with picnic tables and a sturdy pier on the site of the Brown Boar Hotel—the worst dive in the old days. He sat at one of the tables and stared out at the lake, leaving himself open to whatever memories might come.

It had all been so long ago. Across the water lay his old enemy, the line of expensive summer homes on the south shore. As a boy he used to look enviously at those houses, in such grim contrast to the drab and shoddy cabin that his father rented. He wanted to be part of the world across the lake; to enjoy the lawns, the elaborate piers, the speedboats, the sailing craft, the tennis courts, the late-afternoon cocktails, and laughing conversations. Now the homes did not look impressive. He was more successful than any of them. And it didn't matter.

He remembered the last Labor Day dance at the country club. Lynnie wore a strapless light green gown; the skin of her back was smooth under his fingers. She was available now, even eager for him; her radiant violet eyes wide with admiration and desire. They were a handsome couple, very much in love. Every eye in the room was on them. Judge Conroy was the only one frowning. An O'Neill wasn't good enough for his daughter. Lynnie's breasts pushed invitingly against his chest. It was a summer of passionate weekends, of growing self-confidence, of deepening desire. A soft September evening with the half-moon glowing over the lake. The happiest evening in his life.

Then the muttered conversation on the balcony. "He's as worthless as his old man." A slurred male voice. "Same eyes. You watch him turn into a drunk. Crazy ideas about being a writer—who does he think he is? Remember how he blew the championship? Probably going to get her pregnant so he can blackmail the judge. Two scoundrels. They deserve each other. . . ."

Then a woman's voice: "She's a pretty little thing, but no morals just like her mother. She'll run him a merry race."

Lynnie returned, and within a few minutes they were quarreling; later that night they broke up again, she in tears, not understanding why he had turned so sullen and hateful. His teeth were still clenched at the memory. Bastards . . . He'd shown them.

He laughed at himself. Most of "them" were unaware of his success and wouldn't have cared anyway. There is nothing like the passage of time, he thought wryly, to make triumph irrelevant.

The lake looked sinister under the quiet April sky. Although it was not very large and had no tricky currents, hardly a year had gone by without at least one drowning. The lake is evil, he thought to himself, shuddering involuntarily. He stood up and braced his shoulders, dismissing his unease as the sort of thing a writer of entertainment stories would conjure up. No one came up from the city on weekdays in mid-April. Lynnie and the lake. The girl is the lake is the grail is God . . . symbols fit poorly so pedestrian a place as this obsolescent summer resort.

He didn't look back at the lake as he walked away from the park and up the main street. One of the few remnants of the old town was the raised sidewalk in front of Huder's Variety Store and McGaw's Hardware. A very high sidewalk when he was young, now really only a few steps off the ground. He strolled by Huder's, lost in vague images of the sidewalk long ago. He collided with a woman emerging rapidly from the store. Caught off balance, he was sent spinning to his knees against the window of the store. Her packages tumbled over him.

"Oh my gosh, sir, I'm sorry. It was my fault, I wasn't looking. I hope you're not hurt. Here, let me help you." The flow of apologetic babble suddenly stopped as her violet eyes went round in dismay, like a nun who has knocked over the statue of the Sacred Heart. "Jimmy . . . ," she whispered.

Undamaged but barely able to breathe, he stood up, gathered her packages and offered them to her. "Always did say you were a knockout, Lynnie. So, how've you been? I haven't seen you lately."

She put the packages back on the ground and embraced him as though she were going to imprison him on the spot for the rest of his life. A battered hag she was not. Her body pressed fervently against his kindled instant desire. No wedding ring either. Was his heart beating as excitedly as hers?

"Same old Jimmy." She was examining his face. "Broader shoulders, sadder eyes, a little bit of snow in the red hair." The grin had already traveled its route to mischief. "You even hug like you used to."

He was indeed holding her as tightly as she was holding him. "You haven't changed either, Lynnie, or if you have it's all improvement." He'd forgotten the sound of the rich alto music of her voice.

She gently disengaged herself "That kind of compliment, as untrue as it may be, *is* a change for you, sir; nonetheless," her eyes flashed merrily, "I'll accept it and all similar ones."

He picked up her parcels. "Buy you a drink?"

"Sin Lake has reformed, Jim. At this hour it'll have to be something soft. Shall we try the Rose Bowl and see if all the ghosts are gone? My car is down the street. You can dump the groceries in there." The clinical water-ski-instructor expression settled on her face. She was waiting to see how he wanted to play their encounter. There were crow's-feet around her eyes, a hint of softness under her chin, and the gold of her hair was tinged with gray. Nonetheless the fragile loveliness of her face held him in a hypnotic trance. The pencil-thin water-ski scar above her left eye stirred memories he had not felt in two decades.

" 'Scuse my staring, Ma'am," he tried to laugh. "I've just discovered that my childhood sweetheart looks more lovely than she used to. Sure I'll take you to the Rose Bowl, so long as you don't mind the unabashed admiration." My God, why had he said that?

She was flustered. "I bet those are the sorts of things you say to your fancy French broads," she said uneasily, "but stare away. I'll do the same thing, if you don't mind, much more discreetly, though, as befits my Middle-Western provincialism. Here's the car."

A battered Ford station wagon of ancient vintage. Not much money anymore, huh, Lynnie? She opened the tailgate and he neatly arranged the packages in the back of the car. Just like a dutiful suburban husband. He experienced a transient déjà vu. Was he a suburban husband? Had nothing happened in the last twenty years? Was it all a dream?

"Thank you, kind sir; you're just what a suburban widow needs, someone to carry the packages. And now for the concentrated calories," she tucked his arm into hers. "I'll celebrate your apparition—doubtless a figment of my imagination—with my traditional strawberry milkshake. Lent comes tomorrow. And Jimmy, darling," her grip on him tightened, "what the hell are you doing here?" She walked as she always had, shoulders back, with the confident self-possession of the skillful athlete.

"Impulse," he said honestly enough. "I saw the lake when we were landing at O'Hare, got nostalgic, and decided to come here to look at it." His hands were very wet. You wanted this, didn't you? You wanted to see her again. What would Monique say?

"Think you'd bump into me?" she asked impishly as she pushed open the door of the old soda fountain. "Not literally, of course." She giggled like a teenager. Now she had teenagers of her own. . . .

"I'm glad I did." He resisted the temptation to shove her attractive rump through the door. I've got to be careful, he warned himself, not at all sure he'd heed the warning.

The inside of the Rose Bowl jolted him. No more iron chairs and marble-topped tables. The stained glass behind the soda fountain was gone, and the marvelous smell of spoiled milk. All chrome and plastic and polished mirrors. The universal ice cream parlor to be found anywhere in the world. The plush foam cushions in the cramped little booth were as uncomfortable as the old iron chairs. Why couldn't they have left it alone? he thought irritably.

"Yours will be chocolate malt, if I remember correctly. My treat, a welcome-home celebration for the native!" Her hands still moved in rapid feminine ges-

69

tures when she talked, like the women in Rome. Genetic inheritance? he wondered. She was handsome, like a Roman woman, too.

He watched her tall, aristocratic body as she moved easily toward the dark wood counter. The supple figure was unchanged. Underneath the maroon print not-quite-see-through blouse her breasts were elegant and firm, sharply outlined for a moment as she leaned against the countertop. Her hips fit snugly into the brown knit slacks, which showed traces of the scant bikini panties beneath them. His hungry imagination stripped her and delighted in what it found—an inch or two more at the waist, less at the thighs, five pounds heavier, if that much. This quick appraisal awakened the beginnings of desire, but he dismissed his fantasies decisively as she came back with their drinks.

"Do I get a passing grade, professor?" Her eyes were teasing him.

"A-plus," he said in embarrassment. "Sorry, but I told you I'd stare."

"Stare away," she said fervently, sitting down at the table and pushing his malt toward him. "It's all the result of a rigid diet, fierce exercise, and genetic luck. Now drink your milkshake and tell me about Clare." A businesslike tone, getting the conversation organized.

"She's in Rome in school with the Holy Cross sisters, will graduate in June, and wants to come to America for college. For some reason that is beyond me, she manages to tolerate her father pretty well. I'm going to see her in Paris this weekend. She's very pretty, but I think also vulnerable and rootless. Life hasn't been especially nice to her; as you would guess, I was not very good at being mother and father both—maybe not even good at just being a father."

"Doesn't she ever see her mother?" The violet eyes hooded, hiding what she thought of Clare's mother.

"No. Zena didn't want a child, especially a pretty daughter who is bound to grow up. Starlets are not supposed to get old, you know."

"Where will she go to college?" She attacked the milkshake with renewed vigor, but the violet eyes, unhooded now, never left his face.

"You won't believe it. . . ." God, her eyes are beautiful. He couldn't make up his mind whether to look at them or at her inviting breasts.

"St. Mary's!" she exploded.

"That's right." He chose to look at her breasts. Her eyes were dangerous; he couldn't think properly when she absorbed him in her gaze.

"The irony doesn't escape me," she said dryly. "Is she Catholic?"

"By her own choice, God knows. I didn't have anything to do with it. Being Irish, American, and Catholic is very important to Clare. I guess because she wants so desperately to be something. I don't think she really knows what it means, though. St. Mary's may be a shock."

"Different place now." She tilted her head backward as though in thought, again brushing the hair away from her face.

"It doesn't seem to have hurt your mind." His imagination, hardly interested in her mind, was busy unbuttoning her blouse.

"I'm being flooded with compliments. I need them when I learn your daughter is college age."

A reef to be avoided. Better change the subject. "I told you what I'm doing here. It's fair to ask you the same question," he said smoothly, reveling in the chocolate drink. At least that hasn't changed.

She waved a graceful hand as though nothing in her life could be interesting. "My children insisted that I was even more bitchy than usual and issued an ultimatum that I take a few days off during Easter week. We had some of the usual harassment from the IRS and I wore myself out. So I came up here. It's closer than Vegas. For a widow woman with some life left, a lot safer."

"You have the old house?" He shifted back to her violet eyes, now placid and serene. They were less threatening, after all.

"Yep. It's about all that was left when they straightened out the mess the 'old buccaneer,' as you so rightly called him, made in his last years. If he hadn't put it in Mom's name, it would have gone too." She was speaking calmly, almost too calmly.

"And it's safe here?"

Her grin was wicked. "Probably safer than Paris."

"Paris is greatly overrated, I fear. You've been there?"

"No. When Steve was alive, there was the time but no money; now there's no time. I got to Long Island once, though." She finished her milkshake, looked sadly at the empty glass, and shrugged.

She was playing her part in the dialogue with much greater skill than he. His heart was still beating much too fast, despite the chocolate milkshake. The roof of his mouth was dry. There was a muscle in her neck just above the thin brown kerchief she wore that twitched. Somehow it made him feel better. She was anxious too, maybe even frightened. She shifted her position abruptly, and the pressure of blouse fabric against her body momentarily revealed a deep curve of breast. O'Neill felt a sharp stab of desire, so strong that it took major effort to bring it under control. Not just idle fantasies this time.

"Tell me about your kids," he said easily, sensing another reef. "You have five, don't you?"

"At last count. A boy and a girl in college, ditto in high school, and a little fellow in fifth grade." She was playing with her empty glass, not looking at him for the first time since their conversation began. Did she have imagination problems too? Poor woman. "I love them all dearly, and they don't seem to mind me too much."

"How do you survive?" Compassion overpowered desire, much to his relief.

She lowered her head and examined the empty glass somberly. "When my husband died—he got drunk and piled into a lamppost—he left me with $5,000 in the checking account, and a $15,000 life insurance policy—we didn't need insurance, he said—a stock portfolio that had been emptied to prop up his real estate company, a company that was in bad need of more propping, and five children between the ages of four and fourteen. So it wasn't at all clear that we were going to survive."

"My God, what did you do?" A twist of pain for her suffering clutched at his windpipe.

"I decided to make the company go," she said brightly. "The two oldest kids helped a lot, but Loyola was the best we could do for college. The first year we just managed to eat; the next two years we even made a little; and the last two, thanks to some land that my husband forgot about and didn't sell at bargain-basement prices, we managed to pile up a goodly bundle of cash. I don't know what it all proves, except that maybe I am a true pirate's daughter—but you know that." The brightness faded, her voice trailed off as though she was caught in the pains of the past. As she brushed the hair away from her face again, the lines of age appeared.

"Lonely?" he asked gently, wanting to put his arm around her.

"Not exactly, but there's a vacancy. Even though a relationship has a lot of things wrong with it, it's still there. When it's gone, there's a great open space in your life. Activity doesn't fill it up completely." A faraway look of pain and sadness. She absently shoved the milkshake away.

"I know," he said softly, establishing a link of intimacy and warmth between them. "You're afraid to fill it up: but you keep worrying it, like your tongue worries a vague toothache—please excuse my mixed metaphors."

"You do it occasionally, Jimmy, not very often," she

said, the clinical instructor again. "Usually when describing your women." Another teenage giggle.

"You've read them?" he said in surprise.

"You've got to be kidding." She pointed both forefingers at him like they were six-shooters. "I'm afraid I'll encounter myself in one of them. Not yet, though. Worse luck for me."

"What do you think of my books?" His heart was still pounding; he'd almost forgotten about it. Did she really think he might write about her?

"Look, I'm no critic," she began enthusiastically, her face glowing again. "But it does seem to me that a serious writer has to be willing to reveal himself. You don't. You write marvelous entertainments, but James McCormack O'Neill is pretty well hidden behind his characters. Which means that Jimmy O'Neill, the ambitious and talented little boy who was pushed around by so many people, is still afraid to come out into the open and say how much it hurt. Mind you, there's no reason to do that unless you want to write something more than entertainment."

It was a direct and scathing description of his character and his work. Though she had said it gently and playfully, it hurt like hell. "Well, at least you left some of my clothes on," he said, trying to hide his embarrassment.

"Jimmy, I'm sorry." The look of pride which accompanied her lecture was quickly replaced by dismay. "I never should have said any of those things. My large Irish mouth is really worse than it ever was."

"If by worse you mean more accurate, I'll agree. Let

75

me try to recoup my pride by buying you a drink. What would you like?"

She made a face. "One tall and slender Tab, if you please, sir; the lady is not going to push her genetic luck anymore today."

How like Lynnie. Careful attention to calories, but streaks of gray hair. No easy ways out for her. Gray in the hair of his teenage love—he felt a heavy weight of sadness for all that was lost.

When he turned to come back from the counter she was laughing.

"At me?"

"At both of us. This is an absolutely crazy conversation."

"What else could it be?" he asked warily.

They both laughed, relaxing in the knowledge that they had steered by another reef. Lynnie downed most of her Tab in one compulsive gulp.

"You're not going to believe it, but I'm afraid I have to adjourn this session to go to a meeting at the church." She stood up from the table, her figure sending one more spasm of desire through his body. "In my declining years I have grown dreadfully pious."

"You and Clare," he said resignedly.

"This Clare I must meet some day."

"Indeed you must."

As they walked out into the street, colliding with the glare of the afternoon sunlight, Lynnie revived the conversation. "Jimmy, if you want a real live drink, I should be able to find something in the house after the meeting and before supper. I might even be persuaded to warm up some food so you won't starve to death."

Casual and playful—still a gambler.

"Sounds like it might be fun, but I've got to get back to O'Hare if I'm going to get on a morning plane out of New York to Paris."

"Well, maybe next time. When you bring Clare to school, you might stop by and meet the kids. They don't really believe that Mommy ever dated a famous novelist." If she was disappointed she showed no trace of it as she walked briskly down the street.

She took his hand warmly in both of hers. "I hope it isn't twenty years before the next collision." Her eyes were clear, her face serene.

"It won't be," he lied.

She got in the car, started the engine, and rolled down the window. The sun shone directly on her face, emphasizing the ravages worked by age, but somehow making her even more desirable.

"If you get a flat tire or a broken axle or change your mind, we keep a much better quality of booze than we used to."

"I'll remember," he said.

Apparently unconscious of the contradiction between an invitation to a tryst and a religious meeting, she drove away toward the church.

O'Neill collected his car and departed from the town with a light heart. He had disposed of the Lynnie Conroy fixation. She could still stir up some physiological memories out of the past; but she was quite common nonetheless, a middle-class female real estate operator who had never been to Europe and

77

knew nothing of the world in which he lived. Strictly small-time. Not worth anger or resentment or even nostalgic memories.

She was part of the past and had no place in his present—a minor demon, now permanently exorcised.

 6

She closed her eyes and slowly sipped the martini. The alcohol would not soothe her nerves, but the act of slow sipping might calm the racing motor inside her chest. Evelina Brigid, she told herself, you have flipped out. Five years without a man and you proposition this one the first time you see him. No wonder he looked so scared. Then you go to a liturgical meeting in this creepy country parish and daydream about him all afternoon. He won't be back. You're just an old woman out of his past who made a fool out of herself for the second time.

He seemed so gentle and sensitive. All the anger and hatred is gone, now just pain in those silver eyes. Damn it, heart, stop beating like that. Oh God, I love him as much as I ever did. I must have been all of two when my heart started to beat this way every time I saw him. No fool like an old fool. He's lonely. Even when his eyes twinkle, you can see the hurt lurking there. They didn't used to twinkle all that much. He liked the looks of me, too. If he hadn't eaten me up with his damn silver eyes, I wouldn't have propositioned him. I've never propositioned a man in all my life. He's had all sorts of fancy French broads. I'd be a disappointment.

She slammed the arm of her chair angrily and opened her eyes. The miserable son of a bitch! He thought she was an amusing peasant—so what if he didn't show up? Besides, you've got enough trouble with the U.S. Attorney and the IRS. Why add to the mess by getting involved with a man?

She forced herself out of the chair and shook her head in virtuous dismay at the apricot gown she had tossed on the bed. Opaque enough and elegant, but with thin straps, a lot of lace, and revealing more than enough. She bought it on impulse last year just in case the right man, oh, hell, just in case *he* came back. She put the gown on a hanger and carefully hung it in the closet. Frivolous. Loneliness was better than another mistake. She'd fended men off for years, and she grabbed at the one who didn't want her. Real smart businesswoman. You should have known you would never have him. Made a fool of yourself, should have been more coy. He wouldn't come back either way. Might as well give him a good scare. Served the lousy bastard right. . . .

Sighing, she went into the kitchen to get a steak from the freezer. May as well be damned for a goat as a sheep. Gin and beef. Really ought to run this afternoon. It's getting too dark though. I shouldn't have ordered that milkshake. Teenager. Horny teenager at that. She took a small steak out of the refrigerator, hesitated, and removed a second, just in case. Then shoved it back and slammed the door savagely. Damn, damn, damn. I still love him—more than ever. It hurts when I think about him. It's hurt every day since he left—I want him as much as I ever did.

She fumbled for a tissue, found one in the bathroom, disciplined her emotions, thought of the land tract in Delevan they were going to redevelop. Make hundreds of thousands redoing Assembly Park. Get the son of a bitch out of your mind. She looked at her face in the mirror. Stupid old hag. Take a shower and cool off.

She took off her blouse, threw it furiously on the floor, then picked it up and laid it neatly in a laundry basket. A cold, cold shower. What if he came and they both froze up? God, what a comedy that would be—two old polar bears pretending they are young lovers. Absently she tossed her slacks into the basket and leaned against the bathroom door. Stony fear began to creep through her body—he'll come.

As sure as the sun comes up in the morning, he'll stop his car out there on the highway, decide it was all foolishness, then start it up as though he were going to the airport, and come back here. I need another drink. Does he drink a lot? Is alcoholism hereditary? I worry about the kids. . . . good Lord, the kids—I haven't thought of them all afternoon. What would they think? I'll send him on his way, pretend it was all a joke. . . .

She took the ice cubes out of the freezer and removed another steak. The kitchen floor seemed frigid under her bare feet; the ice cubes warmer than her body, though inside a fire was beginning to burn.

I want him. . . . I won't let him get away. This time I'll keep him. She sloshed a large amount of gin into the tumbler and ignored the vermouth.

In the bedroom the gown and the peignoir came off the hangers and back on the bed. The fire was growing hotter. Timidly she looked at herself in the mirror. On the whole, not bad. He liked the feel of you in his arms. . . . As charming as ever, but with more polish and grace.

Grace. She hadn't thought about religion. The gown *was* sinful. She laughed when the clerk at Bonwit's said that. Now the fires of sin were burning inside her.

She held the gown in front of her and looked at the mirror again. Grace. Sin. Which is which? You do look graceful, honey. I hate to admit it, but you're not bad looking at all for a harlot. She laid the gown gently on the bed. It was unreal, a dream. She'd wake up from it. Jimmy hadn't come back. . . .

It wouldn't be a sin. If I'm going to do it, I'd better make up my mind about that. He's my man, always has been. I want him, goddamit—excuse my language, Lord. You've sent him back to me and you want me to get him. You understand what it's like to be foolishly in love. You keep saying that's the way your Father is with us. Anyhow, I'm going to do it. I don't think you'll be mad. Maybe it's a big mistake, maybe I should make him wait. Kid him along, play games with him. Only I can't. I want him so much. Help me. . . .

She grinned. Asking God to make you a good harlot, better than his fancy French women. Oh well, He doesn't mind. You know—she spun around in front of the mirror like a pirouetting dancer—you don't look half bad for someone your age. Ten years— on a good day, maybe twelve. Genes, exercise . . . ugh, discipline . . . all for tonight. Oh, don't be silly, he's not that important. If only you weren't such a sexual inno- cent. She tried to fight back tears and turned her back on the mirror. You should have practiced some the last five years. You almost did a couple of times, even told yourself it was preparation for tonight. You knew the son of a bitch would show up sometime. Why tonight? Well, Evelina, why *not* tonight? Anyhow, you probably wouldn't have learned much from those creeps.

I'll straighten up the house, get the meal started, then take a shower—must smell pretty for your returning hero. She poured the untouched glass of gin down the bathroom sink; heat and cold fought in her chest. Run the vacuum first. The woman in the mirror was blushing. No, you damn fool, it isn't the house or the meal that counts—she tossed her underwear into the laundry basket. Irish cunning and Italian pas- sion—we'll show those French broads. Her heart thumped with terror as the cold shower spray caressed her skin, but it also sang with joy.

He stared at the rectangle of yellow light through the budding trees, drawn to it as though he were a gnat with a fatal attraction for a glowing windowpane. Beyond the trees was the motionless lake, and beyond the lake the disapproving stars. He could not quite believe he was at the driveway of the Conroy property; his hands were sweaty and his feet moved sluggishly. What was he doing here? What irresistible energies had pulled him back? Had someone else taken over his body; had a lurking presence risen from the depths of his soul and turned him into a zombie? He was hungry for a woman. He was bemused, fascinated, dazzled by the woman he had met in the afternoon; he would pursue her even if she were not his childhood lover.

He clenched his fists as he walked around the old house, now painted a light blue-gray with white trim, to the porch on the lakeside. It was a warm evening for April; that's why he felt like he had a fever. He should stop now, not leap into the pit which yawned in front of him. He would get hurt if he went on. He walked up the stairs to the porch reluctantly, still in the grip of the demons which had emerged from the April darkness and taken over his body.

The front porch of the old Conroy house was closed in, but the screen windows were open to the evening air. She lay on a couch, an empty glass on the table next to her, looking like a defenseless child. She wore a low-cut nightgown that clung precariously to her graceful shoulders by thin straps. If Gabya, a friend of Monique's he slept with, was a Titian or a Renoir nude, Lynnie with her lithe, taut body, trim legs, and neatly molded breasts was a Botticelli, seemingly in movement even when in repose. He stood motionless on the steps. He must run. He hesitated, decided to leave, willed himself to go, and knocked lightly on the door, hoping that she would not hear him. "Pardon me, Ma'am, but I'm collecting material for a novel. I hear there is a tragic heroine living here."

She opened her eyes, startled, frightened. "It took that axle a long time to break."

He pulled the door open and stepped into the porch. "I'm sorry if I frightened you, Lynnie, but I don't know how to open a conversation with a woman dressed in a gown like that."

"Standard issue for widow women of my age and infirmity on spring evenings when they're hoping against hope that someone will seduce them." She reached for the robe on the back of the couch, skillfully put it on as she rose, and tied it at the neck. "This protects my sense of modesty without interfering with the view, such as it may be."

"Like French wine, it only improves with age," he responded gallantly.

"Ha," she sniffed. "Note well he says nothing about French women. Anyway, I promised you supper and supper it shall be. Pour yourself a drink and . . . uh . . . you should excuse the expression, make yourself at home."

"Don't bother, please, Lynnie; I'm not hungry," he pleaded.

"The hell you're not. Sitting out there on the highway for half the night wondering whether we're both insane is bound to give you an appetite. You look starved. Eat first, worry about what comes next after supper."

Her gown swishing, she vanished into the kitchen. He found the Scotch bottle and the melting ice cubes, and quickly drained a strong drink.

Lynnie was back almost at once with a cart bearing

a white cloth, an elaborate steak dinner, a bottle of 1937 burgundy, and a single lighted candle. She wore an impish grin to accompany her masterwork. Why had he come? "Lace, candlelight, and wine." She grinned wickedly.

"You really were expecting me?" Oh God, he should get out now.

"I figured there was no harm in being ready if you did," she sighed, standing beside him and pouring the wine. He put his arm around her slender waist; she stiffened.

"Strong muscles still there," he said.

"That's what exercise is all about. Stomach muscles do what girdles used to do. I don't know which is rougher on an old woman." She skillfully slipped away. "Since you will doubtless consume far more than your share of my priceless burgundy, I'll go open another bottle. Don't go away."

"I'd take my life in my hands if I tried."

She returned with an open bottle. "What are you grinning at, mysterious stranger?"

"I was thinking about the Bible."

"Jimmy, darling, I am not Judith. I will not cut off your head. It's so good to have you back, I guess I'm even zanier than usual." Her face softened into sad affection.

"Nonetheless, woman, that is a very seductive scent you're wearing."

"Oh, that. It's called 'Wicked Widow'—no, its name really is 'My Final Indiscretion.' Actually, it is intended to distract a man from my smelly hair. I would have washed it this morning if I'd known you were coming, but it was too late. You remember how hard it is to get it back to life after—but why would you remember something silly like that?" Realizing she had been babbling, she paused, bottle in hand, embarrassed.

Of course he remembered her hair. He almost told her he thought it would look great plastered against her head.

She began to pour wine into his glass. "You sure like this stuff." Her rambling picked up steam again. "I have a whole cellar to trap men who wander by on spring nights. For really good prospects—you haven't earned your performance rating yet, by the way—I have a Neirsteinereiswein that is almost more fun than sex."

"Does this splendid hotel serve breakfast in the morning?" His tongue, acting on its own, cut into the flow of babble. He knew he wouldn't be here in the morning; he was leaving after supper. His hand rested on her buttock. "Tasty as ever. . . ."

"Only to guests who are of good character and well behaved." She skillfully escaped again.

He sipped the wine, then gulped it. Across the table she now seemed restrained, thoughtful, as though some other worry, unrelated to him, had crept into her head.

"Lynn, what is happening to us?" He interrupted her thoughts.

"You were wondering, too." With a start she returned to the present. "We're both lunatics. I think I'm trying to seduce you, which for a widow woman who has had only one man in her whole life is ridiculous. I can't believe I'm doing it. It's spring; we're both lonely and getting old, tired and hungry for affection—sex-starved. At least I am, and judging by the look in your eyes, you are too, fancy French women or not. We shook each other up this afternoon. We want to know more about each other." As she spoke, her voice became uncertain, her frown deepened, the muscle in her neck began to twitch. "We're both drunk."

He put his hand on her trembling neck. "Lynnie, are you afraid?"

"I talk a good game and I act tough; I'm about half an inch from falling apart." She pulled her face from his caressing hands. "Now eat before it gets cold. I don't like to see my cooking artistry wasted."

He ate. Despite the growing warmth between them, he still planned to run. Tomorrow. Lust and weariness wouldn't allow it now. It was hard to think about anything with Lynnie's pale white breasts across the table. He stopped eating to stare at her. She lowered her eyes modestly.

"You're gorgeous, Lynnie," he said, feeling tipsy and foolish.

"Compliments, compliments. Actually, all I am is an elaborately designed baby-making and feeding machine. I'm quite good at making babies, you know. Time was I thought it was all I was good at. Do you want a baby? I'll make you one." She broke off in an embarrassed giggle.

What do you say to that? He was blushing too. "If you were the mother, it would be a beautiful child."

Her smile was now warm and maternal. "I'll get you some dessert, dear." With a swish of her gown she headed for the kitchen. "I think I might bring the Eiswein in after all."

"Woman, come back here!" he commanded.

"Yes?" she smiled archly. "Something you'd like to order for dessert?"

"I'll provide my own dessert. Forget the wine. Come over here." He rose from the table.

She came, slowly, her eyes cast down. Stopping a half-inch from where he stood, her arms crossed in front as though to keep out the cold, she said, softly, "I've forgotten my lines and lost my act, Jimmy."

The last restraint broke; he took her into his arms. "God, Lynnie, I don't know why I didn't do this the minute I got here." His hands, now out of control of his brain, untied her robe and slid it down her arms.

She snuggled her head against his chest. A muffled voice said, "Wondered if you'd ever get around to that."

The skin of her back was as smooth as fine linen. Irish linen of course, he thought irrelevantly.

The wine, the candlelight, her womanliness, the dreamlike recklessness of their conversation, his throbbing head and aching chest all blended into irresistible longing. The last control inside him snapped. His fingers moved to the thin straps of her gown, gently nudging them off her shoulders. She clutched the flimsy garment at her waist, modest and apprehensive. "I talk a big line, Jimmy, but I don't have much experience at these things," she whispered hoarsely. "Don't expect a lot."

He tenderly drew her close and began to kiss her throat, his tongue touching the quick pulse of life. The same satisfied sigh as long ago. She let go of her garment, no longer a mature woman but a young bride, innocent, uncertain, and generous.

The sun was shining through the blinds when he woke up. The woman next to him still glowed from last night's pleasure, now more a Bellini nude than a Botticelli Venus. He found slacks and a shirt that had to belong to her oldest son—big kid—kissed her bare shoulder, touched a lock of gray-streaked blond hair, and went outdoors to absorb the splendors of a morning at the lake.

It was an easy but satisfying conquest. In contrast to her brash exterior, Lynnie was a piquant mixture of modesty and submissiveness as a lover—soft, eager to please, responsive, and pathetically grateful. No huge challenge, but amusing entertainment, until the last few moments when his carefully orchestrated enjoyment was swept away by tempestuous tenderness. He strove for healing love to wipe away the pain of the past. He frowned uneasily. Must be careful not to get too deeply involved. A brief affair that could be conveniently ended. Like the one with Carla.

When he returned, she was just awakening, her face shining with well being, a hand holding a blanket around her neck as modest protection. He stood at the side of the bed, towering over her, again feeling proud of his conquest. Easy lay or not, she was still an impressive woman.

"Something you want, sir?" she asked with a timidity partly feigned and partly real.

"I was told this castle served breakfast."

"What would make me think you wanted anything else?"

Covering herself as best she could with the blanket, she reached for a thin green kimono, turned her back to him as she put it on, and departed for the kitchen. The breakfast she brought back was enormous. "Work up an appetite doing those things," she snickered.

They ate shyly and silently together in bed.

"How do I compare with all your fancy French women?" she asked as she swallowed a piece of toast.

"I don't have any fancy French women."

"Well, your ordinary French women." She eyed him speculatively.

"I don't have any French women at all—or women of any other nationality, for that matter," he said testily. The quiz was annoying. "Lynnie, this is crazy."

Lynnie left the bed and sat down in the old wicker chair.

"Of course it is," she said complacently.

"Aren't we kidding ourselves?" he pleaded.

Her eyes flashed in sudden anger. "Yes, stupid, we *are* kidding ourselves. Most of the things that can go wrong will go wrong; and, no, we ought not to be taking a second chance with our second chance. Does that answer your question?"

She was now striding up and down the room, furious—occasionally turning on him to drive home her point with a finger jabbed in the general direction of his face. "Let me tell you all the things that will go wrong. Clare and I will fight. You will fight with my kids; you and I will fight every day, working out the anger and bitterness we have stored up against one another. You hated your mother; I'll become a substitute mother. I hated my father; you'll become a substitute father. Your friends in Paris will think I'm gross and crude. I'll think they're effete snobs. Sometimes we won't talk to each other for a week. Often we'll both be terrible in bed. We'll get old. Our teeth and bladders and bowels will start giving out. We'll get crotchety and mean. Can you imagine what a bitch I'll be at seventy? Then you know what will happen? We'll die. That's right, we'll die; and you're just the kind of a bastard that will die and leave me a widow again. So what the hell do you want? Life goes wrong."

"Don't be ridiculous Lynnie," he insisted, terrified by her rage.

She ignored him. "You will be furious every day at my loud, obnoxious Irish mouth, and I'll blow my stack at least once a day with your damn stupid fear of strong women. If there's one thing that disgusts me about you, it is that poor pathetic 'don't hit me again' look you get on your face when . . ."

Anger briefly stirred within him. He grabbed her hands, spun her around, pushed her against the wall, and clamped his hand over her mouth. "Will you shut your big, bitchy mouth for a moment and give me a chance to talk?" he shouted.

She went limp against him, all resistance gone. He

took his hand off her mouth but found he had nothing to say.

"Well, what do you have to say, cave man?" All tenderness and affection despite the sarcastic words.

"I've forgotten," he said lamely.

His grip on her turned from restraint to affection. He smoothed her hair. Get out of here before you get swallowed up. His fingers disobeyed him and brushed her lips. His hand caressed her jaw, went to her throat, and then underneath the kimono. He was trapped again. He unknotted the belt on her robe and pressed his fingers against her body, sliding them from shoulders to thighs and back to her flat, warm belly. She shivered and winced. So easy to arouse, my love.

"In broad daylight, Jimmy?"

"With the blinds open," he responded, removing her robe slowly and carefully. "You're lucky I don't take you out on the pier and finish up what I began twenty years ago."

"You won't do that," she said, lowering her head in embarrassed modesty. "You wouldn't have any escape hatches left."

He gulped and took her hands, extended them from her body, and drank her in. No, not a battered old hag at all. One amused, probing eye peered up at him.

He let go of one hand and tilted her chin upward to look at her face. "Thanks for staying a silver goddess, Lynnie," he said, astonished that he was able to dig the metaphor out of his past.

"Hell, in the sunlight, I should be a golden goddess." She was luxuriating in his admiration. "Anyway,

I'm glad you don't mind all the ravages of time. I'm not exactly your exotic playmate type." Her eyes were dull with desire, her mouth open, her body beginning to sag.

Not exotic perhaps. My childhood love, so very easy to possess. "Who's looking for exotic playmates?" The sweetness of their embrace drained his breath.

Afterward, Lynnie announced that whatever other exercise had occurred she was not going to give up her jogging. "Those other activities don't eat up many calories at all," she said authoritatively, as she zipped up the jacket of her jogging suit over a massive and businesslike exercise bra. "Want to join me, darling?"

He pleaded exhaustion, jet fatigue, and a hangover. She shrugged, tied on grimly efficient gym shoes, and briskly sailed out the door. He began to fall back to sleep. She reentered the bedroom, grinning broadly.

"Look, darling, if you decide that the lays are better in Paree and want to leave while I'm running around the lake, I hung your clothes in yonder closet. Never say you were kept here against your will." Then with bright laughter at her own joke she was gone again.

Instead, he dozed fitfully, thinking about how the DuLacs would react to Lynnie if he should improbably bring her to Paris. They would, he told himself, find her coarse and common—an uninteresting American provincial. Clare would hate her instantly.

So the day went: food and drink, laughter and nostalgia, banter and flashes of anger, regrets over the past, and enough sex to last him for a long time. No danger of impotency with Lynnie around, even if he had to pay for his pleasure by having her push him into the cold waters of the lake.

Several times her look of preoccupation returned. Something was eating at her, something that had nothing to do with him. He ought to ask her.

In the evening after dinner he suppressed all fears of being trapped. The joys of the moment were enough.

"I'm an easy lay," she said as he held her protectively in his arms in front of the fireplace, echoing his own earlier silent judgment.

"The value of a citadel is not measured by the ease of its capture," he replied, wondering whether it was his own quote or someone else's.

"Humph," she sniffed. "Literary men are very clever—hey, don't you ever get tired of that?"

His hands were searching her body, now with light and casual playfulness. "Sometimes," he admitted. "But I'll never get tired of it with you." He was so happy that only a small voice in the corner of his brain protested.

She touched his cheek. "I'm not nearly that good, Jim, but it's terribly nice of you to say so."

He would not think about tomorrow, he told himself, not now. Not with her in his arms.

The terror came when he woke up in the middle of the night, as though from a drunken sleep. Where was he? Who was the woman beside him? What happened? He groped for an explanation and couldn't find it. Then he remembered.

She looked like an innocent girl in her sleep; he edged away from her in fear. What had he done?

Carefully he got out of bed and slipped into the parlor. The moon shone on the lake, its light bathing the battered wicker furniture.

I come back to the lake where I spent summer vacations. I meet an old girlfriend, a well-proportioned middle-aged matron, and I jump into bed mostly because of nostalgia and suppressed passion. We make love and act as though we are going to stay together for the rest of our lives.

She's a stranger. I don't know her; she is a creature of my imagination. It's time to leave.

He went back to the bedroom and began to dress in the dark.

Lynnie turned on the light, somberly watched him button his shirt.

"I've got to get back to Paris."

She laughed. "You won't be able to do it. You'll be back. Despite all your fancy French friends—hey, that's alliterative. Maybe I ought to take up writing." Pathos again turning to mischief. Damn her.

She could not be serious even at the most tragic of times. "Every time I'm with you I hurt you worse. I should never have come back."

She sat on the edge of the bed, hair tousled, eyes sleepy, her modest blue gown a deliberate contrast to the previous night's wantonness. "So I get hurt. We've been hooked on one another since we were little kids. Who cares about one more hurt?" Her lips were tight, her eyes flashed, her hand dug into the mattress as she tried to control her temper.

He picked up his coat and left the house. The stern

April moon glared down at him. He leaned against the side of the car, his breath coming in quick gasps. He glared at the moon.

Just get in the car, turn on the ignition, and leave.

He went back into the house. Lynnie was still sitting on the edge of the bed. "Did you find Paris lovely this spring?" she asked.

 7

You have just as much right to sit on this bench as she does, O'Neill assured himself, trying to ignore the old Polish woman eyeing him cautiously as she muttered her rosary. You always wanted to be a suspicious-looking character—what's more suspicious than an Irishman in a Parisian suit sitting on a park bench next to old Polish ladies in babushkas? Still glaring. He wondered if she would complain about him to the police who were sitting in a patrol car at the other end of the park.

In Paris, Wicker Park would be a world-famous landmark—bright awnings, gaudily painted houses with big stained-glass windows, elaborate stone and wood grillwork, soft sunlight filtering through its leafy trees—a picturesque district off a main business street; quiet, quaint, charming. There would be no need for the surveillance of a blue-and-white patrol car. The park's future would not be in doubt, hanging precariously between urban renewal and national landmark status. In a year or two the almost grotesquely playful late Victorians surrounding the park might be burned-out and abandoned hulks, or they might be smart rehabilitated townhouses of the professional class. Idly he thought of buying one. A Chicago house. Ridiculous; but then no more ridiculous than his strange pilgrimage through the city's neighborhoods.

It started the day he and Lynnie walked the streets of their old parish, hand-in-hand, anxiety in her violet eyes, and a lump of fear in his own stomach. When she parked the car by the white stone church—which had existed only in architects' drawings when he left—he was ready for the bittersweet memories to come flooding back. He would feel sorry for himself and resentful of Lynnie as the hurts and humiliations of two decades before rose up to claim their revenge.

There were no memories. The schoolyard, the pool hall, the drug store, the movie theater, the ice cream parlor (now a tavern), the street corners—all still there but no emotional resonance. The neighborhood he ran away from and dreamed of, both loved and hated for twenty years, didn't exist. When they stopped at Conley's Funeral Parlor, plasticized now beyond recognition, he tried to imagine his parents' wakes. Again, emptiness. Lynnie wisely left him with his own thoughts.

Finally, they stood in front of the aging bungalow which had been his home, transformed by yellow aluminum siding. Lynnie put her arm around him protectively. He stared at the house, trying now to conjure up ghosts. The spring afternoon was blandly devoid of psychic energy. Lynnie's arm tightened.

"Where have they all gone?" he asked.

She kissed him on the cheek. There was no one in sight to spoil the quiet privacy of the day. No one since they left the church parking lot.

"The people have moved, darling; it started after the Korean War. The young folks—people like Steve and I—began to buy in the suburbs. Then the older people who had money left too. There's only a few old families left. Ethnic succession, my kids tell me, is what they call it. Disappointed?"

"Nothing left to hate, Lynnie," he murmured forlornly.

"And nothing to love?" She eyed him shrewdly, probing at the weak link in his soul.

He slapped her inviting behind, neatly outlined beneath tight gray slacks; and she laughed joyously.

They walked back to the church in silence, Lynnie now not eager to console him. Where was the young priest? Not young anymore, but probably still a priest. Better not ask her; that will bring up religion.

He gave in to the implacable gaze of the Polish woman and walked disconsolately back to his car parked on a street leading to Milwaukee Avenue. Phone calls to Paris, Rome, New York. He had an idea for a novel about Chicago. Digging into his own past. True enough and a satisfactory enough explanation for everyone, except Clare, who seemed dubious and asked him if he was looking up old friends. He had lied to his daughter without a twinge of conscience.

There were no old friends left.

The first meal with Lynnie's children was a nightmare. He didn't know the suburb she lived in, west of Chicago, and had to ask directions several times before finding her street. The rambling Edwardian house needed painting; autumn leaves still littered the driveway; the doorbell didn't work. After several minutes of furious knocking Lynnie let him in. Inside was a mess—books, phonograph records, magazines, and heaps of clothes littered every available flat place; two large and friendly dogs, a Labrador and a collie; rock-and-roll blaring from a vast stereo system; someone playing a violin upstairs; a typewriter tapping irregularly somewhere else. Everywhere the smell of onions, spices, and Italian cooking.

Lynnie's hair was tied behind her head, her face was smudged, her man-style shirt hung out over her slacks, blotched by some mysterious cooking ingredient. She wore glasses and no makeup, and she smelled of musty kitchen.

"Behold the housewife at work, darling! Don't get too close to me or I'll mess up your expensive Paris suit with a preview of dinner. You can kiss me, though. Don't look so surprised. I told you I was an old woman." She laughed merrily. "Now make yourself at home with the kids while I finish my very special Italian dinner."

There was no chance of making himself at home with the kids. All five ignored him. Marty, a blond-bearded giant who looked like a hippie and allegedly helped in the family business while going to night school, shook hands without a trace of friendliness; Evie, a haunting younger version of her mother, gave him a pretty but fleeting smile; two younger teenagers, Cora and Michael, glared at him sullenly; and Jimmy, the eleven-year-old, didn't even look up from his comic book.

"Jimmy?" he asked in surprise.

"Named after Steve's uncle, silly," she said with a wink. The kids went back to their hi-fi, homework, violin, and comic book, leaving him by himself in the parlor—tall, rangy, blond kids, taking up a lot of space, looking like their mother, and not very eager to have him in the house.

God, how could Lynnie stand such a mess? She was fastidious as a girl.

Dinner was late. Lynnie rushed in from the kitchen to apologize. Last-minute business; she didn't trust Evie with her lasagne recipe. "Not enough Italian blood, you know. Pour yourself a drink and we'll be at it shortly."

The drink mixes were hidden somewhere, but no one offered to find them. He was hungry, thirsty, increasingly angry, and in a lunatic asylum.

Finally supper. More apologies from Lynnie. "No glamorous widow tonight, darling; just don't look at the housewife and concentrate on her food. No time even for a shower. Evie, get the rolls out of the oven; they're burning."

"*Mother*," Evie protested, "it's your fault."

The kids kept up the fiction of his nonexistence throughout the meal. He was sandwiched between Evie and Cora, who avoided asking him to pass anything. The kids talked about school, rock music, the Chicago White Sox, the teen-club dance, exams, summer work, the Chicago Bears, and their friends, who seemed to have only first names. Seven people and seven conversations.

Lynnie didn't seem to notice that he was being frozen out. She carried on conversations with all her offspring at the same time (except Michael, who said absolutely nothing—is he a defective, I wonder?), gave orders for the trips to and from the kitchen, supervised the distribution of food, bawled out those who ate too much or too little, had a minor fight with Evie over the salad dressing, and warned Jimmy that if he didn't take his elbows off the table she would cut them off.

O'Neill, whose elbows were on the table, thought she had meant him and pulled back anxiously. Evie had a coughing spell which led Lynnie to warn her about smoking.

"*Mother*, I don't smoke. Just because you got all holy and gave it up. . . ."

"Darling, be quiet and pass Mr. O'Neill some more lasagne."

She might be a poor housekeeper, but she had learned how to cook.

The fix was in with the kids. They were plotting against him. He wondered how he was supposed to react. Out of the corner of his eye he saw first one, then another, steal an interested glance at him. Baiting me, you little bastards? Well, we'll see. . . .

The table was cleared. He'd eaten too much lasagne and drunk too much wine. The assembled multitude

101

was ordered to stay put while she prepared the crepes. Oh my God, crepes. How do you keep that figure?

"Cora, you help Evie with the coffee cups. Mr. O'Neill has tea." She departed to the kitchen, a whirlwind of harassed energy.

"Well, Marty, you're the head of the family," he said casually. "Do I get a passing grade?"

Five sets of glittering violet eyes riveted on him. "Uh . . . ," Marty stumbled, "gosh, James, I can't say yet, but you sure get higher marks than the last guy." His face was impassive; his eyes still glittered. Evie's smile didn't go away this time.

"I don't care, Marty," Cora blurted. "I think James is kind of cute."

"Cora!" Evie snapped in horror. "Don't be so rude!"

"James," huh? Isn't that nice. Well, I got them on the run. . . .

"I'm sorry, James." Evie's smile was sweeter than her mother's ever was. "Cora's only a sophomore."

"It's all right," he said. Now Marty had the coughing fit.

Cora looked around the table at the others. "Look, somebody's gotta ask him."

"COR-A! . . ." her older sister moaned, covering her eyes.

"Ask me what?"

"Well, are you in love with our mother? Are you going to marry her or what?"

O'Neill slowly scratched a temple. "Well, I don't know, Cora. It's a little early—" He braked himself.

102

"You know I have a daughter in school, don't you?" Try to get out of it, but be diplomatic.

"Did you divorce her mother?" Michael asked bluntly, speaking for the first time.

"James, don't mind him," Evie said, now trying to play Lynnie's role. "Michael is a seminarian—old church." She swept her hair back Lynnie-style.

"That's a fair question, Evie. You're all wondering. Yes, I did; and no, we were not married in church; so yes, I am eligible—even," he added as an afterthought, not knowing quite what it meant, "by the standards of the old church." Why was he saying these things?

Five sets of violet eyes shone. Good enough for them.

"How old is your daughter, James?" Marty asked politely.

"Seventeen. She has red hair just like mine."

"Do you have a picture of her, James?" Evie asked in her small, musical voice.

He reached into his pocket, ceremoniously withdrew his wallet, and gave her a picture of Clare he'd taken at Livorno the year before. "Of course," he said proudly, "she was only sixteen then. . . ."

Evie's eyes widened. "Wow, that kind of competition we don't need around here. . . ." She passed the photograph to her brother as the others leaned over the table, straining to see it.

"If she ever comes to Chicago, James, I would be delighted to show her around, introduce her to some people," Marty said.

"I bet you would," Evie commented.

"Will she ever come to Chicago, James? She could come to dinner," Cora offered graciously.

"I'd just as soon throw her into a tank of piranhas," he said. Five sets of violet eyes riveted on him. He permitted himself a smile.

Their laughter brought their mother from the kitchen, carrying a platter of lovely crepes. "What the hell is all the noise about?" she demanded.

"Oh, we were just looking at a picture of James's daughter," Evie said.

"Humph . . . James didn't show it to *me*. Lemme see." Lynnie took it from her hand and quickly scanned it.

"Incredible," Marty said solemnly, "completely incredible."

He finally escaped with his life. His head was whirling. The last thing he needed was five . . . no, just four more teenagers; a child; two large dogs—a collie named Emily (for Emily Dickinson, "of course, James!") and a Labrador named Archibald ("How did you guess it was Archibald MacLeish?"), a house that desperately needed a coat of paint, and a $750 rock-and-roll stereo system. Buy Lynnie and you get the rest of the package free.

He turned his Hertz Impala into the crowded traffic of Milwaukee Avenue. Some fine, romantic hero he was, mired in his own doubts and hesitations. He was suspended like a spider in a web, caught in his own spinning, weighed down by reflections, self-analysis, doubt, hesitation. The heroes of his stories would not have hesitated five seconds over such a luscious prize.

He turned at North Avenue and drove toward Lincoln Park. He hated Lake Michigan, but maybe today there would be wisdom in its sullen waves.

The paradoxes in her personality were more intricate than ever. She ran four miles a day to keep her figure trim but ignored the gray streaks in her hair; she wore expensive clothes and spent no money on jewelry; she was brash to the point of vulgarity but sexually naive despite her five kids; she was a hard-driving, ambitious businesswoman but as fragile as a glass doll; saw through him but adored him; she bounded merrily through life, but then there were the sudden sentences cracking out at him like a whip: "Still trying to figure out whether I'm death?" she had murmured sleepily one warm afternoon after they had made love in her vast king-size bed.

He drove into a parking lot overlooking one of the Lincoln Park marinas. A few sails were already raised on red and white boats.

He would have to decide soon. June 15 was the target date for going back to Paris—four more weeks. He slammed his hand in disgust against the steering wheel.

After the sweet poignancies of their first times together, he permitted their sex to become middle-aged—efficient, uneventful, satisfying. In his hotel room after a late evening dinner on the near North Side or in her bed when her children were safely at school, he took her with tenderness—you could not help but be tender with such a fragile woman—and

105

caution. As a lover she lacked both inhibitions and experience. Steve must have been an extraordinarily unimaginative husband.

How did she reconcile her piety with their affair? She had disposed of the children last Saturday to spend the whole night in his room—not that there was any more sex than at other times. In the morning she bounded out of bed and cheerfully proposed that he come to Mass with her. He rarely went to church—only for Clare—but if Mama's pet poodle is told to go to Mass, he goes. They did not go around the corner to Holy Name Cathedral. "No good sermons there, and, besides, I don't like the archbishop. It will take a hundred years to undo the harm that man has caused." They took a cab to a little church off the Drive.

At first he paid no attention to the sermon. Then he perceived at the margins of his consciousness that the young bearded man was good. He decided to listen.

"It is not so much the resurrection of Jesus we celebrate during this season, nor even the hope of our own resurrection, which is much harder to believe in. We celebrate, rather, something even more incredible— the mystery of God's passionate love for us, a passion revealed in the blessing of the Easter waters in which the lighted candle is plunged three times. This ancient symbol of intercourse tells us that we are thrust into life at the beginning of a passionate love affair to which we are invited to respond. God loves us with a passion that makes human love look weak by comparison. The resurrection of Jesus and the promise of our resurrection are the signs of this dazzling and terrifying love.

106

To believe in the resurrection is to believe in such love and to believe that in the comforting embrace of God's love our own loves become not only possible but necessary. So we celebrate always, but especially at this time of the year, the possibility of love and the conviction that love is stronger than death."

He wondered if the priest was a heretic. He'd never heard anything like that when he was growing up. What would *his* young priest have said about it? Covertly he glanced at Lynnie. She didn't seem at all shocked or surprised, just thoughtful, a pensive little frown on her forehead. At communion time, with every external manifestation of sincere devotion, she walked up to receive communion—in the hand, no less.

After Mass, the young priest greeted Lynnie by name; he recognized the pet novelist too, but had the good taste to comment only with an extra grin.

"Don't they recognize sacrilege in the church anymore?" O'Neill asked as she linked her arm with his and led him to a German restaurant for breakfast.

"Sacrilege?" She was baffled.

"Unless I have a very bad memory, you were engaged in what we used to call 'fornication' last night," he responded drily.

"Oh, *that!* Don't be silly. Fornication may be something that kids do, but at our age it is impossible. We are trying to see whether we can love one another again . . . canceling out a lot of bad time. It would be sinful not to. You don't really think God minds, do you?" She patted his arm reassuringly and dragged him down Halsted Street.

"I suppose a notorious sinner and apostate like me should receive communion and God wouldn't mind either," he snorted. "What's so funny?"

Lynnie had thrown back her head and was shaking with laughter. "Oh, darling, you are so funny," she gasped between laughs.

He waited impatiently. "My moral condition is funny?"

She gripped his arm tightly. "Of course not, silly, *you're* funny. A great public sinner . . . wild-living reprobate, bloated, pleasure-loving hedonist . . ." More laughter.

Now his feelings were hurt. "Lynnie, I have not been either a celibate or a saint," he said testily.

"Poor baby, I am hurting your feelings and I don't mean to." She patted his arm again. "Anyhow, the church might object if you waltzed up to the communion rail, but God would feel just like I do. That it's nice to have you back. But he'd have better manners than me and wouldn't laugh at you." She steered him into the restaurant.

The warm dining room was crowded and noisy; sunlight filtering through stained-glass windows cast goblin glows on the faces of the waiters. The dense air smelled of spring, or maybe it was only Sunday perfume. Was the ethnic atmosphere authentic or ersatz? The bratwurst was tart and juicy, and the wine sweet and light. After his second glass he began to feel the serene peace of a Bavarian country beer garden. Chicago wasn't such a bad city, after all.

The boats bobbing on the lake blurred into spots of

color. Chicago was a magic city, a Camelot, Samarkand, Katmandu. Lynnie was a magic princess, a modern Guinevere or Delvchaem. He was the knight come to free her from the castle in which she was imprisoned. A fine knight he was.

He started the car and drove onto Lake Shore Drive, back to the Drake and another session of fingers suspended over a typewriter. He and Lynnie were to have supper at La Bastille on Superior Street that evening with Jerry Lynch and his wife. Jerry was a couple of years ahead of him in school, a successful criminal lawyer now, the St. Jude of trial law, Lynnie had called him. She was discreetly bringing back people from the past, hoping, perhaps, to kill off the demons which haunted her hesitant knightly lover.

Superior Street was not a slum anymore. The old buildings were either replaced by parking lots or converted into expensive restaurants and offices. Somewhere along the row of restaurants there had been a long time ago the offices of the Catholic Action organization to which their young priest had been so committed. What had happened to them?

Lynnie would join him at the restaurant. She insisted on driving to and from the West Side by herself. "I'd never forgive myself if you fell asleep coming back from the suburbs," she had explained with a laugh. They would make love in his hotel room afterwards. His heartbeat quickened at the thought.

He recognized Jerry Lynch's crinkly grin immediately. Other than his graying hair, he had not changed in twenty years, and O'Neill knew that they would still

109

like each other. Even in his businesslike manner, Lynch seemed genuinely glad to see him.

"You remember my wife, Margie, of course," he said formally, indicating a small brown-haired woman in her middle thirties with enormous flashing eyes.

"Of course, he doesn't remember me, Jeremiah. Eighth-graders are too big a deal to notice second-grade girls." But she took his hand warmly enough. Her eyes swallowed him, sized him up, and made a decision as to how far she could go. "Lynnie is right. You're still gorgeous . . . and famous too. See, Jerry, there are more honest ways of making money than spending your whole day in a smelly courtroom."

"Darling you hardly know him," protested Lynch feebly.

"There are some kinds of brown eyes you never forget," he replied smoothly. "I remember holding the paten for you when you made your first communion."

Margie Lynch didn't lose a syllable. "Didn't I tell you, Jerry? It just takes bullshit to be a writer." But she flushed with pleasure.

It was going to be an interesting evening. Lynnie was choosing the kind of people from the neighborhood who would demolish his cherished myths.

She arrived just then in a shoulderless black dress and a lace shawl. "My dear," said Margie Lynch, "you look even more devastating than usual. I haven't seen you look so sexy since the last time you chased a man." She kissed Lynnie on the cheek. "Don't let this one get away." She turned to O'Neill. "You are going to make an honest woman out of her, aren't you? We

110

married types can't afford to have this kind of competition on the loose."

Lynnie flushed deeply—something she rarely did in public—color spreading even to her throat and shoulders.

"Don't push him, Margie," she laughed back, not at all displeased. "This kind you have to go after subtly."

"That dress isn't exactly subtle, darling, but I'm on your side. He does have such sad, pained eyes."

"The sad eyes are my defense against housewives who want to talk about my novels."

"This is going to be a fun night. I'm glad you brought up your novels. I've got a few suggestions for revising them. You're really a dreadfully old-fashioned writer, you know. . . ." With Lynnie joining her in reckless enthusiasm, she launched into an elaborately detailed plan for turning *The Parable Problem* into a sex extravaganza. He was no match for them—their conversation was animated and clever, the sort Monique and Etienne would enjoy—more extravagant, perhaps, but definitely intelligent. He began to relax, aided by the white wine which was presentable even by Parisian standards.

Lynnie did indeed look stunning. Her dress, like every piece of clothing in her immense collection was calculated to display her superb body at its best. Still, despite her loveliness and wit, she seemed tired tonight. The lines around her eyes seemed deeper. During lulls in the conversation she seemed preoccupied, distracted—the businesswoman who could not leave her work at the office. He put his hand on her thigh under the table. No reaction. What's wrong? . . .

"What kind of work are you doing now, Jerry?" he asked during a brief moment when both women were silent.

"I'm trying to keep Ted Masterman out of the U.S. Senate," the lawyer responded, filling his wine glass again.

"Who's he?"

"Jimmy only reads the *New York Times*," cut in Lynnie with weary irony.

"The U.S. Attorney in these parts. He's using the immunity provision to build himself a big reputation as a stern crusader for justice. If you get enough big scalps on your lance, then you move on to higher office, perhaps even the presidency."

"Immunity provision?" He knew that he was embarrassing Lynnie by his ignorance, but he was curious.

Lynch patiently explained. "Look, let's suppose that you are a building contractor with important political contacts. You make regular contributions to campaigns. Then the IRS starts an audit, and it turns out they can get you for tax evasion. An assistant U.S. Attorney has a talk with you; he wonders about your campaign contributions. There are broad hints to you or your lawyer that maybe these were bribes. You're told you're going to be called before the grand jury to testify; your lawyer says that you will take the Fifth Amendment. The assistant D.A. says that if you do, they may just grant you immunity from prosecution because they're very interested in your contributions to so-and-so. It's all very indirect and informal, but if you give any sign that you're willing to testify against so-and-so, they'll put you up before the grand jury, give you immunity against all charges, and get you to testify against so-and-so. They indict him, you testify in the trial, he goes to jail on a conspiracy or perjury charge, you get off scot-free, and Ted has another scalp."

"What's wrong with that?" asked O'Neill. "Isn't the politician a crook?"

"We have the odd notion in this country," Jerry went on, his eyes hard, his fingers gripping the stem of the wine glass, "that crook or not, the man has a right to a fair trial. It's not a fair trial when the U.S. Attorney invites perjury against you."

"You mean that the contribution wasn't a bribe?" asked O'Neill.

"Maybe it was and maybe it wasn't," said Marge Lynch bitterly. "Lots of campaign contributions are not. You expect the man is going to help your business, but there's no conspiracy, explicit or implicit. Try convincing a jury of that."

"Jim Thompson used the immunity technique to get Otto Kerner and Eddie Barrett and a lot of policemen," said Lynch, his face grim in the candlelight. "He's governor—maybe he'll be president. Masterman has discovered that you can get an indictment against almost any business or professional man in town. The only thing defense can do is go after the credibility of the immunized witnesses. Damn it, Jimmy, there are people being indicted and sent to jail who are innocent—innocent legally and some of them innocent morally."

"The son of a bitch is a Nazi," snapped Margie.

"You can always plea-bargain and stay out of jail if you're relatively small fish. Masterman is more interested in guilty pleas than he is in jail sentences. Part of the price is usually testimony against someone else. Only you, God, and the victim know whether it's perjury or not."

"This is the United States. He can't do that," O'Neill protested.

"He is doing it, Jimmy," said Lynch heavily, "and the press is letting him get away with it because they figure it's good to see political types go to jail—especially if they're Irish."

"Is he a hypocrite?"

"Was Stalin? I don't know. I suppose he's convinced himself that he's leading a crusade against a graft-ridden society. Oh, we'll stop him eventually, though it may take legislation from Congress. But in the meantime . . . in the meantime, he's ruining people's lives. And some of them, at least, are innocent victims."

Margie saw that her husband was upset and deftly changed the subject to post-Daley politics. Lynch's face cleared and he began to tell political anecdotes. O'Neill wished he had a notebook. Maybe there was a story here in Chicago.

It was a good evening, he told himself as he and Lynnie rode up the elevator to his suite in the Drake. The Lynches were a fascinating couple, the kind of people he would want as friends if he stayed in

Chicago.

"Nice folk," he said, feeling carefree and relaxed from the wine.

"She's crazy, but nice."

"She was right about how sexy you look." He tried to leer.

"A widow woman *has* to try," she answered with a fatigued sigh. Despite his relaxed mood, their love-making was dreary. Lynnie's heart was not in it. Maybe she just kept up the pretense because he was hungry for affection. Tonight she was not up to the pretense. He felt angry and guilty.

"Sorry, darling. Ran out of steam tonight."

He kissed her forehead tenderly. "No complaints," he lied.

"I'd better go." She sat up to get out of bed. "The kids will be worrying."

Impulsively he pulled her back and kissed her again. "What's wrong, Lynnie? Can I help?"

There were tears in her eyes. "You're a darling, Jimmy, you really are. No, you can't help. Poor Jerry didn't know it, but I'm one of Masterman's most recent victims."

He sat up angrily, now wide awake. "The bastard won't get away with it," he exclaimed.

She patted his arm. "Thanks, Jimmy, it's not your fight. You stay out of it. Go back to Paris."

He kissed her again, this time fiercely. "The hell it's not my fight. I care about you; you're not going to jail."

The tears slipped slowly down her face. "Just this moment, Jimmy, I'm hoping that's true." She kissed his cheek softly. "You're sweet and I'm glad you're here. Still, I should go home."

He watched the wisp of the black dress slide over her delectable hips. "Who's your lawyer? Is he any good?"

"Eddie Howard. He's an old-timer and very good. You remember him, he was from the neighborhood. We'll get Jerry, of course, if it goes to trial."

"When do you see him? I'll be there."

She stood at the door, head bowed, looking every day of her forty years despite the bare shoulders. She hesitated, deciding whether to accept his offer of help. Fleetingly he hoped she would reject it.

"Eleven o'clock tomorrow, 111 West Washington."

She rushed back to the bed, covered his face with hasty kisses, then fled the room as he reached out to catch her.

Oh, God, he thought, what have I got myself into now?

After she left he could not sleep. The anguished sirens of ambulances racing through the night on Lake Shore Drive toward the Northwestern University Medical Center shattered his presleep reveries—near-dreams in which he was fighting to escape from Lynnie, often beating her in his desperation . . . more blood . . . Enugu . . . the lake. He got up and turned on the light. He wanted a cigarette despite his promise to Clare; maybe one addiction would cure another.

He got out of bed and sank into a chair near the window. What was the hold she had on him? Why could he not tear himself away? When she was absent he could make his resolutions. Then the sound of her laugh, the touch of her hand, her timid warmth in his arms, her dancing eyes, the skyrocket bursts of her temper, the sad lines on her face when he was silent and preoccupied . . . more powerful chains than his lust.

Wearily he turned off the light and went back to bed, worrying, as he finally drifted to sleep, about the encounter in the lawyer's office a few hours away.

 8

O'Neill twisted restlessly in his deep and uncomfortable chair. Eleven-fifteen and he already needed a drink. He was drinking too much. When this business was over, he would have to give it up completely—the failure of the Irish. He felt like the eleventh player on a basketball team, someone whose presence on the bench is an embarrassment to the coach and the other players.

He only vaguely remembered Eddie Howard, an honest former assistant state's attorney whom his father had liked. O'Neill decided he didn't like him. The white-haired, red-faced lawyer was ponderous and pedantic. His personality fit the dark, old-fashioned office which looked out through dirty windows on the Daley Civic Center Plaza and the bizarre Picasso metal sculpture staring mordantly at the passing world in a heavy spring rain. Howard made it clear that he didn't like O'Neill's presence. His young associate, a sleek, heavy-eyed woman named Nancy Carsello, was equally unfriendly. Affirmative action in a small, prestigious law office, or was she as smart as the old man was alleged to be? She seemed distinctly hostile to Lynnie, too.

"I don't want there to be any doubt about it, Mrs. Slattery," Howard pontificated. "This is a very serious matter. The United States Attorney for Northern Illinois is, ah, a man with a fine sense of the media's importance in his work. You would make an excellent defendant for him. A jury wouldn't like you; the media would enjoy presenting your picture to the public on the ten o'clock news every night."

"Is that what law is about now?" snapped O'Neill impatiently. "Media image and jury reaction? What's happened to such things as justice and innocence?"

Howard glared at him, twisting one of his heavy gold rings. "Mr. O'Neill," he said pompously, "we are not talking about law. We are talking about a possible indictment and trial in the Northern District of Illinois. Law will have little to do with it, and justice is dispensed by juries who separate the innocent from the guilty. Mrs. Slattery is the granddaughter of alleged Prohibition bootleggers; she has cousins who are well-known members of the uh . . . 'outfit'—it doesn't matter if she has nothing to do with them. Her father was a famous political operator whose dealings would not stand the scrutiny of today's prosecutors and grand jurors. Her late husband, God have mercy on him, did some rather foolish things in the last years of his life.

She has made a great deal of money in a very short time; she is entirely too attractive for a woman of her years. She has very serious problems, Mr. O'Neill, very serious problems." He paused to light a cigar which must have been smuggled from Havana.

"This makes me guilty?" said Lynnie in a subdued voice.

"Of course not, darling," said Nancy Carsello acidly, "but it does mean you start out causing special difficulties for your lawyers."

O'Neill almost said that lawyers were supposed to solve problems, not talk about them, but kept quiet. He wasn't helping by reacting to the hostility of Lynnie's attorneys. They had, he supposed, good reason to be suspicious of him, showing up suddenly after twenty years. Besides, Howard probably figured he was as unstable as his father.

"My dear Mrs. Slattery," Howard went on, the slight tremor in his hand appearing again as he reached for an ashtray, "there is a chance you will do so well before the grand jury that the United States Attorney will not think it worth his while to seek an indictment. There is a possibility that he will grant you immunity from prosecution to ask you questions which are pertinent to other, more serious cases. If you are indicted, there is a possibility that we can plea-bargain for a suspended sentence or probation of some sort. If the case goes to trial, there is always the possibility that someone like Jerry Lynch will be able to sufficiently discredit the government's witnesses against you to create a reasonable doubt in the jury's mind about your guilt. Even with a conviction, a sensible judge would hardly want to send you to jail; but in this district we have several judges who believe in giving the maximum punishment to politically related persons. There is, finally, the possibility that the Seventh Circuit Court will overturn a conviction. Thus, as you see, there are five or six turning points, at each one of which, with any good fortune, events could turn in your favor." He paused, his index finger pressing the thumb of his left hand. Having achieved the required dramatic effect, he went on, "But I will not hide from you the possibility—not proximate but not remote either—that you could spend anywhere from one to two years in a correctional institution of the federal government. Do I make myself clear?"

"Yes, Mr. Howard," said Lynnie weakly, "I guess you do."

"And good-looking blondes are just what the butches in those places are looking for," said Nancy Carsello cruelly. Lynnie winced.

Howard went on implacably. "I must therefore stress the importance of this situation for your family. Even without a term in prison, you and your children are going to be exposed to considerable unfavorable publicity from the media. Litigation could go on for years; it will be a serious financial drain on you and an immense personal drain. There is no choice in the matter. It may seem unjust; protesting against the circumstances will not alter them. Do I make myself clear, Mrs. Slattery?"

Lynnie's shoulders were sagging. She looked old

and tired. She would grow old, he thought, under the pressures of the mess she was in. Anger began to stir.

"Yes, very clear, Mr. Howard."

"Very well, I shall proceed. I have been given to understand that Mr. Majorski, the assistant state's attorney, has hinted to you in an elevator at the Federal Building that you might be given immunity if you were willing to testify to the grand jury about the alleged conspiracy concerning the mental health center land, testimony I assume against County Commissioner Donaghey. It was improper of Mr. Majorski to make such a hint, of course; but, unlike his colleague Mr. Ryan, he still has some humanity about him. I must assume that Mr. Majorski was sending me a signal. May I ask you whether under such a grant of immunity you would testify about the alleged meeting between the commissioner and the owners of the land where the Northwest Mental Health Center was built?"

There was a moment of pale silence in the room. It had stopped raining. The Picasso looked distinctly unhappy. "If I were to testify about such a meeting it would be perjury, Mr. Howard," said Lynnie, straightening her shoulders. Howard sighed, either in relief or resignation.

"Please understand, Mrs. Slattery, my position. I will certainly not be a party to suborning perjury. Yet in this kind of case one of the problems of an attorney is to understand what his clients have really done and said. There are people in jail at this moment who would not be there if they had told their attorneys the truth. Legally you are innocent till you are proven guilty; while I see at present little evidence of any wrongful act on your part, I must impress on you again the need to answer all my questions truthfully." He paused, relighting the cigar. Carsello stirred uneasily on her hard-backed chair. Sexy creature. "I have no reason to think you have not done so," Howard went on. "Yet, again, I must ask you, did you indeed never attend such a meeting as Mr. Mannion, one of the other landowners, has apparently described to the United States Attorney?"

There was a quick flash of flame in Lynnie's eyes, a flare of temper which ebbed just as quickly as it had come. She brushed the blond hair away from her face. "Mr. Howard, I know you have to be sure. I know you have lots of kinky clients in this kind of case; whatever kinkiness there may have been on either side in my family, I didn't inherit any of it. I've told you the truth as best as I can."

Again the sigh. "Would you mind repeating it for me? I need to have every detail clear."

Lynnie watched her lawyer intently for a moment and then smiled, lighting up the dark room, even melting ever so slightly the frosty blue eyes of Eddie Howard. "I didn't know, Mr. Howard, that I owned the land until the county started the condemnation proceedings. I had to hunt among the papers my husband left in the basement to find the deeds. I did not meet with any of the other owners before then; I didn't know that Commissioner Donaghey owned shares in the secret land trust holding half the land; I accepted the price settlement between the county and the

122

owners. The money helped put my company back on its feet, but we were already out of the woods when the settlement was made, and it has had little effect on my income since. I gave exactly one hundred dollars to Commissioner Donaghey's campaign the year before the sale of the land. I couldn't afford the hundred dollars, but I wanted to keep something of the family tradition alive no matter how bad things were. Three years after the sale I made a thousand-dollar contribution, but that was much less a proportion of my income than the one before. My family has supported the commissioner since he first ran for public office. The commissioner never spoke to me about the land, never requested a campaign contribution from me. I think my husband did contribute to his campaign before he died, but I can find no record of it. My husband never spoke to me about the land or about the health center. He may have had agreements with the commissioner—though, candidly, I doubt it—but neither of them ever mentioned them to me. I've never met Mr. Mannion, wouldn't know him on the street if I passed him; I never attended any meetings with him or anyone else. As you recall, I was not even in court during the condemnation proceedings." She paused, breathless. O'Neill's heart ached for the pain which was masked by those lucid sentences.

"A conspiracy charge on the basis of trivial campaign contributions—the miserable, lousy son of a bitch, the filthy bastard!" Nancy Carsello exploded, then added in embarrassment, "Sorry, honey, I'm from Taylor Street."

"A generation away doesn't make that much difference," Lynnie said grimly. "I share the sentiments. You just beat me to it."

The woman lawyer softened noticeably; she even smiled.

"Miss . . . er . . . Carsello," Eddie Howard broke in, ignoring the outbreak, "has certain . . . er . . . contacts at the U. S. Attorney's office. She has some . . . er . . . useful background information."

"I keep telling you, Eddie, I don't sleep with him; in fact the bastard hasn't suggested it." The smile broadened. "Anyhow, Mrs. Slattery, you should never have talked to those IRS agents without one of us present. Those two bastards—I'm sorry, I'm fixated on the word—are two of the meanest people in the world. They were trying to trick you into a lie that could serve as the basis for an indictment. Much to their regret they had to give you a clean bill of health. You followed the conservative deduction policies we recommend and there's nothing they can seriously question, which . . . you should excuse me, Eddie . . . is more than can be said for most of our clients in your business. Besides, you have a good memory, so you didn't even make any unintentionally inaccurate statements. They can't get you on income tax. Mannion has testified you were at the meeting of the owners when they agreed to make substantial contributions to Commissioner Donaghey's campaign; no one else admits the meeting ever took place. Ryan is leaning on a number of other people whose slates aren't as clean as yours. Majorski is arguing that it would be a mistake to go after you

124

because the charge is so ludicrous it would discredit the whole case. He's probably right, but we're dealing with slippery characters, goddamn them." Carsello's face was dusky red now, her fists clenched.

"It's a frameup!" exploded O'Neill, no longer able to contain himself.

She grinned. "For a novelist you catch on quick, Mr. O'Neill. Of course it's a frameup, though not completely. That's the damnable part of it. 'Turk' Donaghey certainly had a technical conflict of interest going. He was the chairman of the subcommittee of the county board which approved the selection of the land for the mental health facility, and he owned in secret trust half the land it was to be built on. He should have disqualified himself But he didn't promote the site and all the Chicago papers praised the citizens' committee which recommended the location. It was a completely uncontroversial decision four years ago. Donaghey bought the land in the 1940s, the same time your father did, Mrs. Slattery, knowing that it was an ideal spot for government construction. The expressway plans were on the public record. Anyone could have guessed the property would be valuable. Was there a conspiracy? Who knows? Maybe some of the other owners were discreetly advised to contribute to the Donaghey campaign fund; it wouldn't be the first time something like that has happened; they never had an actual meeting. The Turk is too smart to do anything like that—though," she finished lamely, "that's the kind of thing everyone knows, but you can't argue before a jury."

125

"Hopefully we will not have to argue before a jury. Perhaps we will not even have to appear before a grand jury," Howard said in his pedantic style, as though nothing had been said since the last time he spoke. The girl called him Eddie and got away with it; he even seemed faintly amused by her language—a complicated old guy. "I cannot urge you not to worry, because there are sufficient grounds for worry. I can urge you, though, to have confidence in yourself. There are ample grounds for that. Now if you and Mr. O'Neill will excuse us. And, incidentally, Mr. O'Neill, I cannot tell you how much I have enjoyed your stories. There are few Irish storytellers left, as I have told Miss Carsello. I fear that she has not read your books yet, though I venture to say she will shortly." Even his mirth was frosty.

"I won't call you a bastard, Eddie, because they'll think I have a dumb dago vocabulary," the girl protested.

A strange pair. Lynnie seemed to have won them over. He wanted to take her to lunch; but distant and preoccupied, she insisted that she must return to her office. Had she told her children yet? Poor kids, it would be hell on them. He walked slowly back to the Drake, a deep current of rage slowly building.

Every time he rode up the elevator at the Drake he thought of her waiting in the room for him. After one of her temper tantrums he returned late at night to discover a sliver of light under his door. The wariness from his foreign correspondent days came back. It was not a secret police agent though; rather Lynnie, fresh from the shower, a towel around her waist, smelling of soap and weeping her apologies. He'd entered the empty apartment on the Avenue Kennedy too many times, lamenting that there was no one waiting for him. Now occasionally someone was waiting, even if she had stolen his key. Lynnie with a towel knotted at her hips was worth coming home to.

She was not waiting for him, and he felt foolish for thinking she might be.

 9

"Of course, you don't have to go to dinner at the Sterns," Jerry Lynch said, running his fingers through his gray hair. "I only agreed to see if you would be interested because Stern is the kind of ally Lynnie needs. Besides, he's a nice guy for a liberal Hyde Park Jewish lawyer. His second wife's a bitch, I'll admit, but what the hell . . ."

They were having a "quick drink" at Sherlock's Home, a plush Michigan Avenue pub where the great detective would have felt distinctly out of place, unless he wanted to meet very chic late-twentyish female swinging singles. Sunk deeply into a chair at a table in the dark corner of the bar savoring a bottle of Guinness, O'Neill decided that it was in fact a slave market with some very interesting wares.

"Why should Masterman be worried about Stern's liberal conscience? It seems like a long shot to me," he

127

said dubiously, avoiding the eyes of a gorgeous girl whose hair was as red as his and who had mistaken his discreet appreciation for active interest. Poor girl, with those looks she shouldn't have to be so eager. On principle he disapproved of slave markets. Still. . . .

Jerry sighed. "Keep your mind on the conversation, Jimmy . . . and for the love of heaven, remember the signals have changed since you were that age."

"I never was that age. Anyway, you were just telling me that Stern is an anti-Organization Democrat with lots of money of his own and more available through fund-raising, and that Masterman is counting on his support when he runs. But Masterman is a conservative Republican, isn't he?"

"I'll do it once more, Jimmy, but don't look at that blonde who just came in. You ought to get married real soon if you're going to stay in this city . . . it's a lot worse than Paris. If you're a liberal Democrat of the Hyde Park variety, you end up preferring conservative Republicans to Organization Democrats—even if the Democrats vote your way when they get to Congress—because the Republicans are moral and, more important, they are also against the Organization. The idea is to put together a coalition of Jewish liberals, Protestant Republicans, and the black middle class, and finally turn the Irish out of power."

"Can they do it?"

"Of course not. The blacks don't like us all that much, but they like the other guys less—ditto for the Poles, who the reformers wouldn't take as a gift. Anyway, Stern is a good enough guy—not personally ambitious, though the current Ms. Stern is just out of law school and I think wants to be a state senator herself—and he's troubled about the indictment of politicians for technical crimes other people wouldn't be charged with. He's been doing a lot of crying on my shoulder about it lately. Unlike most of the limousine-liberal types, he figures you should have the same kind of justice for politicians and radicals, black poor people and rich people." Lynch nervously played with his glass of club soda, paying no attention to the young women in the bar. Margie must be all she seemed to be. "Which, by the way, is the good old-fashioned American notion that a person is innocent till proven guilty."

"So why does he cozy up with Masterman?"

Jerry shrugged expressively. "Because in his heart of hearts he believes Irish politicians are guilty, which God knows some of them are. So I tell him that a lot of people who are innocent in every sense of the word are going to get hurt. He doesn't know any such people, but then he wants to have you over to dinner because he fancies himself an expert on literature . . . hell, he may be. I figure you bring Lynnie along, then when her name breaks in the papers—and between you and me it's almost certainly going to—he gets worried about innocent people and has a long talk with Ted . . . follow me?"

O'Neill emptied his bottle of Guinness and debated another. "Yeah, I guess so, but it sounds like a long shot."

Only to someone who doesn't know how things get done in this city," Jerry replied brusquely, tapping his glass on the table. "It's not a long shot; it's a lucky break."

"Jerry, why are they going after her?" he asked as he snatched the bill and gave a ten to their black-eyed and very friendly Cuban waitress. "They don't really think she's a criminal, do they?"

"You know, the funny thing is they probably do." The lawyer ran his fingers through his hair again as they walked toward the door, pushing their way through the incoming rush of customers. "It suits their political purposes. Look at the facts from the perspective of Masterman's crew and the reporters, and there's no way this is going to be kept out of the papers much longer. His office was deliberately created to be a sieve. Her father was a crooked politician; her mother the sister of mob types; her husband was a shady and inept second-rate operator. She makes a lot of money in a few years after his death and cuts quite a figure in the social world. If you're a reformer or a crusader who thinks most Irish people are corrupt to begin with, she's the perfect target. You mix envy with prejudice and political expediency and she's the perfect target."

They were out in the drizzle, caught in the rush of six o'clock pedestrians from Michigan Avenue. "And in most cases with that kind of evidence, they'd probably be right?" O'Neill asked.

Lynch nodded his head grimly. "Precisely."

"Are you going to marry Lynnie?" Lynch asked abruptly as they fought against the flow of humanity on Delaware Place. Like a smart pol he'd waited till the end of the conversation so there would be no long discussion.

"One of the favorite themes of American literature," O'Neill replied evasively, searching for the top of Hancock Center in the mists, anything to avoid Lynch's shrewd little eyes, "is about the middle-aged successful male who returns home with a nostalgic dream of his childhood sweetheart, discovers she was much less than the woman he dreamed she was, then leaves a sadder but wiser man."

"Wiser?" said Lynch skeptically as they huddled in the drizzle at the corner of Michigan, oblivious to the people swirling around them.

O'Neill continued to avoid his eyes and tried to sound like a college professor. "Sure. He learns you can't go home again, you can't become young again, you can't live your life again. So with this wisdom he passes gracefully over the bar, so to speak, and settles down to accept growing old."

"And you've learned all these things, Jimmy?" He sounded worried now.

"No way," said O'Neill hollowly. "I haven't learned a goddamn one of them—not yet anyway."

Lynch found his answer extremely funny, grasped his hand in farewell, and dashed across Michigan Avenue toward the spiral ramp of the Hancock garage.

Now what made me say that? Since when does my story fit the middle-aged, middle-American myth? Why did Lynch think it was so funny? Hell, I thought it was funny. . . .

On his way across the street to the Drake he

regretted that he'd accepted Emil Stern's invitation. In his night school days at Loyola, the University of Chicago types he'd encountered in the Rush Street bars threatened the hell out of him; besides, their crowd had writers who won Nobel prizes. He'd be out of place. It was a long shot anyway, despite what Lynch had said. He'd call him the next day and say he changed his mind.

He thought again of the gorgeous redhead at Sherlock's Home. Why did girls like her have to go out on the prowl? Was that the America Clare was coming home to? Someone ought to talk some sense into the woman's head. . . . She was probably lonely. Loneliness does odd things to you. Should he go back to the pub?

He took his jacket out of the closet, stared at it thoughtfully, then ruefully put it back. No fool like an old fool. He turned on the TV instead.

 10

Rectories, he told himself, shifting uneasily in the deeply cushioned chair, had changed like everything else. The abstract sunburst on the wall was doubtless the Sacred Heart. There was a Bible on the blond coffee table, a modern translation which revolted him—people in the Bible should say "thou" instead of "you." Light beige and cream colors and modern furniture made the rectory office look more like a waiting room of an expensive dentist or the antechamber in a high-class bordello.

It wasn't an office. No grim old desk with a priest sitting behind it like a hanging judge; a couch and chairs were arranged casually around a low table. "You can wait for the pastor in the counseling room," the trim blond teenager had told him when she ushered him into the rectory hallway.

"Counseling room." He wasn't coming to be counseled. Did the priest know he was sleeping with Lynnie? Did he care? Had he ever cared? What the hell? . . .

The girl had smiled warmly as she left him to wait for the "pastor"; she almost slipped and called him "Uncle Mike." He remembered her from the High Club picnic. One of Cora's friends. Did Cora's friends know he was sleeping with her mother? Did they care? Did Cora care? Did anyone care about anything? Did the girl think he was making wedding arrangements? Was that why she smiled?

Impatiently he heaved himself out of the chair—the counselor's chair?—and peered out the window. Big home, old oak trees, kids playing on a warm spring evening. He had looked out on this street twenty-five years before while waiting for the same priest. Now the homes were bigger, the trees older, the street broader, and the cars infinitely more expensive. The neighborhood had moved and repackaged itself, and was now as elegant and permissive as the rectory parlor. Were there any young men who dreamed of adventure and storytelling inside the Tudor and Dutch colonial houses? They were probably getting fellowships from the parish these days. There was nothing left to hate—a neighborhood which doted on writers, a church with a shapely teenager at the rectory door, a pastor called "Uncle Mike," a once-inaccessible childhood sweetheart who was now anything but inaccessible. He wanted to fight the past, only it wouldn't fight back. He didn't like anticlimaxes.

"There's a . . . complication," Eddie Howard had said, pausing dramatically before the last word as he carefully scissored the end off a cigar.

"A great big skyscraper of a complication," echoed Nancy Carsello, exhaling in weary exasperation, which emphasized the shape of her impressive torso under a light spring blouse.

"And the name of the complication," continued Howard, apparently unaware of his colleague's sexual charms, "is the Roman Catholic archbishop of Chicago." He lit his cigar with elaborate care. "May I continue, Mr. O'Neill?" he asked politely, eyeing him over the glowing ash.

"Why not?" asked O'Neill with sinking heart. He stayed away from the lawyer's office because he felt so useless. Lynnie was his woman, in one fashion or another. She was under assault from powerful and implacable enemies, and there had been nothing he could do about it. Now he was being given a chance to do something about it and he didn't like the prospect. He didn't want to be useless, but he didn't want to be too useful either.

"It *is* possible that you may be of some help in the

134

matter, though I do not relish involving you in a project which . . . to put the issue mildly indeed . . . is bizarre." He sighed heavily and looked away from O'Neill.

"I'll be happy to do whatever I can," Jim said lamely.

"Indeed, yes . . . well, Mr. O'Neill, it is, if I may say so, the sort of thing you would not dream of putting in one of your engrossing tales." He paused again, fidgeting with his cigar. "Not to put too fine an edge on matters, we want you to persuade the Roman Catholic archbishop of Chicago to give us an important document which he . . . or, more exactly, his legal advisors . . . claim does not exist, a document which may be critical to Mrs. Slattery's case."

"Poor lovely lady," sighed Nancy Carsello sadly. O'Neill was startled by the compassion in her voice and even more by the sadness in her brown eyes. The girl was still a virgin, he decided.

"You're right," he gulped. "I wouldn't think of putting that in a story."

Howard eyed him speculatively. "Let me briefly outline the facts of the matter. Then my associate will describe the . . . er . . . problems we have with His . . . er . . . Eminence."

He paused again. The man sure wants enough signals to go ahead, O'Neill thought with rising anxiety. "Please do." He tried to sound like one of his resourceful, confident heroes.

"Commissioner Donaghey has no . . . uh . . . issue of his own. Thus he has been particularly concerned about the political and financial career of his nephew,

135

one Charles Stewart Parnell Donaghey, a wealthy middle-aged gentleman who, for reasons which would be obvious if you should have occasion to meet him, is known to most of his associates as Tubbo. He at one time served as the chairman of the board of the Queen of America Roman Catholic Foundation. This was a charitable institution established by the then-pastor of the Queen of America parish, Msgr. Peter Michael Green. To be blunt, the foundation's purpose was to funnel income from his well-to-do parishioners into a place of safekeeping—safe, that is, from the inquiring minds of the chancery office. I might note, by the way, that Msgr. Green, may the Lord grant him rest, was a lifelong friend of Commissioner Donaghey. Do you follow me?"

"I'm afraid so," O'Neill admitted.

"Yes. Well, it would appear that shortly before his death, Mrs. Slattery's husband contributed ten thousand dollars to the foundation with a draft signed by himself and his wife. It would appear that the same week the board, at the suggestion of . . . er . . . Tubbo Donaghey, increased that gentleman's annual salary by the exact same amount. The younger Mr. Donaghey is now under investigation by the Internal Revenue Service and the United States Attorney for other matters, since his administration of the foundation was sufficiently in the past to be covered by the statute of limitations. The information which my young colleague has assembled from her . . . ah . . . sources indicates that the aforementioned Tubbo is now willing to testify for the United States Attorney against his uncle."

"Bastard," snarled Nancy.

You belong in one of my stories, flaming virgin, he thought.

"Now please, Miss Carsello. We must restrain ourselves, though I will concede I do not find his behavior particularly admirable. In any event it would appear from our ... ah ... friends—would that be the proper word, Miss Carsello?" The young woman turned a dusty rose but smiled—so there *was* banter between this bizarre twosome. "It would appear that he is also willing to admit on the witness stand that the check from Mr. and Mrs. Slattery was in fact a bribe to his uncle, made in the guise of a contribution to a religious organization and hence was tax-deductible, I might add. Now this transaction is covered by the statute of limitations and certainly is not indictable; however, if Mrs. Slattery knew of the ... er ... contribution, and Tubbo is willing to testify that she did, then her claim to have been no part of her husband's other dealings with the commissioner, as well as her claim to be the innocent widow, is going to be notably impeached. It will not by itself be of decisive legal weight ... ," he paused ponderously to light his cigar, "but it will have a strong impact on a jury unless I am badly mistaken. I put it to you, Mr. O'Neill, if you were a juror, would you believe a woman who used a church organization to bribe a public official?"

His head was whirling. "Lynnie wouldn't do a thing like that."

"Of course not," Howard went on smoothly. "You know it, I know it, Miss Carsello, despite intermittent

bouts of envy for Mrs. Slattery's . . . er . . . attractive-
ness, knows it; but Charles Stewart Parnell Donaghey's allegation, particularly if the press hears of it
beforehand, as I imagine it will, should have a devastating impact on Mrs. Slattery's credibility. Now, if
you don't mind," he crushed his cigar out in an ashtray, his hand trembling ever so slightly, "let me tell
you of the involvement of the Roman Catholic Archdiocese of Chicago. The late archbishop was in awe of
Msgr. Green and did not attempt to interfere with his
financial independence, which, if my sparse knowledge of canon law does not deceive me, was quite
unusual, to say the least. However, the present incum-
bent of the see cares little for the kind of power the late
Msgr. Green had. He promptly retired the monsignor,
bullied the foundation into turning over its assets and
records to him, and moved the funds into special
banking accounts . . . and I will note, by the way, that
the archbishop has indeed a strong affinity for liquid
assets. One hears that the archbishop's accountants,
who are men not totally unfamiliar with the ways
ecclesiastical finances can be manipulated, were
shocked at the activities of the foundation, made a
quick check of their own, and then locked all the
records in the deepest vaults of the chancery office.
They have responded to the U. S. Attorney's inquiries
and to my own less formal questions with the solemn
word that no such records exist, that the late Msgr.
Green destroyed them all before his hasty exit from
Queen of America. No one credits this denial, but it is
unlikely that either side in the case would want to sub-

poena the archbishop's records, or that even if a sub-poena were issued the records would survive long enough for a U.S. marshal to arrive."

O'Neill was weary of this tale of venality and corruption. "Where do I fit in?"

"We're coming to that," said Nancy Carsello, leaning forward eagerly. "There was a young priest named McCarthy on the Queen of America staff at the time of the alleged bribe. He was smart enough to see what was going on but afraid to do anything about it. However, he kept detailed records of the kinky doings and turned them over to the new archbishop. After that he was assigned to a crazy pastor who quite literally worked him to death—a heart attack at thirty-seven."

The girl's voice, calm at the beginning, rose as she told the story.

"Anyway, we have received an anonymous letter from a priest who knew McCarthy and who has heard rumors about this investigation. He says McCarthy told him about the Slattery bribe before he died and insisted that Mrs. Slattery did not know about it. He also says that McCarthy had written a memo to that effect. So you see," her face was aglow with excitement, her hands moving in quick graceful gestures like an accomplished Shakespearean actress in a soliloquy, "if you can get the memo from the archbishop, we'll be able to protect Lynnie . . . er . . . Mrs. Slattery from Tubbo's testimony."

O'Neill's imagination slowly unbuttoned her shirt. The lucky man who would get her—"Why did Lynnie sign the check?" he asked dubiously, rubbing a calf that had fallen asleep as he listened to the dreamy and confusing story.

Howard cleared his throat, and glanced out the window at the Picasso. "I do not know the extent of your relationship with Mrs. Slattery, sir, and hence I do not know what she has told you about her late husband. I will merely say that he was a man of great religious fervor and a very unruly temper. In the months immediately before his death, his wife often feared for the physical safety of herself and her children. She sensed what was later to become all too apparent— namely that their resources had been shamefully squandered. Yet for the sake of peace in the family she felt she had no choice but to acquiesce in his burst of . . . ah . . . charity."

Howard looked acutely embarrassed, as though he had just told a mother that her daughter was pregnant. Poor Lynnie. Oh God, poor Lynnie.

Nancy spared him the awkwardness of further silence. "The archbishop's lawyers assure us there is no such memo. The archbishop will not return our phone calls or answer our letters. He will not speak to Lynnie . . . oh, damn, sorry, Ed . . . Mrs. Slattery, or acknowledge a letter she wrote him. The psychopathic sonofabitch can save her," now her cheeks were flaming red, "and he won't even talk to her, and goddamn it, there's no reason at all. They can phony up any excuse they want about that memo and all the rest of the stuff—who's going to prowl through an archbishop's file? He's going to let her go to jail, after all the things she's done for the Church!"

O'Neill's restless fantasy began to speculate on Ms. Carsello's wedding night, with himself the deflowering groom. He endeavored halfheartedly to dismiss the lovely pictures.

"Come now, Miss Carsello," said Howard sternly, "we must not let sympathy for the client, however merited, interfere with our legal dispassion. We do not even have an indictment, much less a conviction. Our hope, rather, is to avoid both of these events. If we could obtain Father McCarthy's memo, as I'm sure you realize, Mr. O'Neill, the U.S. Attorney would be reluctant to involve our client further. We could have the ability to impeach Charles Donaghey's testimony. Hence you would be doing all of us a very great favor if you could . . . er . . . persuade our good archbishop to be of assistance."

"Why me?" asked O'Neill weakly.

Nancy was on her feet now, hands on her hips, eyes flaring, a Sicilian pirate princess addressing her forces before battle, totally unaware that his undisciplined eyes were tugging her skirt away from those hips. "Let's not be subtle about it, O'Neill. The archbishop is a flake. He does nutty things. Sure he wants to keep the Queen of America thing quiet, but a lot of it's going to come out in the trial anyway unless the government backs off. If his lawyers were smart instead of proper, they'd tell him to give us the memo. Then maybe the whole Tubbo business would die out because Masterman would be afraid to use him against anyone. He's so goddamn stupid," she paused, breathless.

Howard sat impassively. Does he enjoy the show, too, the old gaffer? O'Neill wondered. "I still don't see where I fit in."

"You're almost as stupid as he is," she said impatiently, and then shut off the flow of words. "Oh, I'm so sorry, Mr. O'Neill, that's not true at all. Mr. Howard, I'm sorry." Her hands rushed to her mouth, but the torrent began again. "You see he's a real flake . . ."

"Miss Carsello is trying to describe a very peculiar man," said Howard from left field. "It is indeed hard to control one's emotions when one discusses him. In any case, the fact seems to be that he is what some would call whimsical and others would call capricious. He makes decisions and unmakes them for reasons which may be known to God but to no one else. In addition he is almost childishly attracted to the famous and the powerful."

"And you're famous, as I'm sure you know," Nancy interjected eagerly. "We thought that he'd be real happy to have a visit from a famous novelist, and then . . ."

"I get the picture," said O'Neill glumly, squelching his imagination. Naked pirate princesses were lovely but not when they sent you to face a flaky archbishop.

"You'll do it?" asked the pirate triumphantly.

What choice did he have?

The pastor charged into his rectory parlor just as in the old days, leading with a barrage of exploding questions designed to throw you off guard. "Back in the rectory, eh, Jim? How do you like the new style? Counseling room, eh? Not bad for an old pastor, huh?

New church, you know, gotta do something when you inherit a palace like this, don't you? Hey, whatta ya think about the new church?"

The wee leprechaun priest, an Irish grandmother had called him when he first came back to the old neighborhood. Old neighborhood—God, he was already sounding like he belonged. Uncle Mike still looked like a leprechaun: short, bouncy, green eyes sparkling with merriment. Though there were lines around his mischievous mouth now, he didn't look much different than he had when he was the "young priest."

"When the 'young priest' becomes 'Uncle Mike, the lovable old pastor,' the new church looks kind of interesting," he fired back.

"Same old Jimmy. Well, maybe not. If you delivered a line like that twenty years ago you would have said 'eccentric' instead of 'lovable.' " He collapsed into the couch as if exhausted. Yet his energy level was as high as it used to be. At the High Club picnic he had easily worn all the other adults—O'Neill most especially—into the ground.

The irony of seeing him at the picnic—his hair dusted white but the twinkling eyes as shrewd as ever—the young priest, the pastor of Lynnie's parish; the shrewd bitch had not warned him.

O'Neill was pressured into chaperoning the picnic in old Potawatomi Park, a few acres of worn grass and baseball field on the shores of the muddy, sluggish Fox River—hundreds of screaming adolescent delinquents, including Cora, muscle-bound lifeguards (both male and female) blowing whistles at the side of a swimming pool which smelled as though it were pure chlorine. The pool wasn't there in the old days. Why did the park look so much smaller?

"Come to finish it up, Jimmy?" There was no mistaking the voice. "I'd figured you'd come back eventually. Took your sweet time though."

"You're at her parish, Father?" he asked hesitantly.

"I'm glad to know whose parish it really is. I'm only the pastor." He winked. "Well, good luck to you . . . if not this time, the next, huh?"

"I don't know what you mean, Father," he said uneasily, wishing the man's green eyes didn't see so deeply into his soul. He threw a softball back to a screaming adolescent.

"Not a bad arm for an old man," said the priest. "See you in church, Jim?"

"Don't count on it, Father."

"Ha," said the priest, walking toward a bevy of teenage girls who were screaming, "Father! Father!"

They still adored him. Some things don't change.

Lynnie appeared, a barbecue fork in hand, breathtaking in a white halter and very tight jeans. "Would you help carry the hamburger buns from the station wagon? Hey, why the faraway look?"

"I think it was here I saw you in a halter for the first time."

Still holding the fork, she extended her arms for inspection. "Well, what do you think about me this time?"

"I think about the same thing I thought then, which was pretty dirty. I bet the girls at this picnic

144

hate your guts."

"You are incorrigible. Didn't I see you talking to Micky?"

"You mean the young priest?" he asked, shocked by her disrespect.

"We did use to call him that, didn't we?" she said with a nostalgic smile. "Time does slip away. Anyway, what did you talk about . . . besides me, of course?"

"Arrogant bitch." He touched her bare stomach, moving his fingers slowly from one side to another.

She put her hands behind her back, turned her head aside in a quick expression of pleasure, then stepped away from him. "Don't do that . . . what will the kids say if they see us?"

"I don't care what the kids will say. I wanted to do that to a fourteen-year-old a quarter of a century ago and I didn't. I'm not going to pass up a second chance."

Lynnie beamed. "Don't be a dirty old man, Jimmy. It's not half as good a stomach as it used to be, anyway. Now go get the rolls before you have an old widow in tears." She brushed imaginary hair out of her eyes.

The captive errand boy, he went to the station wagon, a decrepit Dodge which was called the "second car" because it was even older than the Ford. Cars were in the same category as jewelry. You didn't spend money on them—not like clothes—

Delicious, painful images of the park, the muddy river, the teenage noise, Lynnie's body as a girl and as a woman, the taste of burned hot dogs, and the languid lovemaking after the picnic floated through the back of his imagination as he talked to Uncle Mike. Could he see the archbishop? Would Uncle Mike call and set it up? There was a long silence in the room when he finished. Uncle Mike thoughtfully fingered the buttons on his blue shirt.

"Sure, Jimmy. Lord, yes, I'll make the call for you. You've got to do everything you can to help poor Lynnie. I didn't know about this part of the business . . . only . . ."

"Only what, Father?" He couldn't call him Mike, much less Uncle Mike.

"Only I guess I want to protect you from His Prominence. Jim, it's hard for a priest to admit his diocese is presided over by an archbishop who's quite willing to see one of the finest women in the whole country in jail because he's too damn mean to help her."

"Does he have something against Lynnie?" asked O'Neill uncertainly.

"Who knows? He might. She had some run-ins with him when she was on the Charities board. Or he may just not want to be bothered with her letter. Hell, he may not even have read it. Or he may even be in league with Masterman, for all I know. The bastard is capable of anything."

The "young priest" had been the most gentle and charitable of men in the old days. He would not have used such language to describe anyone, much less his bishop. "How did he get to be archbishop, Father?" he asked.

Uncle Mike ran his fingers through his salt-and-pepper hair. "How? The man could be said to have bought the archdiocese. Oh, I don't mean simony like in the Middle Ages, nothing as obvious as that. Ever since he was a student in Rome he impressed important people with 'gifts,' birthday, anniversary presents, five-hundred-dollar 'prayer offerings.' The more power he got, the more money he spent. People in Omaha, where he was before he came here, say it ran into hundreds of thousands a year. When Chicago opened up he just called in his favors and collected on them, too bad for Chicago. Well, I guess Lynnie is worth the trouble, but just keep telling yourself, as we do, that he's not the Church . . . She drives a man right up the wall, doesn't she, Jimmy?"

"I keep telling myself I should go back to Paris," he said slowly.

The priest shrugged. "Won't help. See, the trouble is that it's all been too easy. If the old neighborhood—now the new neighborhood—and the old woman—now the new woman—had greeted you with hatred or contempt, then you'd have something to fight and you'd be happy. But everyone is pleasant to the famous writer and the girl is available and now needs help, and her kids want to capture you the worst way. So the same old question is still there, only it's hard to hide from it, see?" He leaned back in the couch, pleased with his argument.

A lifetime in the priesthood dealing with adolescents had given the man a permanent adolescent syntax. "Not exactly, Father. What is the same old

147

question?"

"Oh, that. Well, it's how much of an Irish male you are."

Somewhere deep down in his stomach there was a sting of anger. "What do you mean by that?"

"Look, Jimmy, face it. All Irish men . . . well, most of us . . . are scared stiff of women, especially the strong ones. I don't know, maybe it's not just Irish men. Personally, if I were in the marriage market, she'd scare me. What she wants done in the parish she gets done. You got away from her once—now for reasons of your own you're giving her another chance. You get away to Paris, nothing is solved; or you stay and, hell, maybe she does smother you and you die. At forty going on forty-one, maybe even that's better."

"You'd know about loneliness, I guess," he said, trying to fend the priest off.

"Me? Gosh no. A lot of married men in the parish are more lonely than I am. The logistics of middle-aged adultery are not so easy these days. Gotta find the time and the place." Uncle Mike stood up—somewhere else to rush to.

"So maybe I should go back to Paris and resign myself to lust and loneliness, since I'm lonely either way," he mumbled.

 11

O'Neill blocked her exit from the car with his arm.

"No way," he said. "Your dress, stockings, and shoes match your eyes. You're not going to hide them behind glasses just so you can pretend to be a goddamn intellectual." He took the glasses out of her unresisting hand and put them back in her purse.

"You're just as frightened of the University of Chicago highbrows as I am. What are we doing here, anyway?" She wrinkled her nose as though she were walking through the lion house at the zoo, appalled by the smell.

He opened the car door and assisted her out. Lovely, lovely. Even they would have to look twice. He couldn't tell her the real reasons. "I want to meet the Great Novelist," he said evasively. "It may motivate me to work for a Nobel Prize."

She sniffed suspiciously. "I've a hunch I'm being shown off, but turnabout is fair play, I guess." She adjusted the sash on her flowing jersey dress. "Okay, boss, I'll be the mysterious mistress of the Irish storyteller. I hear the Great Novelist has a weakness for women."

"Not Irish women."

They walked dubiously up to a vast, turreted Hyde Park mansion, beaming in the late sunlight like a Tolkien castle. The Great Novelist was not there. "The poor man has a very bad stomach," said Emil Stern smoothly, "and as you can imagine, the ordeal of winning the prize made it worse."

"Nonsense, Emil," snapped his wife. "You know as well as I do that he could not stand anyone else sharing some of the attention. He even does his writing surrounded by mirrors. . . .

Ms. Stern, Marsha, was pretty in a thin, tied-back, ash blond way, but she had the tense narrow lips of a dedicated zealot. She was also at least four inches taller than her lean, tiny husband, whose handsome face and high forehead were locked in a permanent expression of ascetic concern.

"It is very good of you to come," he said gently. "Would you have some wine and cheese while we wait for the other guests? They are so eager to meet you. Chicago is fortunate to have one of its own novelists back in the city again. It is a beautiful sign of our cultural growth to recapture you from Paris."

"I'm only a storyteller, Mr. Stern," he said. A parlor with a four thousand-dollar Oriental rug and furniture that looks like a display in a Michigan Avenue Svensk window, and they serve jug wine.

The wine hour went on unconscionably long, and O'Neill was getting woozy from the cheap wine as they awaited the other guests. Are we ever going to eat? His stomach protested vigorously as he went through half a wedge of cheese. Lynnie, having draped her elegant frame on a white leather chair, nursed a single glass of wine, didn't touch the cheese, and didn't say a word.

"Your writings fit into a very interesting new genre, Mr. O'Neill," began Lawrence Bingham, professor of English literature, without any preliminaries. "I've done a number of studies on such works and must say candidly that they show a good deal more vitality and ingenuity than much of our academic fiction. While I generally don't agree with what John Gardner says about 'moral' fiction, I must also say that I admire the integrity of your work. You make no pretense of being anything more than what you are . . . a popular novelist. I find that admirable." He made a pained face at his first taste of the wine.

"Storyteller," corrected O'Neill, not knowing whether to be flattered or offended. Bingham was a lean, shallow-looking man about his age, with a receding hairline and a pipe which seemed to be built into his mouth. Did he eat with it? He seemed to be the kind of professor who took it for granted that others wanted to listen to his lectures. His wife, an immense and exceedingly unattractive woman in a black sweater and brown skirt, made no attempt to hide her boredom.

"As a recent returnee to Chicago, Mr. O'Neill," interrupted Aaron Goldman, a bushy-haired, bushy-bearded young political scientist who looked like one of the apostles in *The Last Supper*," I would like your objective and candid opinion on a matter of utmost concern. Are you satisfied with the Bears' draft choices for linebacker?" He tried with little success to put cheese on a cracker and hold a wine glass, managing to cover his fingers with cheese, a problem which did not distract him from the earnestness of his question.

"My memory goes back beyond Butkus to Bulldog Turner, Aaron," O'Neill replied, "and I've never seen the linebacker corps look worse."

"Which leads to another crucial question," Aaron said as his wife discreetly handed him a napkin. "In

151

your opinion would a quarterback like Sid Luckman compare favorably with someone like Ken Stabler or Terry Bradshaw? It seems to me that we notably underestimate the skills of the great men of the past who had nowhere near the technical resources of the present signal callers."

As O'Neill tried to explain that while he had never seen him play in his prime, men like Luckman played both offense and defense, he was cut short by Marsha Stern. "Aaron, we are not here to bore Mr. O'Neill with talk about sports," she snapped.

Goldman was totally unoffended. "You're right, of course, lovely lady, but we have located him as an authentic Chicagoan."

Bingham impatiently began his lecture again. The conversation lurched ahead disjointedly to the end of the cheese and crackers and into an appalling curry dinner which Ms. Stern had prepared. Bingham lectured about fiction, Stern asked questions which were designed to be sensitive and intense, their wives occasionally snapped nasty comments, Goldman wondered about the Bulls compared to the old Chicago Stags and "the Bruins, which I'm sure you know were also owned by Papa Bear," and Lilly Goldman simply looked attractive. Lynnie was completely relaxed and mildly amused—threatened by intellectuals indeed—should he try to get to legal issues? Jerry had said it might help the cause to make the matter explicit.

"So you see, Mr. O'Neill," Bingham was finally winding down, "it is the function of serious fiction to reflect the ultimate absurdity of life, and the function of your kind of popular writing to give us temporary but essential solace in the midst of that absurdity." It was, O'Neill was sure, an epigram he had practiced many times.

"An interesting theory, Professor Bingham," he replied, trying to sound lightly academic, "but where does that put our absent friend the Prize Winner? Surely in his later work he comes close to seeking something beyond absurdity; and both Cheever and Updike are trying, however unsuccessfully, to do the same thing. I don't think Gardner is doing that yet, despite his strictures on Pynchon and Barth, though at least he approves of such attempts. So we storytellers are not the only ones who see the outcome of the battle between good and evil as still undecided."

Lynnie's eyes, mellow and placid all evening, widened in astonishment.

"The prize winner is a sexist prig, and you write fairy stories," snarled Bingham's wife. (He didn't know her first name; maybe no one had told him.)

"I won't deny it at all, Ma'am. Still, if I'm to believe your Professor Bettelheim, that's a form of literature with long historical and deep psychological resonance." Great word, "resonance"; stop looking surprised, Lyn, I'm flying on one engine but so far so good. . . .

"The '38-'42 Bears were a fairy-story team," Goldman observed, though no one paid him the slightest heed.

"I'm afraid you may have missed my point," Bingham observed, nibbling a piece of meat. "Surely you can't equate Cheever's response to evil with your own?"

"I hope not," said O'Neill airily. The curry was inedible and the cheap burgundy didn't help much to wash it down. Well, that shut the bastard up; let's see him write a story.

"Where did you receive your education, Jim . . . if I may call you that?" asked Emil Stern solicitously, his brown eyes glowing softly.

"Two years of night school at Loyola and then Dien Bien Phu," he said, knowing he was being backed into a corner. The embarrassed pause around the table told him that he had definitively stigmatized himself.

"And what do you do?" Marsha barked at Lynnie, her voice shrill, her eyes concrete hard, the prosecuting attorney beginning the feminist catechism.

"Oh, I sell real estate and things like that in the suburbs," replied Lynnie in a soft, carefully modulated voice, which made real estate sound very sexy.

"Must be quite dull," decided Marsha. "Don't you find it boring?" The young woman's not-unattractive body was coiled spring-taut.

"Sometimes it is, of course," said Lynnie with a gentle, immensely secure smile, "but sometimes it is very interesting. A remarkable opportunity to watch the variety of people. . . ."

"Not very relevant socially," accused La Bingham.

Now an amused and unthreatened little laugh from Lynnie. Emil Stern seemed to have discovered her for the first time. "What company do you work for, Mrs.—?" he hesitated, turning pink with embarrassment.

"Northwest Realty." Lynnie said.

"Yes, indeed," said Stern, now quite interested in his intense, concerned fashion. "A remarkable organization, some extremely interesting notions of suburban development. Been nominated for a national planning prize, I believe, for a concept of a 'ready-made neighborhood.' Headed by a woman, too, as I recall, though I'm afraid I can't quite remember her name. . . ." Again the embarrassed tinge.

"Slattery," the grand duchess laughed graciously. "All Irish names sound alike. *C'est moi*," she laughed again.

"How very remarkable." Now Stern sounded like Studs Terkel doing an interview. Was the imitation deliberate? O'Neill wondered. "Would you mind telling us how you conceived the beautiful idea of the 'ready-made neighborhood?' It's extremely exciting."

Lynnie shrugged her shoulders and glowed. "I grew up in a neighborhood on the West Side which all of us, even our errant novelist—oops—storyteller here, dearly loved. I noticed how many people tried to turn suburbs into neighborhoods despite their physical layout, so I wondered if you couldn't design a community in which the physical layout made it easy for them. I found a young Italian city planner at IIT who also grew up in a Chicago neighborhood, and there we were. I do hope we win the prize; he worked so hard on it."

Who was this strange woman? She had never told him any of this. Of course he resolutely refused to ask about her work.

"Very, very exciting." Stern beamed triumphantly.

He had found a new celebrity, one more exciting and surely prettier than the returned storyteller.

"I imagine it's an all-white suburb," challenged La Bingham, her voice loaded with venom.

"Oh, not at all," Lynnie laughed again. "I'd bet we have a higher proportion of nonwhites than you do on this block."

"You ought to run for the United States Senate," said Aaron Goldman, who had been consuming the unbearable curry with great fervor.

The men and Goldman's wife were delighted. Marsha Stern's body coiled even more tensely, like a viper preparing to strike.

"Do you have children?" she demanded imperiously.

Lynnie's eyes narrowed, then regained their steady glow. "Indeed, I do—five of them. That's why we're so happy with the success of the ready-made suburb. I'll be able to send them to college—though unless we make a lot more money, I'm not sure it will be the University of Chicago."

"I don't see how anyone can justify having that many children, even if you *can* justify bringing children into the world when things are as bad as they are. That many make the population problem worse. How do you justify them?"

The woman was a heresy hunter, a nasty mixture of arid legalism and self-righteous moralism. Watch it, Lynnie, we can't have them angry at us.

"The U.S. birth rate is below replacement," Lynnie responded easily, determined not to lose her temper.

"We're really not a threat to anyone."

"But don't you feel that your children are taking food away from children in India?" The triumphal question which would bring in a guilty verdict from the waiting jury.

Lynnie raised her glass and carefully sipped some burgundy. "If I understand international economics at all, they are not," she murmured.

"It simply isn't right for some children to enjoy wealth while others go to bed hungry," Marsha insisted brusquely.

Lynnie set the crystal goblet back on the table. "Maybe, but then it wouldn't be right to live in a house like this when others live in mud huts." Her coup de grâce was delivered in the same mellow, friendly voice that she had maintained through the whole argument. What the hell does she know about international economics?

"Bravo." Stern clapped his hands enthusiastically.

"Touchdown," announced Aaron Goldman, throwing his hands into the air and knocking over his wife's wine glass.

In the confusion of cleaning up the mess, O'Neill found time to feel sorry for Stern. He was a man of too delicate manners not to be acutely pained by his wife's rudeness. In the first pleasures of a new marriage he had not yet found a way to restrain her. A dangerous situation, and I haven't found a way to bring up grand juries.

The after-dinner liqueur was astonishingly Napoleon Reserve. "I'll drive home," Lynnie whispered in his ear. "Go ahead and drink it, darling."

He insisted on only half a glass. He was drinking too much almost every day.

"It has been perfectly delightful having you here, Jim," observed Stern with passionate sincerity, as he carefully poured the precious fluid. "I can't tell you how important it is to all of us with literary interests to have you back in Chicago."

"Your books lack social relevance," Marsha put in, returning to the attack. Did he hear a suppressed sigh from Stern?

"As I understood Professor Bingham," he said, sniffing the brandy and trying to sound as easily confident as Lynnie, "one would not look for social relevance in my kind of writing, but I don't know . . . *Black Holocaust* was about Biafra. Some of the reviewers thought it demonstrated compassion for victims of genocide."

"That was black against black, not whites oppressing blacks; and besides, the central government was merely engaging in the necessary task of nation building," she shot back, proud of her knowledge of the forgotten civil war and of her correct analysis of what happened. From *Time*, he wondered? A cold fury began to build in his stomach. He put the brandy snifter down.

"A million deaths is a pretty high price for nation building. Besides, the Ibo had at least as much right to break away from Nigeria as we did to break away from England. The fact that the world community betrayed them didn't make their cause any less just." His voice

158

was rising.

"Some must die in order that the people may be born," she protested.

"I think it was George Orwell who wrote, and correct me if I'm wrong, Professor Bingham, that if one sorrows for the death of some children, one must sorrow for the death of all children who are snuffed out by war. I saw hundreds, maybe thousands of dead children in Biafra."

"That's a very moving and beautiful statement, Jim," Stern said piously, trying again to shut his wife off.

O'Neill saw an opportunity. Should he, would it be better not to? . . . He took a swig of brandy and decided to give it a try before Bingham could launch into a lecture on Orwell. "Thanks, Emil. My father, who was a lawyer like you, taught me that freedom and dignity are indivisible." Why should he remember that long forgotten saying of his father's? "When a child dies in Nigeria a little bit of my daughter Clare dies; when freedom is suppressed in Chile we Americans lose some of our freedom; when someone is tried and convicted in the press before an indictment is brought, I lose a portion of my right to be considered innocent till I'm proven guilty. Selective outrage is a contradiction in terms."

He took another swig of brandy. Lynnie looked intrigued. Was she guessing why they were here?

"Very well said, Jim," said Stern, rubbing his hands together anxiously. "I worry about that problem every night. As you may know, though there's no reason you should," he smiled modestly, "I sit on a committee of the Chicago Council of Lawyers which is concerned about political rectitude. A number of my friends say that we are watching passively a mammoth misuse of the grand jury system. I know in my heart that I would object to some of the tactics used if it were a civil liberties case or a political trial. Indeed I have protested violently against much less serious abuses in the Chicago Seven case. Yet the political corruption in this city is so evil I find myself convinced that technical indictments and immunized witnesses are a necessary aberration we must permit for a short time until . . ."

O'Neill finished the brandy, filled the glass again to the rim, and jumped in. "When a politician or a Mafia don gets any less of a fair trial than a political radical," he quoted Jerry Lynch verbatim, "you and I lose some of our freedom, Emil. There is always the danger that someone later on will think we are so hopelessly 'corrupt' that we, too, deserve the same—what do they call it?—'functional justice.' It would scare the hell out of me." Stick it to him good. And his wife has finally shut up, she looks almost lovely when she relaxes.

Stern buried his head in his hands. "I know, I know, Jim. Believe me, I know. And I always agonize over the possibility that some innocent person may suffer. Most politicians in this city are intolerably corrupt; yet I have to believe that it is better that hundreds of the guilty should go free instead of one innocent suffering. Still. . . ." He shook his head uncertainly.

Well, I did it, O'Neill thought dubiously. I wonder if it will help or hurt. . . .

"Come now. We all know Irish politicians are crooks,"

observed La Bingham maliciously.

"Forgive me, dear lady," Aaron Goldman was puffing enthusiastically on his cigar, "I disagree. On the whole they are no more corrupt than university faculty. I trust I need not mention in this room what are normal practices in the matter of research grants. 'Robin-Hooding' is a term which was not developed by Irish politicians but by very moral university research scholars."

"It's not that simple, Aaron," said Stern, anguish twisting his face into an expression of great sadness.

"Besides, you're a student of Jon Hawkin," said Marsha Stern listlessly, the fight gone out of her.

"Indeed yes, dear lady, but if I may go on. . . . Candidly, Emil, you do not believe . . ." he was now a Jewish radical arguing at Bug House Square, his eyes shining, his cigar waving, "in your heart of hearts that the Irish are fit to govern." Goldman tapped his cigar ash into a brandy snifter, which his wife attentively emptied into an ashtray. "They lack what you take to be the deep moral concern required of those who have public responsibility, the agonized pondering of the ethical implications of all public decisions. The Irish govern with a casual flair that seems quite indifferent to ethical dilemmas. As one of my Irish students put it: 'The Irish are guilty about having let their mothers down and nothing else.' " Lynnie's laugh was quite unladylike. "I'm sure, Mrs. O'Neill," Aaron diverted his attention for a moment, "that no child would ever let you down."

"Slattery," Lynnie muttered, trying to hide a grin.

161

"Yes, indeed. Well, to continue my first week of the second quarter lecture, Emil, I would only insist that at the present time the Irish are the only ones around who can direct the music for the delicate minuet between the blacks and the Poles. Neither likes the Irish very much, but both like their partner even less. Emil, should you succeed in using the immunity provision to put every Irish politician in the city behind bars, you would have an ungoverned and ungovernable metropolis. Consider New York, you should excuse the expression." More ash went into the brandy snifter and was transferred to the ashtray.

"That's too easy, too easy," Emil Stern shook his head disconsolately. "We simply cannot go on tolerating civic corruption."

"Look, Emil," Aaron said as he unsuccessfully tried to relight his cigar, "I am a good Hyde Park liberal. I voted for Leon Despres and Bob Mann; I support Richard Newhouse and I campaigned for Barbara Flynn. I am committed to the political ethics of this university community; yet I put it to you this way, sir. With the exception, I daresay, of a couple of your guests and an occasional young mick like Bill McCready over at the National Opinion Research Center, there is not a single person currently within the boundaries of this neighborhood who could deliver half a precinct anywhere else in the city. We want to govern. Oh, we want to govern so badly because we are smart and moral. Should we ever gain power, I personally would migrate to California or some other safe place. I fear the rule of Robespierre . . . oh, thank you, darling. . . ." His wife had lit another cigar for him.

There was a long silence. Finally Emil Stern shook his head again, sadly and helplessly. "I don't know, Aaron, I just don't know. Sometimes I think you may be right."

"That's what I keep trying to tell the management of the Chicago Bears," Goldman proclaimed triumphantly, knocking his ashtray on the floor.

They left with the Goldmans. "You must not mind poor Emil," said Lilly Goldman, now talkative. "His first wife got into consciousness raising and walked out on him after twenty years of his adoration; now he's married to that awful bitch and doesn't know how to handle her."

"I felt kind of sorry for her," said Lynnie. "She really doesn't want to be a bitch, poor girl, but she's so much younger and so much taller, and so afraid of his intellect that she doesn't know what else to do; and he's so pathetically sensitive about his height. Hey, who's Jon Hawkin?"

They were standing under one of the leafy trees lining Woodlawn Avenue, near a brightly lit playground. A Chicago PD patrol car was parked just down the street.

"Oh, he's a government professor at Mother Harvard who used to teach here. He holds, though not nearly so flamboyantly, the same view of urban politics as the one I defended tonight," Aaron said, trying a number of different keys in the door of his Volvo.

"I guess I never expected to be defended by the University of Chicago," Lynnie admitted ruefully.

"Indeed, Mrs. O'Neill, but that's because you don't understand this university. I put it to you, dear lady, there is at least as much pluralism in this community as in the Cook County Organization or the Roman Catholic Church, though I will admit that it may not be nearly so interesting a species of pluralism . . . now isn't that remarkable?" One of the keys opened the door of the Volvo, an event Goldman considered almost unprecedented.

Lilly and Lynnie exchanged phone numbers and promised to stay in touch. O'Neill told himself that he would indeed like to meet the young couple again even though he was leaving Chicago immediately after the investigation.

He surrendered the keys of the station wagon to Lynnie's outstretched hand and got into the car. "Drive home slowly, my dear. I have a headache already," he joked.

"You ought to," she replied. "It was worth it, though."

God, we're driving home like we're a married couple who've been together for years. What would Jerry think of the evening? They had made an impression on Stern. He seemed to like Lynnie and to respect him. Well, it didn't do any harm. On the whole it was probably more successful than the meeting he would have with the cardinal the next day, but he had no way of appraising the moral agony that seemed to grip Stern.

Lynnie was superb. Couldn't have been better if she had prepared beforehand. Unflappable, no temper tantrum despite the pressures, gracious—a real archduchess. Where did she find out about international economics and population replacement? The planning prize.

"You know, O'Neill, there are times when you interest me," she said thoughtfully.

"How am I supposed to take that?" he asked, wondering whether he should be angry.

She turned the car down Lake Shore Drive after the stop light at Fifty-Seventh Street turned green. "This is going to sound bad, but I don't know how else to say it. I'm beginning to like you. I mean, I've adored you and loved you and lusted after you all along, but there are times when you're really impressive. I wonder . . . I don't know, maybe it would have been better if we'd met as strangers, or at least begun the whole thing like we were strangers. You're really quite fascinating at times. Maybe we—oh, hell, maybe *I* made a mistake by starting again the way I did, should have been more cautious. Too late now, I guess."

He evaded her like an infantryman jumping into a foxhole at a sudden burst of enemy fire. "Hey, where did you learn about international economics?"

"Anyone can read *Business Week* and the *Wall Street Journal*," she said impatiently, swerving skillfully to miss a slow-moving Datsun. "Damn intellectuals don't know how to drive. . . . And while we're at it, where did you learn all that civil liberties stuff?"

"I'm a writer," he said stiffly. "I make it up as I go along."

 12

Victorian fog oozed in off Lake Michigan and turned Lincoln Park into gloomy moorland. Well, it seemed Victorian or even Holmesian as it slipped past the archbishop's multi-chimneyed house—he counted twenty-six of them. Someday he would have to write a Holmesian story; the gloom fit his mood. What better place than a moor to treasure guilt feelings? He rose from the park bench and walked along North Avenue toward Clark Street, glancing at his watch again. Why had he come so early? Another half-hour to go.

According to the young priest—Uncle Mike, Micky, whatever—the archbishop had tried to sell the house as part of his continual financial maneuvers only to discover that the land was owned by the Mercy Sisters, bought for a previous archbishop by his sister who was a mother general. The modern Mercys didn't object to building a high-rise condo on the land, only they wouldn't give the money to His Prominence . . . stalemate. Somehow an angular condo wouldn't look nearly so appropriate across from the park as the old Victorian monstrosity.

Archbishop Fogarty, born in New Jersey, trained in Rome, three different dioceses before he came to Chicago. "Each time," Uncle Mike had said, "he got out one step ahead of the bailiff and left his successor holding the empty bag. We don't follow the Peter Principle in the Church; you can get promoted way beyond your level of incompetence."

For a long time there had been a variety of rumors in Chicago about the contents of annual diocesan audits, O'Neill learned. According to Uncle Mike, a member of the archbishop's staff who left the priesthood had whispered to him that millions of dollars had been lost in bad investments, "gifts" to Rome, and grandstand efforts to bail out financially troubled dioceses and religious communities all over the country. The priest who had done the whispering had long since moved on to another place.

"He can't keep staff," Mike said. "Lives and works all by himself. He frequently travels, but it isn't clear sometimes where he's going or why. Funny thing, but people have reported seeing him at places like the Royal Hawaiian when it was thought he was somewhere else."

"What does he do there?" asked O'Neill, frowning at the telephone.

"No one knows. Just holes up and answers the mail that the couriers bring him from Chicago. Could just as well do that on North State Parkway."

Still, Uncle Mike had no trouble making the appointment for the "famous novelist" though it took a week after the request. "Don't expect that he's read you, Jimmy me boy. He doesn't read anything, not even the breviary."

O'Neill turned back from Clark Street and walked toward the lake.

How can people like Uncle Mike and Lynnie still

believe in a church which gives such a man so much power? It shakes what little faith I have left, he thought. He looked at his watch again. Time to try the archbishop's house . . . God knows what's going to happen. *If You exist at all, how do you explain Daniel Fogarty?*

The deity offered no explanation, so O'Neill pushed the doorbell. Chimes sounded somewhere deep in the house. After a long wait, an efficient-looking thirtyish woman opened the door, told him dourly that the archbishop would be late, showed him to an ornate parlor, and departed in severe silence. He heard a typewriter somewhere down the high-ceilinged corridor. Mike had said the archbishop never was on time and he might have a long, long wait. He settled back in an overstuffed chair and tried to sort out his thoughts.

The waiting room was as tasteless as the old-fashioned rectory parlors, only monumentally so, as though someone had set out to prove that if you had a lot of money you could be breathtaking in your bad taste. The heavy green carpet clashed with the dark red fabric wall covering, and the hideous brocades didn't fit with either. Expensive chairs; antiques probably. Four popes frowned disapprovingly at him from the wall. Pope John, he noted, was not one of them. Just as well. Who was that pope who seemed particularly unhappy with his fantasies? He walked over to the pictures. Pius XII. What was the old line Etienne had told him? Pius X was a saint and didn't know it, Pius XI was not a saint and knew it, Pius XII was not a saint and didn't know it. Not very funny just now.

Idly he watched the raindrops on the window merge

into little rivulets and slide off the sill onto the ground. A pool of water lay beneath the window and from it a small stream ran across the sidewalk toward the street. In his mind he traced the progress of the drops into the sewers, down the sanitary canal into the Illinois, and then the Mississippi, and finally, a hundred miles below New Orleans, choosing one of the many paths through the Delta into the ocean.

The drops on the window, each one a different woman. His mother, Zena, Clare, Lynnie, Mary, the Ibo nurse, Monique, Carla. So many images, so much quick pleasure, so much pain and guilt; like the chocolate he liked so much as a boy, tasty in the moment but strong and harsh afterward—all these sweet and bitter memories flowing together into rivers, then a vast ocean of tantalizing and tormenting chocolate drowning him with pleasure and pain. Who was that early Christian—Tertullian? Cyprian? Origen? One of them had castrated himself to avoid the pain and the madness. He could see the man's point. Yet there were moments of quick ecstasy—Lynnie the night he came back to the lake—like cool water on a humid day, when it seemed worth all the trouble. No, he would not follow the Church father's example quite yet.

What do you know about it? he mentally asked Pius XII, who seemed to be watching him through his rimmed glasses, shocked at witnessing such thoughts in an archbishop's house. Was there ever a woman like Lynnie in your life? Someone you couldn't keep your hands off of?

Then he remembered that at the end of his years

that aloof old Roman aristocrat had been kept alive by the tender care of a woman, who also ran the Church for a few months and didn't do such a bad job either. Hell, maybe you do understand. Still, you never wrote an encyclical about her, did you? What was the Latin for bittersweet waters? Make a great title for an encyclical or even a book.

He went back to his chair to wait for the archbishop.

It was another forty minutes—well into the supper hour—before the archbishop finally appeared, resplendent in red buttons and sash, doubtless dressed to impress the famous novelist.

"Sorry to keep you waiting, Mr. O'Neill," he blustered like a tornado as he swept into the room, "but those of us who deal with worldwide issues know what time is like, don't we?" Tall, thin, with an egg-bald head and hawk face, the archbishop reminded him somehow of the scarecrow from *The Wizard of Oz*, a scarecrow with red buttons.

He did not need to fashion an answer to the bizarre first question. The archbishop roared on, a whirling storm of words. That's why he was like a scarecrow—a body swept by the wind. "I've got to tell you how much I like your stories." His thick Jersey accent had not been eroded by his years in the Middle West. "I had an incident happen to me in Berlin just like the one you describe in one of your books." So Micky had been wrong; he did read something. "I was flying into Tempelhof in '45, on the first DC-6 to land there after the Potsdam conference . . ."

The rest of the long story was a detailed repetition

of one of O'Neill's early books, *Encounter in Berlin*—
the man actually thought the whole plot was an experience of his.

"I didn't think they had DC-6s in the ERO that
early," he said weakly.

"Sure they did," the archbishop insisted, not in the
least bothered by accurate military history. "It was a
top security secret—well kept, too, like those things
rarely are. Oh yes, I've had some interesting experi-
ences. The secrecy is still good on my trip to Vietnam,
though I suppose those journalist fellows who are
always trying to track down my adventures will
unearth it one of these days; but first of all, let me get
you something to drink. Scotch?"

He swept out of the room like a headwaiter with a
big tip and was back almost instantly with two very
large glasses, still talking. It was the finest quality
Scotch, Jim noticed appreciatively.

"Yes, that Vietnam affair was a near thing. The Holy
See wanted me to go into Saigon right before the fall
to ordain bishops for the Catholic underground there.
The Navy flew me in on a chopper from a carrier
while they were evacuating the embassy . . . smooth
operation, that. Anyhow, things got confused and I
thought for a while I'd spend the rest of my life as a
jungle archbishop in Vietnam." He guffawed. "A lot of
my priests would really like that, Jim, let me tell you."
He gulped half the Scotch with a single swallow.
"Anyway, we finally got to the coast and were taken off
by night on a landing barge. Just barely made it. Rome
is going to have to find someone else to do their nasty

work the next time, but none of the younger fellows would volunteer." He paused long enough to consume the rest of the Scotch.

Possibly true but not likely. And the evacuation of the embassy in Saigon had not been a smooth operation at all but an awful mess.

"Well, Jimmy, enough of this talk. Let's go have something to eat. After keeping you waiting so long the least I can do is put something in your stomach."

The winds continued to roar at the dinner table, interrupted only by the pauses necessary for the archbishop to wolf down two steaks and most of a bottle of 1964 burgundy. The efficient-looking secretary doubled in brass as a waitress in the mahogany-paneled dining room. Was she the cook too?

The stories rolled on through the plots of several other books. The archbishop had assimilated a vast literature of adventure stories and made himself the hero of them all.

"You certainly have had an interesting life, Your Excellency," he said cautiously.

"It all started when I was in Rome, Jim. I worked with three different popes on a close personal basis, you know. Got quite a reputation for being a man that is good in a hot spot. That's why they sent me to Chicago to clean up the mess here. It's been a rough job, let me tell you."

The conversation then turned to Chicago, stories of his enemies in the city and their plots, his close personal friendship with Daley, the mayor's dying words to him, the citations he had won over his opponents, the sexual failings of many of his clergy, and all with hints of how much more he knew but was not free to say. O'Neill was both appalled and fascinated. How could you sort out the truth from the lunacy?

In a confused daze, numbed by the archbishop's nonstop conversation, and the wine and whiskey, he permitted himself to be led back into the parlor for brandy, which must have cost a couple of hundred dollars a bottle. With such an appetite for food and drink, how did the man stay so scarecrow-thin? He must burn up calories through the sheer vigor of his speech. Lynnie wouldn't believe it. Lynnie. My God, that's why he was here. He had forgotten.

"Your Excellency," he began hesitantly, "I've really come to ask for a favor."

"Ask away, my boy. No one ever said Danny Fogarty wouldn't help a friend. What can I do for you? By the way, how does your daughter like the school in Rome? The Holy Cross Sisters are very good. Their cardinal protector, Consalvi, is a good friend of mine. Be glad to help there whenever I can."

How did he know about Clare? The comment had been deliberately made to impress O'Neill. Mad but shrewd. Tread very carefully.

"Well, it has to do with the Queen of America Foundation and the memo from Father McCarthy about Mrs. Slattery," he began, deciding to be straightforward.

"Bad business, Jimmy, bad business," said the archbishop brusquely, draining the brandy tumbler and filling it again. "If I could tell you all the things I know about that case. I know a lot about the FBI, you know. Always have. Did poor old J. Edgar some favors a long time ago before he turned sour. If I could only tell you some of the cases I've heard about."

"But Mrs. Slattery is innocent, Your Excellency. We're old friends from school days, and I thought a personal appeal to you might—"

"Can't do it, Jimmy, just can't do it. Poor woman made some mistakes. Too bad, did things she never should have done. Sorry about it. She's a good Catholic laywoman otherwise, but it seems the government has the goods on her and there's nothing I can do." He sighed expansively and drained the second tumbler of brandy.

He felt his anger rising. He'd been patient with this freak long enough. "Still, Your Excellency, the memo from Father McCarthy would be a big help. A person's innocent till proven guilty."

The archbishop guffawed. He dismissed the plea with a wave of his elongated hand. "People like you and me who've been around a lot know that isn't so. She's guilty all right. We can't help her. It's a shame— lovely woman, I'm told. Probably can buy her way out in the end; most of them do, you know. Let me tell you a story about. . . ."

"You goddamned psychopathic bastard!" O'Neill could not believe it was his voice, or that he had risen threateningly from his chair. "I want that memo and I want it now! If you don't give it to me, I'll ruin you; and I know just how to do it!" He had not the foggiest notion how to do it.

The archbishop was serenely unperturbed. "Well, why didn't you say you really need the memo in the first place, Jimmy? You know Danny Fogarty always helps his friends. Just a second, I'll get it for you." He exited from the room with his usual speed, if on a somewhat more erratic line.

O'Neill crept to the doorway and watched the archbishop in an office down on the other side of the corridor. He was shuffling rapidly through several stacks of paper at least a foot high—unanswered mail? Finally, he triumphantly pulled out a sheet of paper from the middle of the third pile. O'Neill quickly faded back into the parlor.

The archbishop burst into the room, excitedly flourishing the paper. He waved the paper enthusiastically. "See, Jim my boy, a good administrator can put his hand on anything he needs in a matter of seconds. Here it is, just what you wanted. You and the lovely lady are welcome to it for whatever use you may make of it. Poor Joe McCarthy. Wonderful young priest. Worked too hard. Too conscientious, don't you know. I always told him to slow down. Sent him to an easy assignment, but he just couldn't change his way, poor man. Now I myself have always made a practice myself of taking vacations when I need them. Sometimes they become very interesting too." He relaxed comfortably. "I remember once when I was staying in one of the out-islands of Hawaii. . . ."

The paper did indeed seem to be the memo, a document which was almost a matter of life and death buried in a stack of unanswered mail. Had he held out on it before because it was too much bother to hunt it down? O'Neill interrupted the maelstrom of words, expressed immense gratitude and apologies for having to take his leave, and hastily eased toward the front door of the archiepiscopal mansion. They parted with boisterous good fellowship. Jim slipped out into the rain and the mist, which were transparent in comparison with the fog inside the house.

He looked at his watch. 9:15. More than six hours in that insane asylum, four of them with Daniel Fogarty. He was too bemused by the experience to try to make sense of it. Walk back to the Drake, call Lynnie with the good news. It *was* good news, wasn't it? The man was evil, a monster; yet, like running water, he had followed the path of lesser resistance. A slight threat and he caved in. He was supposed to be vindictive. Would he try to get even? How had he found out about Clare?

Back in his room O'Neill put off calling Lynnie. He had to try to straighten out his wits. Ten o'clock. Absently he turned on the TV for the news. Odd that the Chicago custom was to have the news on an hour earlier. . . .

Lynnie's house was on the screen, she and the kids coming down the front stairs, reporters all around with microphones, Lynnie splendid in a flowered sundress and jacket. A close-up of her face—tight, haggard, her upper lip trembling. What were they saying?

"I haven't committed any crimes; I haven't been charged with any crimes." Her voice sounded flat and taut on the TV soundtrack. "I have nothing to say other than I wish my family had been spared all of this."

"Are you denying the charges in the *Star* article?" demanded a bitchy-voiced woman reporter.

"There are no charges in the article to deny." She spoke slowly, but there was a flash of anger in her arctic eyes; he had not noticed the ice before. "Only rumors and innuendos, on which my lawyer has advised me not to comment." She pushed her hair away from her face in a gesture which was both nervous and graceful. The camera panned to the kids' faces, the younger ones confused and frightened, Marty scowling angrily, poor Evie strained and nearly hysterical.

"Do you expect to be indicted?" A black woman journalist had asked the question, her tone accusatory, as though she were the United States Attorney.

The upper lip trembled again as Lynnie reached for words. She swallowed. "I don't know what will happen," she said very carefully, straining for the last crucial sentence. Then a smile. "But innocent people have been indicted before, haven't they?"

The white woman again. "Do you deny that your husband and father were criminals?"

Oh my God, how could they get away with such questions?

Again the smile. "I don't think I should try to answer any more questions."

A cut to a picture of her father, then Steve, then a portly balding man, doubtless the estimable Tubbo Donaghey. He could hardly understand the words. Then some dark-skinned faces. Had the anchorman really said "Mafia connections"? Was this still America? He stood up angrily, his fists clenched. He wanted to smash something. . . .

Then a corridor in an office building; a lean stringy-haired man, the U. S. Attorney, speaking like a grim avenging angel. "I have no comment on this particular investigation, but the people may rest assured that my office will prosecute wrongdoers no matter how high their social status." Then a tire commercial.

My God, all of a sudden it was a populist crusade against the rich, against a woman who had earned all her money by her own hard work. They hadn't missed a thing.

As though in a trance, he turned off the TV and went down to the lobby to buy the *Star*. He stood transfixed in front of the newsstand staring at the headline "Report 'Merry Widow' Indictment," unable to pick the paper up from the counter. Finally he shook himself free of his paralysis, bought the paper, and returned to his room as though he were slogging through thick snowdrifts.

There was a picture of Lynnie amply filling a swimming suit on the front page, with no hint of where the picture was taken. Inside, pictures of her father, Steve, Charles Stewart Parnell Donaghey and his uncle, her cousins, who were "reputed" to be involved in "organized crime," a number of men who had been her "constant companions."

"Well-informed sources" predicted the indictment of a "well-known socialite" with crime syndicate "connections." Lynnie was depicted as a rich woman inheriting ill-gotten wealth from both sides of her family, and the widow of a wheeler-dealer with his own political connections. His death was described as an auto accident in "unexplained circumstances"; it was hinted that after his death she had emerged as a "swinging socialite," active in fashionable causes by day and popular with men at night. Were they suggesting that Lynnie had arranged Steve's death? You could certainly read the piece—by two "Pulitzer prize-winning reporters"—that way. The Queen of America affair was related in details which only Tubbo's testimony could provide. Her children attended exclusive suburban private schools, an inventive way to portray parochial grammar and high schools. No mention that she had only a few thousand dollars to her name when Steve was killed. Just a spoiled rich girl with crime in her past and rumors of crime in her present. A superb job. Had the reporters or the leak at the U.S. Attorney's office determined the line? Must have been the reporters.

He turned the page. A picture of Emil Stern, chairman of the Chicago Council of Lawyers' Commission on Urban Government. Gravely disappointed to hear of the involvement of the Church in political corruption, result of a long era of dishonesty in Chicago politics. Church authorities would have to exercise greater vigilance. No comment on Mrs. Stephen Slattery. Many victims of the system; victims must pay the price of their wrongdoing.

His stomach turned. He hesitated, then rushed to the bathroom. The dirty little phony, he thought as he retched into the silently protesting toilet. Drained and shaking, he picked up the paper again, tried to read through the story.

Why the leak? he asked himself, staring at the letters crawling on the newsprint. Did they know he went to see the archbishop? His heart sank. Maybe he was responsible. The archbishop was quixotic. Rather than have their witness destroyed on the stand, they would get his testimony into the papers and turn every prospective juror in the county against Lynnie. Sure, her lawyers could issue a statement the next day quoting the McCarthy memo, which lay where he had dropped it on top of the TV. That would be fifth-page news, reassuring to some of Lynnie's friends but of little use to her butchered reputation. She would have to live for the rest of her life with that story and so would her kids.

He let his head sink into his hands. Somewhere in the depths of his personality there was anger, but it could not surface. It swirled around, spreading poison through his veins. He ought to call her, he ought to find Howard and give him the memo, he ought to do something. He couldn't move, couldn't think, couldn't rise from the chair. The newspaper slipped to the floor. Eventually he fell into a heavy, druglike sleep.

 # 13

"Where were you last night?" Nancy Carsello snapped as he entered her tiny windowless office. "We tried to get you on the phone all evening. Howard's at Lynnie's right now."

He gently placed the McCarthy memo on her desk. Mr. Howard was not in the office, the receptionist had said, but "Ms. Carsello will see you."

"Having dinner with an archbishop, lovely lady," he said, "which in case you haven't heard is an all-night, you should excuse the expression, affair. I didn't see the papers till this morning." Only a little lie . . .

She grabbed the memo like a hungry woman snatching for bread. "You did get it!" she smiled happily. "Mr. O'Neill, my apologies. Excuse me, I've got to tell the old man about this. Have a seat."

O'Neill eased into the one chair in the office as she frantically dialed the phone, swore when she got a wrong number, and then dialed again more cautiously. "Hello, Cora honey, this is Nancy from Mr. Howard's office. Could I talk to my boss for a minute, please? . . . Hey, Eddie, your client was right. O'Neill was with the maniac all evening and got the memo. Well, it's better than nothing . . . that bad out there, huh? Poor kids. Look, the *Herald* will do the story. I'll show the memo to the reporter and point out the lines to quote." She looked up at Jim, who was beginning to wonder how large his little lie was. "Mr. O'Neill, did the archbishop put any restriction on the use of the memo?"

"I don't think the idea even occurred to him. It was just a favor from one man of the world to another."

She frowned, not quite sure how to take his answer. "No restrictions, Ed. Yeah, sure, we shouldn't get into the news management business, but we're fighting people who use the media to convict our clients before they come to trial. No, I won't teach a course in it at law school. How is she? . . . yeah . . . When will you be back? . . . No, I'm not going out to lunch, I'll be here. I'll see you." She put the phone back on its cradle. "My boss," she said to O'Neill, "has ethical problems about an article in the *Herald*." She grinned owlishly. "Like a lot of other ethical problems, he's managed to overcome this one."

"Will it do any good?" he asked, his head aching and his mind still blurry.

She held the memo lightly in her lacquered fingertips. "It won't undo all the harm," she shrugged. "Nothing can do that, but it will help. Hell, I don't know how much. The *Star* reporters will begin to wonder whether they can trust Masterman's honchos. Her kids will have a much better image of their mother to remember. Prospective jurors may recollect that there was another side to the 'Merry Widow' headline."

"Where did they get that damn picture?" he sighed.

"You wondered about that too? First thing I thought of. God forgive me, I should look that way when I'm that old." She turned dusty rose. "Sorry, Mr. O'Neill, she really isn't old. . . . Society swim meet for muscular dystrophy victims, a perfectly innocent picture on the society page taken out of context. Clever boys, our friends at the *Star*." Her oval face knotted in anger.

He stood up to leave. "I'm angry deep down inside," he confessed, "but still too confused to know what to do with it." May as well tell part of the truth. "I can't believe something like this is happening in America."

She shook her head dejectedly. "I'm afraid there's going to be a lot of other un-American things happening before it's all over. How is she today? How did she seem when you talked to her?"

"I haven't talked to her yet." The girl's disapproving frown reappeared. He gulped. "I've got to do it personally; there's too much to say on the phone . . ." he trailed off lamely. One more lie didn't make much difference.

The frown vanished. "Yeah, I know what you mean. Anyhow, give her my love and tell her that she'll really like the early edition of the *Herald*. They've got a picture of her tutoring deaf kids. That should knock the props out of the Merry Widow bit."

"I'll tell her, but I don't think I'll put it quite that way." They both laughed nervously, and O'Neill made his escape. No pirate-princess fantasies today, anyway.

His emotions grew more tangled as he fought heavy truck traffic on the Congress Expressway. The Irish, he had learned, simply refused to call it the Eisenhower,

183

just as they still called Pulaski Road "Crawford Avenue" forty years after the name had been changed. His head pounded as if a dentist's drill were working on it. He couldn't label the mishmash of feelings which were hassling him, but one of them was fear . . . coupled with a strong compulsion to run.

He worried about the TV cameras in front of her house. His name hadn't showed up in the papers yet. No point in adding a famous novelist to the list of her constant companions—a momentary pang of jealousy—she had not told him about those men. "Novelist Rides to Rescue of Merry Widow." But there were no trucks or reporters in front of the house, no living creature in sight. A quiet, respectable residential street on a gentle May afternoon. The old trees were turning green.

Michael was at the door before he could knock, grave and self-possessed. "Am I glad to see you, James!" the normally taciturn seminarian exclaimed, shaking his hand solemnly.

"What's it like, Mike?" he asked, not wanting to sound like the head of the family.

"Not good. Cora came home from school at ten o'clock hysterical. She's up in bed. Jimmy didn't want to go back after lunch. Kids get pretty cruel, you know." Suddenly so mature, too suddenly.

"What about your classmates?" he asked.

"We're off today. Anyhow, they're different." He grinned. The first time he'd ever seen Michael grin. "A couple of them called, wanted to organize a demonstration against the *Star*. Future clergy are into demonstrations, you know. I told them to cool it for a

184

while. Mom and Marty and Evie are in the study. I know they're waiting for you."

Lynnie and the two kids sat like a three-judge panel behind the vast mahogany desk—solemn, somber, impassive. Lynnie was wearing glasses, her hair was awry, she'd had no time for makeup. Still she looked cool and efficient in a brown jacket and slacks, the slim warrior queen in command of her troops during a lull in the battle. He moved a cactus plant off the only other chair in the room. The smell of newly blooming roses drifted in from the French windows facing the garden, for a moment reminding him of the DuLacs' garden. Roses and account books—all you needed were tennis shoes to complete the symbolic triad of Lynnie's complex life.

"Sorry I'm late," he mumbled, feeling like a subordinate commander tardy for a conference. Emily, the Labrador, who had been behind the desk, padded sleepily toward him and sat at his feet, her muzzle resting on his leg. He patted her absentmindedly.

A bear hug and tears from Evie, a relieved smile and a warm handshake from the bearded giant, and a chaste peck from Lynnie, her eyes a frigid glow.

"Why, Lynnie, why, why, why?" he asked, squeezing her shoulder with what he hoped felt like affection.

She seemed surprised. "You mean why would the *Star* do it? Oh, that's easy. I keep forgetting that you were away. Funny, it feels like you never left. Anything you can do against the Organization is fair if you're a Chicago reporter. It's adversary journalism; they have nothing against me personally. The two of them were out there this morning, as friendly as can be. It's all a game—Get the Organization—and for present purposes I'm part of the Organization. 'No hard feelings, we hope, Mrs. Slattery.' " Her voice was dangerously calm, just as it had been on TV the night before. Close to explosion or collapse, maybe both.

What do I say next? He was saved by the telephone. "A lot of our clients are worried," Marty explained as his mother made reassuring noises into the phone. "The office is screening out the minor problems and sending us the big ones. We were afraid there'd be too many people at the building this morning. If we don't show up today, they'll lose interest and we can do business as usual tomorrow."

The same frozen calm as his mother. Twenty was too young to be head of the family. Poor Marty, he had to play the role when he was fifteen. Did he have a girl friend? Was she serious about everything too? What would he and Clare think of one another?

Lynnie was off the phone. "I guess Howard told you about the memo," he began hesitantly.

"Oh, *James*, you've got to tell us all about it." Evie's teenage exuberance rose from the dead.

"Every detail, James," said her mother, a glimmer of thaw in her eyes. "Lord knows we need some good news and some laughs. Tell it like a master storyteller."

Archibald wandered into the room and settled on the other side of his chair. The master storyteller had two dogs in attendance, chaplains at the throne of an archbishop. "Only way I know how to tell it," he mumbled, feeling his face grow warm.

186

As an audience they were irresistible. Assuring himself they needed the laughter, he recounted his adventures with the archbishop, embellishing the tale to make it even funnier. He cast himself as a straight man who had stumbled into the archbishop's manic world, and climaxed the story with a reenactment on Lynnie's disordered desk of the archbishop's desperate search for the memo; and they laughed until they protested their sides were aching. The worship in three sets of violet eyes made him uneasy, but he enjoyed it.

At the end of the tale it was Lynnie's turn to give him the bear hug. "Oh, James, when you write your novel about this, you've just got to make yourself the hero."

Her body was disturbingly soft. "Please, Madame," he said, his face now very hot, "you must realize that I am a tragic hero, not a comic one."

Lynnie then discovered that he had not eaten lunch, reprimanded herself for not asking him before, and with Evie, Archibald, and Emily in tow, went to prepare it.

Did she want to leave him alone with Marty so that the two senior males of the family could consult with one another? They had apparently assigned him a role, he was "James"—even Lynnie called him that now. What was a "James"? Surely he had to do something besides telling funny stories.

There was a gnawing in the pit of his stomach. He thought of his mother for the first time in years. "How bad is it, Marty?" he asked, hoping he had struck the right man-to-man note.

"Pretty bad, James," the blond kid replied, the strain

showing in his voice and in the knotted arm muscles beneath his T-shirt. "Mom's tough; she can survive almost anything. She's had to, God knows. But it's terrible on the kids, and it could wreck the business."

"The business?"

"Sure." The shoulder muscles were knotted too. "The headlines cost us clients and customers. More headlines will cost us even more. Mom, as I don't have to tell you," a quick smile, "is a gambler. Construction, speculation, other businesses—nothing too dangerous. Hell, we survived last year's soft market fine, but in an operation like ours you stay just ahead of the cash-flow problem. It's usually not difficult. Our credit is good and our clientele has always expanded, but if you start sinking or even lose momentum the cash-flow thing can drag you through the floor in a hurry. You've got to sell and sell and sell, always at a loss. Add a fortune in legal bills, and we could lose it all even before a trial."

"All because of one story?" he asked incredulously.

"The story we can live with, especially when the *Herald* sets the record straight tonight—and God, James, that was spectacular getting away with the memo from the archbishop." The blond giant's face shone with admiration. "The kids will get over it eventually," he went on. "Mom knows how to absorb her pains. The clients, most of them anyway, will forget. We can put the pieces back together—some losses but nothing disastrous. If there's really an indictment, though, there'll be coverage on TV night after night after night. It will do us in."

Lynnie was back with several elaborate sandwiches, a huge bowl of fruit, and a bottle of the same burgundy they drank the first night at the lake. "Gotta get rid of this stuff before it goes sour," she chuckled, winking at him. "I knew I shouldn't leave you menfolks alone; you're as somber as though you were at a wake—a non-Irish wake. James, do you remember the wakes in the old neighborhood?"

A signal for more stories. That's what "James" was—the family comic storyteller. Well, he had chosen his profession, but he didn't like the comic role in it. He began to tell the stories, getting an idea for a book in the process. He was running out of wake memories when the phone rang again.

Lynnie's face turned pale. The tundra was back in her eyes; her fingers tightened around a pencil. "Of course we will cooperate. We have always cooperated, haven't we? What makes you think we wouldn't this time? Come now, Mr. Blucher, you don't expect me to believe that this is not connected with the story in this morning's paper, do you? . . . Of course I know you have a job to do, especially when *Star* reporters call to ask if you've looked at the company's performance lately." Her face tightened with rage. "Have you ever found anything illegal before? You know as well as I do that our operation is just about the cleanest your inspectors ever looked at—you said so yourself, didn't you? . . . Oh, you do remember. Didn't tell the *Star* that, did you? . . . Yes, of course, Mr. Blucher, send your inspectors the first thing in the morning. We will be as cooperative as always, and you'll find us as clean as always. And the papers will give the same prominence to that report as they will to the announcement of your investigation? . . . Oh yes indeed, Mr. Blucher, I do understand that you have a public responsibility. Let me just make clear," her voice turned cold and threatening, "that I have a very long memory." She slammed the phone down.

"State Revenue Department," Marty explained unnecessarily.

"Bastard!" shouted Evie, the tight anger in her face making her look even more like her mother.

"Evie," said Lynnie, abstractedly brushing her hair away from her face, "don't use such language. James will think you are as common as your mother."

"Call Nancy," said James O'Neill.

"Huh?"

"Have her tip off the *Herald*. They can get your friend Blucher to comment about your company being the cleanest in the profession. That will pull the ground out from under . . ."

"You really do amaze me, James." She was already dialing the number.

"Thank God you're here," Evie breathed.

More worship. Admiration was a trap just like love.

"The first of many vultures," Marty said, angry again. "They'll all be on us before it's over."

"Will they find anything?" It was tactless, but the question didn't seem to offend anyone.

Lynnie hung up the phone. "Not a thing, Jimmy, oddly enough. No use in pretending that my father was not a . . . a product of a different era; he was—but

190

there was too much suffering for others in that route. Even if it were still safe, I figured time was running out on the old style. So I decided to stay clean as a whistle." She shrugged her shoulders. "Hell, maybe I even believe in virtue, a terrible WASP thing to do. So they won't find anything at all." Lynnie hesitated, frowned, looked at him thoughtfully, and then, making a decision, added, "Well, they won't find anything indictable anyway. Still . . ."

"Still what?" he asked harshly, feeling somehow very self-righteous.

"It's complicated. Sometimes I don't know myself. Do you try to get friends to review your books?"

"What does that have to do with it?" he asked impatiently, his chin sinking into his hands. "I don't do it myself, but I suppose the publishers do. They sure as hell ought to. Better friends than enemies . . ."

Marty played nervously with a pencil, Evie pleaded with her eyes, but Lynnie went on. "And sometimes don't you wonder why the big law firms downtown hire Harvard, Princeton, or UC graduates instead of Loyola grads with the same marks? Well, you wouldn't wonder since you've been away for so long, but wouldn't it make someone who knew about it wonder?"

"I guess so," he conceded, realizing he was in deep waters, in a troubled sea. Damn it, the woman was so beautiful—head high, shoulders back, trim waist. . . .

"And the presidents of banks have trustees who went to Yale with them . . . ," she went on implacably.

"Where is all this heading, Lynnie?" he asked impatiently, his head sinking even lower into his hands.

Marty took over, his face wrapped in the serious expression of a young business school teacher. "It's not a matter of corruption, James," he said with calm authority, as though he were explaining a complicated accounting problem. "When you put up something like our ready-made neighborhood, you need permits, licenses, zoning board approvals, reliable contractors and subcontractors who finish on time, good legal advice, foolproof insurance, even a caterer who will serve warm food instead of wilted sandwiches at the groundbreaking party. It helps a lot if the people you do business with have political connections. No bribes necessarily, certainly not from us; no exorbitant fees, nothing like that. Still, if you want to finish on time, you'd better hire the right people."

"I think I know what you mean," he said slowly. "Favors passing all around, like an Indian potlatch."

"Whatever that is," said Lynnie, her shoulders slumped wearily, her eyes on the desk, her voice flat. "Look, we needed a major zoning change to try our new neighborhood plan. Nothing which wasn't proper or socially beneficial, whatever the hell that is. If I had gotten one of the big-name law factories to handle the case, we'd still be before the appellate courts and not a spadeful of ground would have been turned. Harvard degrees or not, get an Irish firm with a ward committeeman on it and we have no trouble at all. No one is bribed, I probably pay less than I'd pay the Harvard cats, the legal advice is every bit as competent and intelligent, and the suburb is finished and up for a

192

prize. Maybe they're just really good at wording zone requests, specialists . . ." She still wouldn't look him in the eye.

"And," he said unsteadily.

"Well, suppose one of the state highway inspectors is harassing us about a right-of-way. It's a marginal case. He could decide either way, but we've got the law on our side if we go to court, only it would take months. I call a friend who is higher up and ask him what the hell we're being hassled about. I don't tell him, but I think the guy is too dumb not to know his man is probably on the take. The hassling stops. Is that wrong?" Cloudy violet eyes in a very pale face watched him intently.

"It's not against the law," he said dubiously.

"Only the greedy ones break the law, and the stupid small fry, and a few old-timers like the Turk who don't know the rules have changed since . . . since Daddy's day."

"Do you think it's *wrong*, James?" Evie's voice was anguished, her fingers moving nervously on the big desk.

He smelled the roses outside the window, leaned across the table, and patted her hand, turning her face crimson with delight. "Tell you the truth, honey, I'd sooner see Irish lawyers from Loyola get the money than WASP lawyers from Harvard. There's still a lot of catching up to do."

Lynnie was giving him a chance to get out—the clearest, most obvious chance he'd had yet. "Anyhow," he went on, "they're after us not for things we did but

193

for things we didn't do." Why had he said "we"?

"There's nothing to worry about from all these inspectors? They won't find us breaking any laws?" The damn first person. Would those violet eyes please stop shining at him?

"Time, money, legal and accountant fees," Marty said, "but that's the cost of doing business, I guess." He didn't add, O'Neill thought, that each new investigation, elaborately reported in the *Star*, would build up a little more the prejudices of prospective jurors. Maybe he didn't know it yet.

"I should leave and let you folks get back to work." There was no disagreement. Lynnie's farewell embrace was much more than a chaste peck. He could not respond to the invitation, not tonight, maybe never again. "I'll call you again tomorrow," he said at the doorway. If she was hurt there were no signs. A third bear hug, this from a tense, wild-eyed Cora, a manly handshake from a troubled Jimmy, a final kiss from Lynnie, and he was on his way.

He didn't return to the Drake but drove south, through the Polish and Lithuanian suburbs where the impeccable neatness of the square, light-colored brick bungalows and small front lawns made it believable that the housewives did indeed scrub the sidewalks every night; then through the shady, curving streets of Beverly, the "magic" neighborhood where some of his classmates now lived; next the ravaged two-flats and apartment buildings of Englewood and Woodlawn, as devastated as any air-raided landscape; and down the Midway with the ugly, haughty university looking down its supercilious gray nose at the rest of the city. What was he doing in this crazy city? Why couldn't he get out of here? Why not leave for Paris tomorrow, fly to New York, and take the Concorde? . . . Only three hours. He couldn't help the Slatterys; they were demanding the impossible of him. Families always demanded the impossible—that's why he never remarried, why he shouldn't have married in the first place.

He drove south down Stony Island, onto the Skyway, out of the city on the Indiana Tollroad into parts of Chicago he had never seen before. The oil refinery haze of Hammond, the fires and chaste white smoke of Gary, the great, black steel mills were a surrealistic painting on the sky over Lake Michigan; in the May setting sun, an intensely vital kaleidoscope of color, light, and energy.

He finally stopped for supper at a lakeside restaurant just outside of Michigan City, and watched the waves roll onto the beach and lap up at the foot of the restaurant's sea wall as the sun slipped under the haze at the other side of the lake. The haze over Chicago was appropriate . . . that's the kind of city it was. He was halfway to Notre Dame in South Bend. His father had always wanted him to go there; probably his own self-education was better. Still, he ought at least to look at the place. Not tonight, though. Plenty of time. . . . What did he mean by that? He was going back to Paris as soon as the investigation could be cleared up. . . .

He permitted himself dessert with his coffee, chocolate-chip ice cream with chocolate sauce. Maybe it was the taste of the chocolate; desire for Lynnie flooded

195

back. She needed reassurance—that was one thing he could do for her. He felt she would be waiting for him again in his hotel room. The image made his heart thump and his blood flow swiftly. Damn testosterone—He broke the speed limit all the way to the entrance of the respectable old Drake.

There was no sliver of light beneath the door. Inside, the room was dark and empty.

 14

He parked his car two blocks away from the "Taylor Street Café." Despite vast acres of parking lots, the cars drawn to the University of Illinois at Chicago Circle filled the streets around the campus like filings drawn to a magnet. The university's drab concrete buildings loomed at the end of the street, squat foothills to the Alps of the Sears Tower and the Standard Oil Building towering behind the university against enormous thunderheads. Pink-and-lemon sky, "tornado weather" his father used to call it. There were tornado warnings on the car radio. Despite the sunlight, which made the storefronts of Taylor Street look like a set for a technicolor musical, it was raining. He hoped he could make it to the café before a downpour.

"1162 Taylor Street," Greg had told him. "You can't miss it; it's right next to 1158, only it doesn't have a number on the door."

"I can probably find the sign," he had replied to the

mysterious voice on the phone.

"Jimmy, man, it doesn't have a sign. No street number, no sign, nothing. You couldn't tell it was a restaurant unless you knew. That's the idea, see? Remember the Taylor Street Café. You can't miss it!"

Obviously you could miss it. That, indeed, was the idea, see; and there was no point in remembering the name, since it didn't have a name.

The building between 1158 and 1164 was an old Greek revival two-flat covered with aluminum siding. An addition built in front of it reached the sidewalk; a narrow window in front, rendered opaque by several years of dirt, displayed a battered sign that read "Open at 11:30." On either side of the window were two doors, one leading to a stairway to the second floor, the other opening to a tiny corridor and another door. He hesitated, thought of Clare, felt the rain come tumbling out of the sky, and walked through the corridor.

That morning he had been sitting in his room picking at breakfast and reading the *Herald* story. The lead was the memo from the chancery office which disproved rumors reported in "another Chicago newspaper." Lynnie was portrayed this time as a serious, responsible businesswoman who had put together the pieces of her shattered family wealth and still found time for charitable and civic service. Her children were honor students at "parochial schools"; Blucher had been made to concede that her company's real estate procedures had always been "beyond reproach" and had insisted that the new investigation was purely routine. The chancery-office press spokesman had refused to comment on the "McCarthy memo"; poor devil probably didn't know a thing about it. There were even two pictures of the development which had been nominated for the planning prize.

So, a point for our side. I hope that Carsello woman knows what she's doing. What if the *Star* tries to fight back? Probably won't just now, but it's no good to get caught in a fight between two journalistic giants. And how do you balance the good effect of a favorable story against the bad effect of being the subject of press controversy for two days running? He still had a lot to learn.

Impulsively he punched out a private phone number which Jerry Lynch had given him with great solemnity.

"Emil Stern," the soft, sincere voice said at the other end.

"Did you have any second thoughts this morning after you read the *Herald*?" he barked without preliminary.

A silence. "Yes, I did. I felt deeply troubled, doubly pained—"

O'Neill cut him off. "Would you have said what you did to the *Star* if you'd known about the McCarthy memo?"

Another silence. "No," characteristic anguish, "I have thought about it with considerable pain and I don't think I would have."

"Are you going to retract?" Let him feel what it's like to be under cross-examination.

"I've weighed that issue very carefully, and I do not

198

think any useful purpose can be served by it." No sign of anger from Stern, just suffering patience. "I really was deeply pained when the reporters approached me yesterday. I have the highest respect for you. Mrs. Slattery is a most accomplished woman. Your relationship with her is transparently beautiful. I did not want to say what I did, yet I felt morally obliged to speak out against corruption."

"Did you stop to think about how much pain your premature moral obligation might have caused Mrs. Slattery's children?"

"I am well aware, Jim, of those implications. Yet a man has a duty . . ."

"You miserable little sawed-off hypocrite! It's your conscience that always encourages you to do what is politically expedient for your side! Who's going to run for the Senate on Lynnie's corpse? You or that castrating bitch you sleep with? Why don't you be honest with yourself, Emil? Admit you hate the Irish with a fervor as strong as anti-semitism. You're not going to get away with this, I promise you." He realized as he said the words he would never try to get even. "And I hope that wretched neurotic drives you out of your mind before you work up enough courage to get rid of her!" He hung up before Stern could answer.

And was promptly disgusted with himself. Fine, marvelous speech. Save it for one of your books. You had to work out your responsibility and guilt on someone, so you picked an easy victim. Bully. Emil will agonize for days before he can fit you in one of his moral pigeonholes, and he's not going to be able to forget what you said about the girl because he's already thinking those things himself. Besides, you might have been able to exploit Stern's guilt. . . .

His musings were interrupted by the phone. "Hey, Jimmy, it's Greg," said a deep, raspy male voice.

"Hello, Greg, it's good to hear from you again," he said dubiously.

"Not again, Jimmy. You never met me. Don't know that I exist."

"All right. Then I don't know you. Who are you?"

"Oh, I'm lots of people, but as far as you're concerned, I'm one of Evelina's Italian cousins . . . hey, man, how about them apples?"

"If you're a relative of hers, you must be all right," he said manfully, wondering if that was the right reply to a Mafioso.

"Don't get me wrong, Jimmy boy; I'm connected, all right, but I'm clean, know what I mean? You didn't see my name in the papers, did you? No outfit stuff at all."

"I don't know whether I saw you in the paper because I don't know your name."

Laughter at the other end of the line—sinister laughter? "Nice, Jimmy boy, real nice. You and me are going to get along fine together. But just so you know I'm clean I thought I might tell you that I really liked some of those stories about the Irish wakes you told the kids yesterday. Poor kids, they really need some heavy laughs, eh, Jimmy boy?"

"You win, Greg, you're clean."

More laughter and then the luncheon invitation. "There are one or two things about this whole mess we could talk over, know what I mean?"

Casting caution to the winds on Lake Shore Drive, O'Neill figured that it was probably better to have the "outfit" on your side than on the other side.

The "Taylor Street Café" reminded him for a moment of a bar he occasionally went to in a Paris suburb.

The bartender and the three dark-skinned men sipping at the bar eyed him suspiciously. Sicilians, he told himself, not Corsicans. The bartender saw the red hair and smiled. "Hey, Jimmy, good to see you. I'm Larry." He extended an immense hand. "Good to have you here, real good. Greggie is at the table in the back."

The back room bore no resemblance to Paris. It was an American ethnic family restaurant: wood tables, unsteady chairs, sausages and cheese hanging from the ceiling, the menu chalked on a blackboard. If they served what they promised it might be a superb meal. The only man in the room wore a light tan suit, white shoes, and dark sunglasses. His long black hair was neatly arranged in sweeping waves, part Valentino and part Stallone. Rings, cuff links, carefully tailored suit all said big money. Taking a deep breath, O'Neill said, "Hey, Greg, I'm Jimmy."

"Hey, Jimmy, good to see you. Hope to see more of you. Good to have you back. Any friend of Evelina's is a friend of ours." The handshake was friendly but overlong. "Sit down, boy, sit down. This place might not look like much, but it's the best in town. Makes those places like Alfredo's or the Tre Scalini look like tourist traps. The only real Italian food is Sicilian food

201

anyhow, just like the only Italian women are Sicilian—isn't that true, eh, Jimmy boy?" He playfully punched O'Neill's arm and knocked the wind out of him.

It was a potentially dangerous situation. A gangster and four hoods and help a long way off. "I can't claim to be an expert on either, Greg, but I like Sicilian food and there's one half-Sicilian and half-Irish woman that's like hot spice in the blood."

He was punched again. "Hey, you really talk like a writer, man. I never met a real writer before, unless you count that Saul what's-his-name who won the prize. He doesn't much like guineas if you ask me, but what the hell? Say, did you know that the blond hair is on our side of the family? Every couple of generations it turns up—Norman blood. There was a Norman kingdom in Sicily for a long time, crusaders and that sort of operation. I got a kid, little guy, whose hair is even lighter than Lynnie's. My poor wife thought I'd be suspicious; we called him Reed."

"Reed?"

"Sure, short for Tancredi, a real good Sicilian name; but it comes from Tancred, which is Norman, of course, so it all figures out. You and Lynnie have a kid, you ought to give it a Norman-Irish name like Seamus, maybe. That's short for Jacques, which means James. I did a paper once on these things in college."

"I don't know about kids. Anyway, where did you go to college?" A Mafioso who studied history.

"The golden dome, where else? Hey, man, didn't you see the class ring? Then an MBA from the god-damn University of Chicago. Say, do you mind if I take these shades off? I figured I'd put on my Godfather duds so you'd know who I was. Well, suit yourself about kids. She's a real woman, that lady. Great mother. Her father and that goof she married didn't want to have anything to do with our side of the family. By damn, when I got married she showed up with all the kids even if her old man, Steve, I mean, didn't like it. Class lady. Boy, I bet she's good in bed, eh, Jimmy?" Another punch. "Yeah, I still see her around. She and my wife are on the woman's symphony board together."

"Symphony board?" The disbelief showed in his voice.

Big laughter from Greg: fine, even white teeth, handsome character, a Sicilian lover from a Mastroianni movie. "Doesn't fit the stereotype, eh? Yeah, Ernie, my friend Jimmy and I will have the works and the reserve chianti too. What was I saying? Oh, yeah. Hey, man, let's be straight about it. Sure, I'm connected, but I'm legit. Couldn't say the same thing for some of my cousins, to tell you the truth, and I'm not sure where all the money that comes into my bank is from; but, hell, neither is the Citibank in New York, and I don't think the Rockefeller money got started any cleaner than did some of our family money—only thing is we still know our roots, know what I mean?"

Greg's flashing brown eyes turned serious for a moment. His thin lips drew tightly together. "Look, Jimmy, big-time crime is as American as blueberry pie—maybe I should've said as American as pizza. The outfit has done nothing that the Jews and the WASPs and you micks didn't do, except maybe add a few colorful names like Big Tuna and Paul the Waiter and Jackie the Lackey. You need an organized national crime conspiracy to sell movies like *The Godfather*. Sometimes I wish the mob *was* that efficient; I wouldn't lose so many loans—no, I'm kidding about that."

Jim felt a surge of sympathy for this strange young man. He thought he'd like reporters from the *Star* a lot less. Maybe he was rationalizing. The hands of the Irish were not exactly clean either.

The food was indeed as good as promised—the best calamari he had ever eaten, and the *chianti classico riservato* made him forget Lynnie's burgundy. He complimented Greg on the meal.

"Yeah, you see, the thing is this boy Larry doesn't want anything but a neighborhood restaurant. He won't let the newspapers in to take pictures, he doesn't want any articles, he doesn't want to be big—he just wants good food for the people from the neighborhood, know what I mean? You can't get reservations, and you come in here, Larry doesn't know you, you might have a hard time getting waited on. Now he knows you, you come back any time, you get the best Sicilian food in the city—that's a good deal, isn't it, Jimmy boy?"

There was almost a plea for acceptance in the young man's voice. "I'll come back with Lynnie," O'Neill replied.

"Oh, you couldn't do that!" Greg was horrified. "She's a class lady, you couldn't bring her into a joint like this."

The chianti had loosened O'Neill's tongue. "Whattya mean? A class person brings class. Besides, this is a class place. You bring your wife here, I'll bring Lynnie here. What's the difference?" Had he begun to sound like a character from *The Godfather*?

"Sure I bring Gina here, but, hell, she grew up in the neighborhood." Greg sipped his chianti nervously.

"Hell, Lynnie grew up in a neighborhood too." He had consumed a lot of wine since he came back to Chicago, more than in Paris.

"Different neighborhood." Greg waved his hand vigorously as if to fend off the sacrilege of confusing neighborhoods.

"When you've been away as long as I have, Greg," he slapped the pockmarked table decisively, "you realize that a neighborhood is a neighborhood."

"How about them apples?" Greg beamed proudly. "You writer fellas sure can write."

O'Neill was not sure whether his leg was being pulled.

They talked about fiction through the meal. Greg's taste was broad and his judgment solid. He also was a man of fierce prejudices. He didn't like Saul what's-his-name one bit. "A goddamn Hyde Park snob," he exploded. "Can't handle women either."

O'Neill wondered if Irish-American storytellers were any better with women.

"Hey, after all this stuff is over, would you and Lynnie come and have dinner with me and the wife? Never had the nerve to ask her before." There was a touching pathos in the request.

"We sure will," he returned, the warmth of the second bottle of chianti loosening his tongue and self-control even more. "Tell you what, the next time you're in Paris you and your wife will have to have dinner with me in my Paris apartment. It's right on the Seine."

"Hey, Jimmy, that's great." Repeated handshakes had replaced the punches. "We'll be there. XVI Arrondissement?"

Nothing about Greg surprised him now. "First of all, though, I've got to get this mess cleaned up with the goddamn U.S. Attorney," he said, swallowing half a tumbler of chianti.

Greg turned serious. "Yeah, that's what I really wanted to talk about. Two things, Jimmy. First of all, me and the big blond kid get along pretty well. I throw them a little business now and then and I don't want to embarrass herself—how about that for knowing the Irish idiom? How about them apples, hey, Jimmy boy?" Another handshake and then serious again.

"So I call him yesterday and say, 'Marty, boy, tell me about this guy Jimmy O'Neill that's hanging around your mother. Is he okay?' Well, let me tell you, Jimmy, the kid just about wanted to canonize you on the spot. So I says to myself, here's a guy I can deal with."

O'Neill began the handshake this time and poured both of them some more wine.

"So what I want to say is there's going to be a lot of money trouble if this thing goes on. I don't want that poor girl liquidating all her stuff just to pay lawyer bills, and I don't know what you got that's loose . . .

206

and, hell, man, you're in a real awkward spot too . . . so, no sweat, no strain. It gets tight for cash, you let me know, you got it?"

They were both embarrassed. "I got it, Greggie. If we have trouble, you and me will get together and work it out—right?"

Greg beamed. "Got it. Man, you Irish learn quick. Now the other thing. I'll say it real fast and let you think about it on your way home. Why don't you put out a contract on Masterman?"

O'Neill almost choked on the wine in his mouth. "To get rid of him?" he sputtered.

"Nothing crude like murder. There's lots of ways you can do a hit job on an ambitious politician like Teddy baby, especially if you're a writer, get me?" He was back to the arm-punching routine. Suddenly sober, O'Neill wondered about black-and-blue marks.

"Give me a few more hints, Greg," he said carefully.

"Look. I says to myself when Gina and I are reading the morning paper—that's short for Regina, if you want to know—I says, if this guy is such a hot-shot writer, he can get stuff printed about a guy like Masterman. Only he's been away from Chicago for a long time and he's forgotten a lot about politics, and he's thinking of the woman's tits a lot of the time, so he doesn't see the connection between getting into print and knocking off Masterman. And he's not likely to know anyone smart enough to see the connection— your goddamn Irish lawyers are smart, but not as tough as their fathers were. So I says to myself, maybe I'm the one to drop him the word. So I drop you the word. It's in your court, Jim baby."

O'Neill wasn't sure what he meant. Too much wine. Too much calamari. Too much hot spice in the blood. He shook hands with Larry and the three guys at the bar, a different threesome, he thought, but he wasn't sure. "You bet I'll be back, Larry . . . bring the little woman along the next time too." He tried to ignore the drenching rain as he walked back to his car.

Greg insisted on walking with him.

"Hey, Jim boy, don't tell herself about this little lunch, huh?" Greg pleaded, oblivious to the damage the rain was doing to his suit.

"Don't worry a minute about it, Greg." He punched his host again, figuring he was still way behind. "We'll work it out, we'll work it out." It occurred to him that he didn't even know Greg's last name.

"One more thing." The water was running down the young man's face as though he were standing in a shower. "Take real seriously what I said about doing your kind of contract on Ted baby. Those guys are evil; I mean, worse than the worst enforcers in the outfit. They're out on the street now, hunting and digging— nothing's too old, nothing's too irrelevant for them to use or slip to the *Star*. They're out to get her, Jimmy. They're out to get her. And when they find out you're involved, they'll try to get you too."

An ominous feeling of doom chased the wine-warmth out of his blood. The rain seemed bitterly cold. Was the worried, dark-skinned young man speaking literally? "What do you mean, Greg?" he asked softly.

208

"I mean," Greg hunched his shoulders as if to fend off the rain, "that those lawyers of yours are real smart. Howard and Lynch. And Anna Maria Carsello is a real good girl too, real good—I know her mother and father. They're not hungry the way Masterman and his bunch are. Every damn law school graduate who is too low in his class to get a good job thinks he can be president of the United States, and the U.S. Attorney's office is the way to go. Look at Jim Thompson. And every punk kid who is sworn in as an assistant thinks he's going to be a goddamn Jody Powell someday. Jimmy, they're bad news. Already this morning I get calls about the kinds of things they're asking, digging way, way back. . . ."

The chill spread through his body. Wine must be wearing off. So Greg was talking literally. "Thanks for the warning, Greggie." He shook hands for the last time. "We'll beat the bastards."

"That's my boy," beamed his host, his good mood restored. O'Neill wished he didn't sound so much like a fight manager.

What the hell was Greg baby talking about? A contract against Masterman with the printed word. It was only when he got into the elevator at the Drake that it all fit together. His head cleared—God, how long had it been stuffed? He was suddenly sober and deadly. Poor Masterman.

He called New York and informed a delighted editor of his plans, dragged out his small portable typewriter and began to pound it vigorously. The story took possession of him, its characters weaving a spell around him. Never before had he had a motive for finishing so quickly. It was long after midnight before he fell exhausted into his bed. The next day he began another chapter. He was interrupted halfway through the second page by a jangling phone. He leaped from the chair as if he had been stabbed, and snarled into his phone.

"Am I in trouble . . ." Lynnie, sounding very unsettled.

What the hell was the woman bothering him for? He almost screamed at her. In the last half-second he caught himself. "Oh, gosh, of course, Lynnie. I'm sorry, really I am. I've started to write. When that happens I just drift away from everything. I'm terribly sorry, I should have called you."

She accepted his explanation without the challenge it deserved. Slade Mannion had now testified that she was at the conspiracy meeting. There didn't need to be a meeting to establish conspiracy but it helped. She had been called before the grand jury. Tomorrow after lunch. Yes, Eddie Howard was worried. No, he could not come. She had to face the grand jury alone. Her lawyer could wait outside the room, and she could consult with him before answering a question. No, she didn't want him with Howard; but if he didn't mind meeting her at Howard's office afterward, she probably would need a quiet, low-calorie supper. The kids were still wonderful; she felt so sorry for them.

He stared glumly at his typewriter for a few moments. He was a dolt for not thinking about her.

He began typing again, his fingers slashing at the keys.

Nancy Carsello was waiting for him in the 111 West Washington Building. He remembered it had been the Conway Building long ago when his father worked at City Hall. He mentioned it to her; she shrugged her shapely shoulders. Youth's disdain for history.

"What's going to happen today, Miss Carsello?" he asked.

"Call me Nancy. Eddie loves to be pompous, but he's disappointed when he's not the only one doing the act." She grinned like a belly I dancer at a Greek restaurant; a very dangerous woman, he thought uneasily. "Okay, Nancy, do we win, lose, or draw today?"

"I don't think we'll lose. Your friend is too smart and too articulate to make any real mistakes—though you watch, Eddie will be mad that she doesn't come out and consult with him. There won't be anything to consult about; they don't have any tricky questions. They'll go through her life history—tax stuff and all—and then ask about the land and the meeting. She'll tell the truth about everything; they may still indict her for perjury and conspiracy, but only because Masterman will be able to find another perjurer like Slade Mannion who would implicate the pope if he thought it would save his precious hide." She leaned back in her chair, looking even more attractive.

"So we can win or draw." He reined in his imagination.

"We win if she's so good that Masterman, who will

be there, by the way, decides that she's too smart a witness to try to go against before a jury of her peers, especially if a smart trial lawyer can get her case severed from the others and put together a jury which doesn't mind that goddamn body of hers. Your friend Jerry Lynch could probably put together a jury which actually liked it—which would mean a vote for the psychic health of juries, wouldn't it?" Then, with a quick, blunt thrust she added, "Do you really love her, O'Neill?"

"I don't think I'd want to be on the stand with you appearing for the other side," he answered, laughing easily. "Yes, I may be a bastard beyond your Taylor Street dreams but I really love her. Always have." He could hardly believe that his enthusiasm had carried him that far.

"Lucky devil."

"Which one? And what if it turns out to be a draw?"

"Both of you. And me on my virginal couch every night. Oh well. A draw, anyhow, is what probably will happen. Majorski, who is trying to persuade himself that he's really not a Nazi, will urge that they leave her alone. That fat little toad Ryan, who will be a disbarred alcoholic by the time he's forty, will push for an indictment, pointing out how she'll attract media attention and how reporters hate women who are rich and beautiful; shrewd old Masterman will stall, waiting to see what comes up. He's a bad man, O'Neill, but he's not dumb. There's a fair number of very bright politicians in the slammer just now because they thought he was."

"How long a stall?"

"Days, weeks, months. He's got till October before the statute of limitations covers the sale."

Time was on their side. The story was the magic sword by which the magic princess would be freed.

Finally Lynnie and Howard came into the office. She wore an almost dowdy gray suit and white blouse, her glasses, and looked exhausted. So that's how beautiful and rich widows dress when they are invited to perjure themselves before the grand jury. Howard's fluffy white eyebrows were pulled together in a thoughtful frown as he eased into his vast leather chair and began the usual lecture.

"On the whole, Mrs. Slattery, I am not unfavorably affected by your account. Let me emphasize once again that I was dismayed that you didn't consult me once. On the other hand, I tend to agree that the questions were relatively straightforward. From your description of your answers I would venture to guess, subject to later correction, that you would impress even the . . . uh . . . uninspired folks who sit on grand juries. Mr. Masterman will have doubts about taking you on in court. Most trial lawyers in cases like this want to keep their defendants off the stand. I presume that Mr. Lynch will want to pursue the opposite strategy."

He reached for the humidor in which his expensive cigars were stored and carefully examined a number of them before making his choice. His lips pursed thoughtfully; you couldn't tell whether he was thinking about cigars or the case.

"It would also appear that Mr. Mannion cannot recollect the exact day of the alleged meeting. That, of course, eliminates the possibility of alibis for the alleged conspirators, but it also casts even more doubt on his credibility. Mr. Lynch will be able to make much of that, particularly if he can get the trial severed. Furthermore, an intelligent federal judge, and there are one or two of them still on the bench in this district, would throw your indictment out of court after a preliminary reading. If you believe in prayer, you might ask the deity to get you the right judge. It would help even more if the case did not fall into the hands of someone whose experience of life comes from lecturing a law school class."

"We don't even have an indictment yet, Eddie," Nancy Carsello hastily reminded him.

His frosty eyes probed her for a moment as he put his cigar clipper back into a desk drawer. "Are you suggesting, young woman, that in addition to being pompous I have reached the age in life where I begin to rave on?"

"It was so . . . so degrading," said Lynnie, as though she hadn't been listening. "That vile little Ryan boy prancing around, insinuating, leering, acting like I was an evil woman . . ."

"And Majorski waxing philosophic while that bastard Masterman just stared like a dead fish and all the time the jurors were trying to stay awake," continued the Carsello girl angrily.

Lynnie looked grateful for the sympathy. "How can evil be so bland?" asked Lynnie.

"My dear Mrs. Slattery, evil is always bland. You are too young to remember much about the late Chancellor Hitler, but—"

He was cut off by a buzz on the intercom. Nancy grabbed it without asking. "Yes, put him on," she snapped.

She listened intently, muttering an occasional "yeah." Finally she grimaced. "About what we'd expect . . . huh? Don't be sexist . . . yeah, okay." She hung up.

"You will think it irregular that we accept such communications, Mr. O'Neill," began Howard, "but these are not ordinary cases. Normally there are . . . uh . . . sources by which rumors can be tracked down and checked; there are many federal government personnel in this city who, particularly in the wake of the recent scandals in the national government, would very much like to see Mr. Masterman come a cropper. I cannot judge them guilty of violating the spirit of their oaths of office under such circumstances, though I'll grant you that it makes an interesting ethical point."

"Like I say, Eddie, I don't sleep with him. He knows that if I ever get him to bed he'll never get away. I'm sorry, honey, I'm in a horrid mood. You were great. You knocked them dead. Even that insect Ryan is hesitant. Old Ted is hedging his bets till they get another witness ready to perjure himself, some poor fool who doesn't want to go to the slammer for his income tax games. They're going to need a really good witness against you and they know it."

The girl's eyes were glistening. Damn it, she's proud of Lynnie. The woman wins over everyone.

"Excellent news and, I suppose, as always reliable,"

Howard commented. "I would observe, Mr. O'Neill, for the sake of the novel you will undoubtedly write about this event," his shrewd old eyes boring into O'Neill, "that while I would certainly applaud the success of my young associate in winning herself a spouse, by whatever measures her culture and our era deem appropriate, I would draw the line at using . . . uh . . . bed partners as a source of information, unless, of course, it were truly an extraordinary set of circumstances."

The clever old goat, how did he know about the story? Probably just guessed.

After two drinks and some very high-calorie pasta at the red-and-black-lacquered Como Inn overlooking the Kennedy Expressway, Lynnie relaxed enough to laugh about the grand jury experience. He led her very carefully through the story, wishing he could take notes or use a tape recorder. Once he probed a little too hard about one of the questions asked by Assistant U.S. Attorney Ryan.

"Are you really writing a book?" she asked angrily.

"Don't be silly," he answered. "Eat your Ravioli alla Como. Revert to Taylor Street."

"Yes, isn't she cute? I bet that boy wants to marry her and even wants her to have a career, and she's frightened." She speared a ravioli. "Are you writing a book about me?"

"Someone frightened of marriage? I don't believe it. And you still have time to play matchmaker?"

"I'm an Irish mother with five kids to dispose of. I can't help myself. You're ducking my question." She put the fork down with determination.

"Do you really think I'd exploit you, Lynnie?" He pretended to be hurt.

Her expression changed from suspicion to sorrow; she touched his hand. "I'm sorry, darling, of course not. I guess I'm just an emotional wreck today. Too many ambitious young men without any morals. I really am sorry. I shouldn't take it out on you, of all people." She tightened her grip on his hand.

He dismissed it lightly. "Eat some more pasta, run an extra mile tomorrow morning."

Guilty now. "Oh, Jimmy, I hate to admit it, but the widow woman's falling apart. I haven't done any running in a week. I mean, why worry about your figure, if you're going to . . ." She fought to hold back more tears. "I can tell from the expression on your face that you're disappointed in me. I'll go back to it tomorrow, though . . . ugh . . . it's hard after you stop."

"Not displeased at all." He took her hand reassuringly. "Just kind of glad to find that the widow woman has a few flaws around the edges."

"Stay around, darling, you'll see that there are a lot of flaws, and not all of them at the edges." She paused; then contemplating the candle glowing between them, she said softly, "You're grace for me, Jim. God sent you as grace just when I needed it."

She began to reverently kiss the tips of his fingers, oblivious to the rest of the Como Inn. "I was beginning to feel like a weary old bitch and you showed up on an April morning to make me think I was young again. Then this terrible investigation; I'm ready to fall apart, and you're here steady as a rock."

He felt himself tumbling into darkness, a deep, dank pit. His halfhearted lovemaking and thoughtless support hardly made him a messenger of grace. "You don't value yourself enough, Lynnie," he muttered. "You deserve a lot better than me."

Now her face registered surprise. Her vast purple eyes grew even larger. "I don't know what you mean, Jim. Anyhow, you're the best I've ever had or am ever likely to get, and I love you so much I turn to mush every time I think of you."

He brushed her lips with his knuckles. "We can't stop each other from growing old," he said, trying to feel tragic.

"We can help each other grow old gracefully," she insisted.

More religion. "Are you grace for me too?" he asked skeptically.

Her eyes widened in surprise. She patted his hand like an affectionate parent. "Of course, dear," she said as though she were explaining the obvious. "I'm God for you."

O'Neill clumsily withdrew his hand from her grasp. What the hell did that mean? He was afraid to ask.

He drove her down Milwaukee Avenue into the crowded Loop where her car was parked. She was probably ready for bed, but he had to get back to his story; he insisted that she go home to cheer up her children.

Back in his room, with the windows open to catch the soft lake breezes, he sat down to work. He hesitated as he put a new sheet of paper in the typewriter. His fantasy was the knight saving a magic princess. Once the magic princess was saved the knight might not want her. The fantasy was only a temporary energy source. Her fantasy involved grace; she took it seriously. It was a dangerous comic fantasy. He began to type, then paused and rubbed his chin thoughtfully. *A Comedy of Grace*: a title like that deserved a story.

 # 15

He put the phone back on its cradle. A brisk, chilling wind blowing off the lake through the open window added to his exhilaration. His throat was dry, his pulse rapid, his senses acutely perceptive, adrenalin raced through his veins. Battle lust. He had forgotten what it was like. The last time? A touch of it in Derry, the real thing in Enugu during the final phase of the Biafran evacuation. Before that, Kurdistan and Bangkok; then the first time in the mountains beyond Dien Bien Phu. Nothing like it—lust for a woman could not compare with the anticipation of battle—fear so strong you could taste it, eagerness for the risk, the excitement, the danger, the toss of the dice.

Now another battle here in Sarnarkand-on-Lake Michigan. His last battle before he became an old man, a battle for a magic princess he didn't really want. No matter, it was now the battle he wanted, not the princess. He would feel guilty afterward, as he always did when the battle was over; now all that mattered was the battle. The self-analyzing skeptic in the corner of his soul could watch and wait; his day would come later. Now the warrior's turn again. This time the battle was one of words, not guns or plastic explosives, and words were his best weapon.

His fingers drummed the telephone. He'd better check his strategy with someone who was better informed. Recklessness had almost cost him his life in Enugu. Call someone, Howard? The pompous old goat would read him a lecture. Who then? He grabbed the telephone book, impatiently searched for the L's and then fiercely punched out the number on the phone.

There was no delay in getting through to Jerry Lynch. "Jim, I was thinking of calling you this morning. It's a damn shame. It makes me want to get the hell out of this lousy country—the man is a rotten little Hitler!"

He was momentarily taken aback. "What?"

"I mean about the indictment. I just heard they're going to hand it down the day after tomorrow. If ever there was a misuse of prosecutorial power, it's this time. I'd like to nail that guy into a coffin and keep him there till Judgment Day."

So Masterman had finally found his second witness. Well, small good it would do him. "If it comes down to it, Jerry, you'll get a chance to. I'm sure Lynnie will want you."

"Oh, hell, I wasn't thinking about getting a case. Yes, goddamn, I was. She's my friend. I . . . well, I can't tell her this, but I won't take a fee. I couldn't. That son of a bitch has bitten off more than he can chew this time. Lynnie will cream him when she testifies." Lynch's voice was tight with anticipation. So there were other kinds of battle lust.

"That's not why I called, Jerry," he said coolly. "I've got a little legal . . . uh . . . problem of my own."

"Oh my God, not you too. What is it?"

"It's more of an opportunity than a problem, I guess. I've just been invited to lunch at The Attic tomorrow."

"High-class place. Who's the invitor?"

"Theodore F. Masterman." He relished every syllable, picturing Lynch's open mouth.

There was silence at the other end of the line. A soft voice, "Why?"

"He's got an idea that I'm writing a story with a character that is rather like him."

"What the hell ever gave him that idea?"

"I suspect that someone at my publisher's has trouble with the IRS and makes part of his payments by being an informant. I sent a hundred pages off to New York a week before last. I rather imagine Mr. Masterman read a Xerox of them last night." He was enjoying himself immensely.

"You mean you *are* writing about him? Wow . . . Jimmy," alert and decisive now, "are you clean? Have you been in any scrapes they could get you on?"

He shifted his position in the chair. There were big whitecaps on the lake now, crashing on the breakwater. "I've had scrapes in lots of places, Jerry, but

221

nothing indictable by the United States government."

"Taxes?"

"An American self-employed writer living out of the country? I get audited every year and they don't have a thing. I didn't want to take chances with my daughter's future," he added lamely. Poor excuse from a warrior.

"Is the character readily identifiable as Masterman? Could he get you on a libel charge?" Lynch was running down his check list.

He shrugged his shoulders even though Jerry couldn't see him. "I've changed enough of the details so he'd have a hard time proving identifiability. Anyhow, let him sue. It'd sell a lot more books and would finish his chances of getting into the Senate."

"You know, Jimmy, you could be a real menace. Remind me to stay away from your women. A book of yours is a cinch to get on the bestseller list, and the Chicago papers would go wild. You'd kill the poor son of a bitch."

"Before you get a chance to."

Again the pause at Lynch's end. Was Jerry shocked? Good for him.

"And the informants at your publisher's did you a favor by tipping him off. Raises the issue even before an indictment. Were you counting on that?"

"There was bound to be a leak. I've got another hundred-fifty pages I'll bring along to lunch tomorrow. That should give him indigestion."

A low whistle at the other end of the line. "You do play rough. So the deal is he drops the charges and you drop the novel. Have you told Eddie Howard or Lynnie?"

"Are you kidding? Poor Eddie would have a stroke."

"Yeah. No, it's a good idea to keep them out of it. Masterman's a tough bastard, Jimmy, really tough," Lynch warned him sternly. "He's not going to give up easily."

"I hope he's tough. There's no fun in beating a pushover, is there, Jerry?"

"I guess not. I feel kind of sorry for Masterman. You got him in a corner; he'll fight like a caged tiger, but I don't see a way out for him."

"I wanted to hear you say it. You want to bet on their handing down that indictment?"

"No way, no way . . ." His voice trailed off thoughtfully. What was Jerry thinking? Scheming a back-up plan? Thinking of who he could talk into a bet about the indictment? No, more likely imagining another nail in Masterman's coffin. "Just be careful. He's a really vicious character."

"I've known a few in my life. Don't worry, I'll be careful—for Lynnie's sake, if not my own."

The phone conversation increased his excitement. He shed his shirt despite the lake breeze. He could hardly wait till the next day. The phone rang. Rome calling. Clare. Had anything happened? Of course not, but she hadn't heard from him in ten days. Was he all right? He was into a story. She knew what he was like at those times. Besides, some friends of his in Chicago were in legal trouble. Bad case of government oppression. He'd tell her the whole story when he got back in

223

a couple of weeks. Yes, he had finally found some old friends. It was good to see them, much better than he had thought.

"Have you seen *her?*" asked Clare, her voice hard and suspicious.

"Who?" He felt his intestines twist in surprise.

"You know who I mean. The girl from your past. The one you're carrying a torch for all these years, your childhood sweetheart."

"You're bluffing, Clare. I've told you twenty times there isn't any such person. The man I'm working with is a lawyer named Jerry Lynch. I was just on the phone with him before you called."

Grudgingly she retreated. "Okay, Daddy, you haven't really convinced me. I love you anyhow, and I know I'll just hate her when you finally bring her around."

He laughed as though she were a little girl refusing to disbelieve in Santa Claus. He would call her in a few days and she should keep out of trouble. Sure he loved her; the book he was working on would pay her college tuition. Bell-like laughter, then the disconnected line. He was shaking like a man with palsy. Brave warrior terrified by a seventeen-year-old.

He got up, closed the window, shook the memory of Clare out of his mind, and went back to the typewriter. He forgot about lunch, devoured a hamburger at four-thirty, and plunged on in his story, his battle with Masterman blending with the conflict of the story and the reality of the story shutting out the world beyond his imagination. He did not notice the bellman who brought his steak for all the ruthless, corrupt young assistant United States Attorneys who crowded his imagination; they were real and he was not. The brooding, sinister presence of the U.S. Attorney lurking in the background of the story, manipulating his victims like an evil puppetmaster, was more immense that the vast lake turning golden and rose in the spring sunset outside his window. His war was no longer with the real Ted Masterman but with his fictional counterpart, his own creature whom he would ultimately destroy. Storytellers played God with their characters.

Then sexual arousal, peremptory, implacable. So it had often been in the thrill of war, the lust for a woman and the lust for battle mixing in confused but irresistible desire. Lynnie would still be at her office in the shopping plaza, finishing up her work before the ordeal of indictment and trial began. No better way to prepare for the joust tomorrow than by possessing a woman tonight.

Late rush-hour traffic surged ahead as his Citation sped west on the Eisenhower Expressway. He drove steadily, his hands sweaty on the wheel, his body tense with anticipation. No middle-age sex with her this time. Using her? What else were women for? His grip tightened on the wheel.

The lights were on in her office. As he expected, she was clearing up her desk, an efficient woman for all her untidiness. He knew nothing of her work, had deliberately stayed away from her office and avoided questions about the business. He was astonished to learn at the

Stern dinner party that Lynnie would probably win a prize for building a "neighborhood suburb." The successful businesswoman with civic and social concerns was a stranger to him. There had been no hint of it in her youth and there was not much talk of it even now. Did she think it would bore him? Maybe it would. She was a mystery, he told himself as he rode up in the slow elevator, but a mystery he wanted very badly. Find out about the company some other time.

She was wearing reading glasses and a thin blue dress with a floral pattern—almost a house dress. Her hair was tousled, and she hadn't made up her face; she looked tired, every day of her forty years. But still delicious. Lynnie, you'll look delicious at seventy. Tenderness mingled with desire, making his hunger even greater.

The office was as cluttered as her house. No onion smell, though. She looked up, saw him standing silently in the doorway, smiled her sun-dimming smile. "I thought maybe you had gone back to Paris." A jest, no trace of anger.

"I'm sorry," he muttered through tight lips, "it's what happens when I get carried away by a story."

"No problem, Jimmy, I've been busy."

"You shouldn't be here alone this late; someone with rape on his mind might come along."

"I should be so lucky." She missed his intention, then saw the hard look in his eyes and turned away unnerved.

He took her into his arms, a captured princess now to be used savagely and to be awakened to savage response. She was astonished by his fury, then terrified. He would smash into the inner secrets of her body and soul, invade, possess, absorb, blend her into himself so that all that she was depended on him for its existence. He would force her own fury to explode and consume him. They were two firestorms sweeping through a forest to merge into one roaring inferno, two wild animals locked in writhing combat, two swirling rivers rushing together into a tremendous waterfall roaring toward the sea.

At the end, it was not conquest that made him shout with pleasure but a terrifying tenderness, a warm flash of incandescent light. He held her gently in his arms after the fires had ebbed and the light faded, affectionately reassuring her as they clung to one another on the office couch; her hair disheveled, her clothes in rumpled disarray, she glowed happily. "So that's the way the French make love," she murmured. "Sure is an interesting use of office furniture."

"No." He caressed her hair. "It's the way the Irish make love when they finally get wrought up."

"Then give me the Irish love any day, in fact every day." She nudged her head more deeply against his shoulder.

"We don't get wrought up every day," he laughed. "But once we do . . ."

"I can believe it. Today was a good day to begin the widow woman's postgraduate education in Irish lovemaking."

"Why today?"

"I feel guilty even mentioning it just now, but dear

Mr. Masterman finally got his second perjurer. They're going to hand down an indictment the day after tomorrow."

As if from a distance he contemplated his cruelty. He had taken advantage of a woman with a terrible worry, had known about the worry, and hadn't even bothered to mention it. Well, worry made her an even more cooperative lover. "Lynnie, I know it's hard not to worry, but don't. I told you that he'd never put you in jail. Believe me." He began to kiss her again. She touched his lips in weak self-defense.

"Just now, darling," she said breathlessly, "I'm prepared to believe anything you say."

He ran his fingers back and forth on her lips, reveling in the glow of her wide, soft eyes. "I suppose you think God sent me to assault you tonight," he laughed.

"Of course he did, darling. He knew I needed you and he put all kinds of terrible dirty thoughts into your head, bless him."

"So even this is grace?" he asked skeptically, touching her.

"Wow . . . yes, of course. What else could it be?"

"It won't stop us from growing old, Lynnie," he murmured in her hair.

"Nothing can do that, silly; at least we grow old being grace for one another." She snuggled even closer to him. "I like this kind of grace."

"And then we'll die." He was suddenly grim.

"Until we die, we'll laugh at death every time we screw. You see, you were wrong long ago, Jimmy. Loving a woman isn't death. It's cheating death."

"Death has the last laugh," he sighed heavily, pulling away from her.

She drew him back into her arms and kissed his throat. "Well, we can somehow face his laugh gracefully and tell him that we lived till the end. Can you enjoy me the way you just did and not think for just a moment that we'll finally laugh even at death?"

"You deserve a lot better that I can ever give you, Lynnie," he said morosely.

She sat up, rearranged her rumpled dress, and put a clenched fist against his jaw. "You know, I might just slug you if you say that again. Every time I try to thank you for loving me, you tell me how I deserve someone much better. Now be quiet and let me finish." She put her hand over his mouth.

"I've loved you since I could talk. I lost you once, and now, thank the good Lord, I've at least got my claws half into you. I've never had much love in my life. If God sends me grace like you to make up for what's gone wrong before, I'm not going to send you back for a newer model and," she took her hand off his mouth and dug her fingers into his thick, kinky hair, "there may still be some reasons you should sneak off to Paris without me. I'm willing to listen to them when the day comes, but don't try to tell me that the reason is you're not good enough for me. Maybe you're not, but I'll be the judge of what is the best I'm ever likely to get."

He stripped away her remaining clothes and rolled her off the couch to the floor. "Not again, darling," she protested weakly, "I couldn't take—"

His hand muffled her protest as with quick, confident movements he pinned her to the floor. His kisses assaulted her breasts and his hands roamed over her docile body, challenging, teasing, cherishing. Her response now was different. The first time, she had been frightened, then submissive; now she was an active participant, ravaging as well as being ravaged, forcing him to the depths of his passion just as he was forcing her to the depths of hers. In a quiet corner of his raging brain a laugh took shape. He remembered racing her on the beach, challenging her only to have her challenge him. Invade her and she invades you. Tear away all her self-control and she will strip you of yours. He could no longer tell which of the merging avalanches dominated. Nor did he care. His final moment of pleasure was flawless, so perfect that it was painful, so exquisite that for a moment he thought he would die.

The laugh wrenched free from its quiet corner and exploded almost at the same time as his pleasure. She was laughing too. In their shared laughter they embraced.

On the expressway he permitted himself to admire his male powers, if only to blot out the implications of his joy. In the endless primal struggle between man and woman, he had won an exultant victory. He played the scenes back in his imagination. He was a wandering samurai who defeated his enemies and took whatever woman he wanted. He vividly imagined all the things he would do in future triumphs.

A half moon was rising over Lake Michigan as he turned onto the Drive at the end of Congress. The moon again. An ugly, fearsome, lifeless satellite. Why did anyone ever think it was romantic? Lynnie's absurd superstitions about God sending him were not to be taken seriously either. He was acting on his own. He was no puppet of a conniving deity. His lust for her was his own, not God's. God, if there was one, didn't feel lust.

How can he possibly know? she asked herself, wrapping a towel around her body . . . dratted kids always taking the robes. . . . He knows when I need spectacular sex without even seeing me or talking to me. He's got my body figured out perfectly, can make me do anything he wants. If he ever gets over being afraid, he'll own me.

Dear God, I liked it. Am I kinky? Maybe our kinks match. It really wasn't kinky, just passionate. The old widow's learning a bit about passion—better late than never.

She sighed and lackadaisically began to hang up her clothes. He may have me figured out, but I don't know what to do about him. So dour and timid some of the time and a conquering warrior other times. He's afraid of me and afraid of getting involved and afraid of death and hangs around like a worn-out puppy dog. Then he comes into my office, his eyes burning with arrogant confidence, and makes me explode. I'm as much a coward as he is. I didn't do too badly tonight, though.

Turned into slapstick comedy—even more fun. He's not witty with me much, with the kids all the time.

Why so damn serious about me? Why can't I make him laugh more?

She sat dejectedly on the side of her bed contemplating her toes. It was *so* good. Her body's rhythms had meshed with his. She had lost control of her own rhythms. The volcano that had exploded within her was unlike any . . .

She got up from the bed and turned off the lights in the bathroom. No point getting yourself worked up when your man ravages you and goes back to his book. Dear God, what should I do?

The exclamation became a prayer. She was on her knees in front of the old Sacred Heart statue hidden behind a Kleenex box on the vanity. It's all your fault, you know. You put us near one another in the world. You made us fall in love, you brought him back, you got me in trouble with the law to keep him around town. You must have something up your sleeve. Let me know what it is so I don't mess up things for you again. How should I handle him?

The room was silent, the statue implacable. I tell you what, I'll make a deal. You let me have him and I'll promise you one first-rate Irish Catholic novelist. What do you mean you don't make deals? Sure you do. Well, I'll do my part anyhow. . . .

She made the sign of the cross mechanically and dragged herself off her knees. Getting out of shape already. Gotta get back to the running tomorrow. She turned off the light, threw aside the towel, and snuggled under the sheets, telling herself sternly that tomorrow was a critical day and she should not stay awake fantasizing. She remembered something she'd left out of her prayer.

Oh yes, please keep me out of jail. If you want me to take care of the poor man, I can't do it behind bars. . . .

 16

His sleep was deep and undisturbed, his dreams filled with slender limbs and full breasts. He awoke at nine-thirty, relaxed and refreshed; ate a huge breakfast, and impulsively called Monique in Paris. She was in one of her ironic, professional-psychiatrist moods. No blatant charges like Clare's. She was so glad to hear from him. The children were home from school and asked for him every day. Etienne was busy with a case of immense importance, or so he said; "There was a widow involved whom, my dear, I simply do not trust"; the advocate Leclerq had invited them to Saint-Tropez at the end of June to sail on his pig of a yacht. He insisted that "*le bon* Geemie and his lovely daughter" join them; doubtless the advocate's son found Clare interesting. "Of course not, he is far too shy to even talk to her much less make love to her. If your 'work' in Chicago is finished you must come, of course, though not to protect Clare; that one can take care of herself. But of course, darling, we will eagerly await your return. You love me?" Now flustered. "It is nice of you to say it. It must be pleasant in Chicago."

The last sentence the most ironic and suggestive of all. Damn, why had he called her?

A brisk shower, a careful selection of the most conservative suit, one that would be appropriate for a prestigious old club in the Field Building; 175 more pages of the novel Xeroxed the night before, packed in a sleek leather case; then a walk down Michigan Avenue under the clear May sky, a faint recollection of the *High Noon* theme echoing in the back of his head.

The Attic was so distinguished a restaurant that it could afford to be plain. Simple white china, serviceable old silverware, sturdy but inexpensive tables, gleaming tablecloths which made up in cleanliness what they lacked in expensive thickness—not one of your plastic new clubs in the lake-shore skyscrapers—old men in five-hundred-dollar suits, ancient waitresses, an imperious Hungarian maitre d'. The ethnic neighborhoods of Chicago spread out to the west beyond the river until they lost themselves in the suburban distance on a rare smogless day. Ideal time and place for a conflict. Masterman would be late, of course, a way of throwing his adversary off base. A foolish ploy with so skilled a warrior as James McCormack O'Neill. He picked up the *Wall Street Journal* calmly and read slowly and carefully an article about the problems of the plastics industry. His heart was beating rapidly, his head was clear, the adrenalin was working again. He was eager for the battle to begin, but not too eager. He could wait; he held all the cards.

Finally Masterman came, twenty minutes late, filled with apology. No trouble recognizing him; he had seen him enough on television. Masterman himself doubtless knew that there would be few six-foot-two, red-haired Irishmen waiting in the tiny lobby of The Attic, even if the FBI hadn't found a picture of him on a dustjacket in a local bookstore.

The United States Attorney was even taller than he was and much thinner—a lean, hollow face; long, thinning, lifeless blond hair; deepset, clear blue eyes like the icy waters of the fjords; high-pitched voice; tense, sharp features; long, nervous fingers playing with the silverware. Theodore Masterman reminded him of the Evangelical Lutheran pastor in the church down the street when he was growing up: an aloof, intense, dedicated man, unmarried, totally committed to the pure principles of the Reformation—so dedicated, in fact, that he embarrassed his well-to-do parishioners. After a year and a half he left for a small congregation in rural Nebraska.

O'Neill began to be afraid. Masterman was a totally dedicated man too, a true believer, a deadly and dangerous foe. He had made a mistake in underestimating him. He stirred uneasily; the balance of strength had shifted to his enemy.

Masterman seemed to sense his hesitation. He was brisk, friendly, intelligent, radiated energy and strength. Their conversation during the meal was quick, wide-ranging, and sophisticated. Literature, art, music, French law. He professed to be greatly interested in the changes going on in the French pretrial processes, the new functions of the *juge d'instruction* (with a faint hint of the similarities and the differences in the American grand jury system, a nice preliminary blow). O'Neill quoted his friend Etienne DuLac at great length.

"DuLac, oh yes, I've heard of him. Specialist in international corporate law, isn't he? Very famous man. Married to a lovely psychoanalyst, as I remember."

An ice-water voice to match the cold eyes. So they had found out that much about him in such a brief period of time. The taxpayers were getting their money's worth. There was probably little about him that Masterman didn't know. He began to worry that he had forgotten something that they could use against him. Masterman had won another preliminary round.

"So lovely that I wouldn't ever want to be on her couch," he laughed back, defying the U. S. Attorney to make what he could out of such a comment.

There were other hints. Biafra. The Nigerian government would certainly like to have him back, but no American court would extradite, at least he didn't think so. Derry. He had broken British law, but there was no way the English would want that story to become public. No mention of Bangkok. Well, they missed something. He thought fleetingly of the lovely Thai girl he had pulled out of the flaming boat. Where was she now? Was she well? God knows she was the kind to survive, come what may. Such lovely legs . . . then Lynnie's legs and a calming of his nerves.

Neither had dessert. Both ordered tea, a faint smile from Masterman at the common order. "You liked the corned beef?" he asked cordially enough.

"For the Irish there is only good corned beef and better. This was better." He laughed again. Masterman had the FBI; he had his tongue. We beat you bastards at Clontarf and we'll beat you again, he thought to himself.

The real battle was about to begin. "Well, I was fascinated, as you can imagine, to learn you were writing a novel about federal legal procedure," said Masterman, briskly clearing away any preliminary fencing.

"I don't write novels, Mr. Masterman," he responded meekly. "I don't have that kind of talent. I just write stories."

"Please call me Ted. Everyone does, and I'll presume the right to call you Jim?"

He nodded his assent.

"Those who have seen it tell me that you have been remarkably successful in capturing the flavor of our business—ambitious young lawyers, dubious politicians, clever, high-priced defense attorneys, Mafia dons. They felt you must have lived in the United States Courthouse for months to soak it all up."

"Never even been inside a federal office building. It's all a work of the imagination." Again he carefully down-played his achievement—must not appear too eager.

"I thought I'd offer the cooperation of our office if you were interested in getting a look at the inside, though from what I'm told your imagination is very good." He was playing nervously now with a fork. Smooth voice or not, fella, I've got you worried. "You never have been investigated, then, I take it?"

The bastard knows my whole history; he also knows that I don't believe that he hasn't read the manuscript. "Never once. I've led a remarkably dull life as far as the law is concerned."

"Not even on income tax?" So that was the threat. Go back over the old returns. Fine, go right ahead. Let my tax people earn their retainers. A faint tinge of doubt. Maybe they *could* find something but it would take a long time. "Come on, Ted, a self-employed writer living out of the country, the IRS folks go over me with a microscope every year. They grudgingly tell my tax lawyers in New York that I'm as clean as a whistle. I don't even see them, so that's hardly an investigation I could write about in one of my stories."

Masterman nodded sympathetically. "There's a hell of a lot of inequities in the tax code. All the reforms I've heard about would just make more inequities."

"I'm not complaining. I was born during the Depression. I'm glad to have the income to pay taxes on."

Masterman smiled this thin, tight smile. "Yes, it certainly has changed since then, hasn't it? I imagine neither of us ever expected to be eating lunch at The Attic."

He gave away very little. Much more clever than O'Neill had expected. Maybe they already had something on him from the tax returns. Fear began to clutch at his windpipe.

"Of course, anyone who tries to write about a real situation runs the risk that some damn fool will enter a libel action against him," Masterman went on with the same tight smile.

Preliminary relief. He was firing all his guns; perhaps all he had were blanks.

O'Neill shrugged. "You know how hard it is to get a libel judgment, especially when you have to prove malice. Personally I think writers have too much leeway nowadays. All libel suits do is sell more books."

"They can scare off publishers though." A quick, deadly parry.

So that was it. The informant was pretty high up. Masterman must be desperate to be trying something that silly. O'Neill began to feel better. He laughed easily. "The best thing that can happen to a book is for the word to get around that a major publisher was afraid to touch it. The other big companies line up to get it, each one with a bigger promotion budget. Practically guarantees that a movie will be made." Slowly, ace, slowly; he must still have a big card to play. That was a throwaway.

"Of course, you would know a good deal about our work from the Evelina Slattery investigation, I presume?" Fog settled over the ice in his eyes.

How long since he had heard her called 'Evelina'? Her poor mother, surely—no, he'd forgotten Greggie baby. A warning gong in his brain. "I've only met with Mrs. Slattery and her lawyer once or twice." Careful, Jimmy, careful.

"Yet you are very good friends, I take it." A slight emphasis on "very." So that was it. He had never thought of that angle. How much did Masterman know? Had they been watching last night? Did they have pictures? His mind raced. He had to think.

"We've known each other a very long time."

"Your fathers were friends too, as I remember. Political standards were different then, of course, though I must say it is only federal prosecutors like my predecessors and myself who have managed to change the standards."

What was the threat? A leak to the *Star* about his affair with Lynnie coupled with a reexamination of their families' pasts? More than enough scandal to mess up five young lives. Check, O'Neill, you're in check. Desperately he reached for a response, struck out blindly. "My father had the misfortune to be honest even in those days, Ted. As for Mr. Conroy, he was indeed a product of another era, poor man. I think my father died happier than he did, though it's hard to tell. In any case, Lynnie and I were caught in too much when we were growing up. In God's providence we end up middle-aged with a second chance. We're going to be married soon, after we get my first marriage straightened out with the Church."

He enjoyed the immensity of his lie. Would Lynnie say that God had whispered it in his ear? The line about the Church was bound to throw Masterman; a leaked scandal about people who might actually be married before the leak or whose marriage was being delayed by the Church could ricochet dangerously. The chilly fog in the U.S. Attorney's eyes lifted enough to show uncertainty. Lucky stab in the dark.

"I certainly wish you all the happiness in the world. I can appreciate that these must be very trying times for you." Masterman's words were tumbling out now;

he'd lost his composure. "I haven't watched the case very closely, but I assume there are lots of extenuating circumstances—a young widow caught without any money or experience, not understanding the implications. I hardly imagine there is any question of serious guilt. Extenuation would be very important in any decision."

So the tide of battle was turning. It had been a narrow escape. Masterman didn't have quite enough guts. He said nothing, letting the extenuation option hang in the air.

Masterman lumbered on. "My two young assistants on the case are very dedicated men. Frankly, I've been a little ill at ease with their zeal. In fact, I've been meaning to take a good hard look at the whole matter. I don't think I can resist their pressure for an indictment, but I would imagine that I'll be able to work something out with Ed Howard so that it doesn't go any further than that."

Aha, a deal. Don't jump at it. "An indictment would be a serious mistake, Ted. I wouldn't do it if I were you."

Masterman shook his head sadly. "I can understand what it means to you, but you know what it's like in an organization. Candidly, if I turn down my assistants on this one, it'll be a devastating blow to morale. I can't afford to have them quit on me."

O'Neill shrugged and slowly poured himself a second cup of tea. "It will still be a mistake. First of all, Lynnie is innocent. There's enough evidence for Jerry Lynch to prove that in court. It would not only be unjust to indict her, but it would badly affect the rest of your investigation when they prove that Slade Mannion is perjuring himself." It was another immense lie, a diversion to shake Masterman. No deal yet.

Masterman's hand drummed a spoon softly against the table. "The evidence will have to be worked out in a court of law, but under the circumstances I value your insight. You've seen more than a little of life, Jim; and if you're convinced, quite apart from your relationship with her, that there's a chance of serious injustice being done here to Mrs. Slattery and her family, I would be remiss in my oath if I didn't take that insight into account when I exercise my discretion in seeking an indictment."

Bullshit. He was backing down. "I wouldn't try to tell you your business, Ted. Nor would I say that Lynnie was innocent if I knew better. I wouldn't say anything. Probably I wouldn't even be here. I know guilt when I bump into it, God knows. Someday I'll tell you about some of the murders in Biafra."

"Yes, I will certainly have to take a closer look at the case. If your insight is accurate . . . well," he grinned, a weak attempt at suggestiveness, "there frankly won't be any obstacles to a happy wedding day from my office."

Victory if he wanted it. It wasn't enough. There would still be clouds over Lynnie's life. You didn't settle with a man like Ted Masterman by letting him off easily. Beat him into the ground just to play it safe.

He waited long enough for tension to build. Masterman dropped the spoon, his jaw tightening.

"I've had a strange life, Ted," he began slowly, savoring every sweet drop of the triumph about to be his. One last toss of the dice. "I gave up a lot because I wanted to be a great novelist and managed only to become a successful storyteller. I've been in some odd places and seen some terrible things. There's only two reasons for me to bother to stay alive—my daughter Clare in a convent school in Rome and Mrs. Slattery. I'd stop at nothing to destroy anyone who threatened the happiness of either of them."

Tiny red spots glowed in each of Masterman's hollow cheeks. "Such love can get a man into a lot of trouble, Jim," he said, tightening his fist around a knife. "I think you can be confident that the U. S. government will do nothing to interfere with Evelina Slattery's happiness."

He forced the excitement out of his voice. Evenly, matter-of-factly, he said, "I sure hope not. Still, as long as the Donaghey thing hangs fire, she and her kids live under a cloud. It's the kids I worry about; she's a tough woman. They grew up in a different era. People can get at Lynnie through her kids. . . ." He let his voice fade.

The red spots grew larger. "There can be no question of dropping the Donaghey investigation." His voice was harsh and brittle. "He is a corrupt politician who belongs in jail. We have spent too much time on this case to let it all go down the drain."

The mask had slipped away. Good, now the final blow. "I can see your point, Ted. I don't know much about law though. I can't help thinking that if Slade Mannion lied about Mrs. Slattery, he may have lied about all the others. You certainly know about the dangers of using immunized witnesses. . . ." Again he let his voice fade off.

The sun's rays were now coming directly through the windows of The Attic, forcing his eyes to squint. Another trick of Masterman's . . . too late now. The man's face blurred.

"It's always a possibility, Jim. We've got to watch it in this kind of case. Frankly some of our immunized people get really kinky, spin out all kinds of tales." He was sweet reasonableness again. "I don't think Mr. Mannion is one of those."

"You may very well be right," he responded, picking up the leather case from the floor. "Well, I should be getting back to work. Once you get caught up in a story, it's an agony till you get it out on paper. Incidentally, I brought more of the manuscript along if you want to read it." He stood up from the table.

Masterman hesitated in the chair a little longer, his jaw tense, his eyes flashing hatred. "I'd like to, Jim," he said, his words coming hesitantly as he fought to keep his anger under control. "I've got a couple of hard weeks ahead of me. I'll wait till it turns up in print, paperback maybe." A feeble attempt at a grin.

You're coming apart, man. "Well, you never can tell. I've had it happen before that I get two hundred pages done and then run dry. Toss the thing in the waste-basket and start over with a brand new idea." The two of them were now walking toward the elevator, the last ones left in the dining room. "If I get distracted with a wedding, I might run out of steam on this one."

They rode silently down to the street. The last

exchange. He felt reasonably confident that Masterman would cave in, but still, he might foolishly call his bluff.

He shook O'Neill's hand as they parted on LaSalle Street. "Fascinating lunch, Jim, fascinating. We'll have to do it again after you get back from your honeymoon." The same weak leer.

"Great idea," responded O'Neill with equally phony enthusiasm.

"Give my best wishes for your marriage to Mrs. Slattery. I don't expect I'll be seeing her in court." He released Jim's hand and blended quickly into the flowing crowd on LaSalle Street, only the thin blond hair visible for a few extra moments above the mass of bustling people.

You get no extra points for acting like a good loser, O'Neill snarled to himself. Like a knight swaggering away from a joust he walked north on LaSalle Street. When he reached the Chicago River looking down at the dirty waters cracked his self-confidence. Pride in his success ebbed like life from a dying man. He found a liquor store on Rush Street and bought a bottle of twenty-two-year-old Chivas Regal. You may as well get drunk with high-quality booze. He thought briefly of his father and the cheap liquor he had to drink. Some things had changed.

Back in the Drake he ordered a bucket of ice and systematically drank himself into unconsciousness, savoring the waves of humiliation as he sank beneath them. You always forget during the battle what the aftermath is like, he thought sullenly to himself. Each time the letdown is worse.

Still fully clothed, he fell into a drunken sleep, waking intermittently to vague terror as ambulances made their noisy nightly trips to the Northwestern University hospital. In his confused dreams he was in the ambulance, his lifeblood pouring out on the drive, turning the black water of the lake a glittering red.

 17

He woke in surprise, jumped out of bed, and looked around, groping for where he was. The sun had been shining in his eyes. He was hot, sweaty; his head was a solid lump of pain; his stomach was twisted with sickness; his legs wobbled and trembled. He sat slowly back on the bed. Chicago, the Drake Hotel, clothes still on—he must have slept in them. A hangover, a massive hangover. The room smelled of whiskey. An empty bottle, ice bucket with water and melted ice.

He rose to stagger to the bathroom, glanced at his watch. Eleven o'clock. Was he supposed to be somewhere today? God in heaven, the indictment's today. He promised to meet Lynnie at Howard's office at eleven o'clock. He fumbled in his memory for the phone number, misdialed it, tried again. Mrs. Slattery and Mr. Howard were out to lunch.

He shaved, showered, dressed quickly, and on unsteady limbs navigated his way down to the lobby and into a taxi. He got out at Michigan and Washington, noticing for the first time that it was a hot day, the beginning of the terrible Chicago humid summer. He must leave soon. The walk down Washington might clear his head. What would he use for an excuse?

His head was still whirling; his ears were buzzing; he was unsteady on his feet; his arms were shivering despite the heat of the sun on his back. Twice he was close to vomiting. Would have were it not for the humiliation. How often had his father felt the same way?

He leaned against a store window, trying to settle his body, calm his nerves, catch his breath. The glare of the sun stabbed at his eyes. He did not want to have to face Lynnie this morning. Sick or well, he was no match for her. "*La femme paradigmatique,*" Monique DuLac had called her—God, how he wished he were back on the bank of the Seine with the Eiffel Tower instead of the Sears Tower regarding him with contemptuous indifference. Eiffel. Sears. That was an immensely important symbolic point.

Reluctantly he pushed himself away from the window. A jeweler's. Hell of a place to almost pass out. He glanced at the window and then impulsively went inside and made two purchases. The owner didn't seem at all hesitant about taking his check. He asked why.

"So a writer like you should cheat me?" said the old man. Fame even in Chicago. It made him feel better.

Although the air conditioning was working in Howard's office, he looked wilted, discouraged. Lynnie, on the other hand, was the picture of spring loveliness—a peach dress, sleeveless V-neck, belted to emphasize her figure; shoes, gloves, and hat to match; gold on her neck, new hair style, careful makeup, even jewelry on her fingers. The twenty-five-year-old socialite going to a garden party. His stomach turned in protest against such charm.

"Sorry I'm late," he murmured.

"Not to worry," replied Lynnie airily, smoothing an imaginary crease out of her dress. "We were just discussing the pleasures of sailing on Lake Michigan. Mr. Howard is an incorrigible navigator, would you believe. I think I'm going to have to take it up; it sounds like more fun than selling land." She laughed gleefully.

So Howard was discouraged, and probably so was his Mafiosa aide. Lynnie was ready to cheer them up.

"Sometime we will have to go sailing in the Mediterranean. I know a French lawyer. . . ."

Her eyes focused on him for the first time since he entered the office. "You look terrible, Jimmy. Are you sick?"

"Nothing that changing my drinking habits won't cure," he said bitterly. "Any news?"

Howard sighed. "Nothing yet. The grand jury was supposed to act this morning, but its session was postponed. It will probably hand down its indictments this afternoon. Miss Carsello is . . . uh . . . continuing her intelligence research and should have the details for us shortly. I will not hide from you, Mr. O'Neill," he plowed on, his voice turgid, "the seriousness of the matter. Another landowner, a certain Mrs. Jakobowski, has heavily implicated Mrs. Slattery in her grand jury testimony. Our preliminary information is that there will be nineteen counts, including conspiracy, perjury, and mail fraud. They may even include tax evasion, though I will confess I do not see how. The legal position is no worse than we thought it might be, and I still have confidence in Mrs. Slattery's skill as a witness and Mr. Lynch's as a defense attorney; candidly, I am disappointed. I had hoped to be able to spare Mrs. Slattery and her family the pain." The old man stopped speaking.

"You tried, Ed," she said gently. "No one could do any more."

O'Neill was dizzy. He *had* won yesterday, hadn't he? What was going on? "How recent is your information about the indictment?" he asked sharply.

"Yesterday," said Lynnie, her verve slipping.

"*When* yesterday?" he snapped.

"Nine-thirty in the morning, to be precise," said Howard. "I fail to see why it matters . . ."

O'Neill relaxed. So. The grand jury had not met this morning. Good sign. They would wonder why. Well, they would never hear about it from him.

The door swung open. Nancy Carsello in a dark blue pants suit walked in unsteadily and collapsed into her usual hard-backed chair. She was pale, shaken. "Mr. Howard," she muttered weakly, "I want a tumbler of your brandy."

"My dear Nancy," said the lawyer, "certainly; though I thought you didn't drink the stuff. I take it our worst fears are justified?"

A bottle of Napoleon Reserve emerged from the

bottom drawer of his desk, and with it four Waterford crystal snifters. O'Neill almost tore the bottle from the old man's hand. He was the one that needed the hair of the dog.

"It's all over," said Nancy, gulping a substantial portion of the brandy in her tumbler. "Finished."

Lynnie was on her feet, nervous now. O'Neill discreetly poured himself a very large shot and began to sip it blissfully.

"Surely that cannot be the case," fretted Ed Howard. "An indictment isn't a conviction."

"Oh God, I'm so sorry, Lynnie darling. I'm all mixed up. There is no indictment. Nothing. There won't be any indictment."

"Hooray," said O'Neill quietly, his nerves already relaxed under the prospect of the Napoleon's soothing effect.

"Are you sure?" exclaimed Lynnie in joyous disbelief, on the verge of becoming an adolescent hoyden, Cora at a picnic.

"I'm sure, all right." Nancy poured herself another glass. "It's the craziest thing I ever heard of. They've dropped the whole investigation. It was all ready to go yesterday morning, then late in the afternoon Ted Masterman called in his staff and told them that they had to abandon the whole investigation. Tore the hide off Ryan and Majorski for suborning perjury, said the witnesses were worthless—regular temper tantrum. All a big secret till this morning. No one knows what the hell happened. They think a payoff somewhere. Masterman is going to lose a lot of chips on this. I can't imagine . . ."

Howard was alert. "Sometime, then, between nine o'clock in the morning and five in the afternoon—come now, Mrs. Slattery, I am entirely too old to be hugged that way, grateful as I may say that I am for such a display of confidence from a client—as I was saying . . ."

"They think it was something that happened at lunch. He was enthusiastic about the case till he went to lunch—didn't tell them where or with whom—came back, locked himself up in his office, and then broke the news at the end of the day." Nancy considered a third glass and put the bottle aside. "Oh, Mrs. Slattery, I am so happy for you." The brandy made her teary.

"So if we knew where he went to lunch . . . ," Howard insisted.

"I know that. I had a hunch," Nancy broke in. "Sometimes when he wants to avoid his staff he goes up to The Attic in the Field Building. I have an uncle who is wine steward there."

O'Neill finished his brandy with a single swallow and wondered whether he could make it to the door in time.

"We progress. Excellent." Eddie Howard poured himself a very small portion of brandy. "Was your uncle able to describe—?"

"A tall, nice-looking man in a gray suit with wiry red hair and sad eyes." She stared straight at O'Neill.

"Oh my God," said Lynnie.

He had intended to keep it a secret and now would have to expiate his folly for weeks, but at least he could

251

enjoy the few moments of glory. That's what life was about, a few pleasurable moments now and then. Three sets of eyes were focused on him: frosty blue, smoldering brown, and dazzling violet.

"I'm sure, sir, you will want to explain," said Eddie Howard formally, sipping nervously from his brandy glass.

"I made a deal with my friend Ted," he said casually, as though he made "deals" every day.

"You'd better tell us all about it, Jimmy." Lynnie's face was a harsh mask.

Hey don't go getting mad at me, woman. "I agreed, implicitly, mind you, and with a lot of double talk, not to publish the novel . . . uh . . . story I was writing about him if he'd kill the whole investigation. Didn't have much choice, poor man."

"*All* about it, Jimmy," ordered Lynnie, but with a hint of a grin.

So he told them, using all the skill of his storyteller's art in the process. Beautiful women in the audience always brought out the best in a storyteller, he rationalized to himself as he heard the words tumble out.

The office was silent when he finished.

The old water-ski scar on Lynnie's forehead colored slightly. "My God," she said again.

"Wow," said the Carsello girl, "you're absolutely crazy."

"Mr. O'Neill, in all my years of practicing the law," another courtroom speech from Howard, "I will admit I have never heard of such cool and daring ruthlessness. I am impressed, sir, indeed awed. I must remark that you certainly should have told me, as Mrs. Slattery's lawyer, what you were about. I would strongly have urged you not to take such action. I would have been wrong—an admission which your young admirer from Taylor Street here will testify I seldom make. I can, sir, only congratulate you and hope that you are not associated in such an . . . ah . . . intimate way with any other case for which I am counsel."

Again silence. He felt his heart sinking. One more display for which he would have to feel guilty. Lynnie's eyes were glowing, her lips parted. Sexual hunger, he thought bitterly. "I think we'd better be going," he said sheepishly.

Howard shook hands formally, and wished him well.

"Hey, what about the book?" said Lynnie at the door, remembering the loose end. "You can't let him stop you from publishing it."

"I made a deal, lovely lady, and besides, I can use most of the material anyway."

"What if he runs for the Senate?" She was frowning, displeased that her freedom had been purchased at a cost. What the hell do you expect, woman? "He'll lose, I'll see to that," said O'Neill grimly. "The statute of limitations will run out next fall."

"I wouldn't want you on the other side," breathed Eddie Howard fervently.

"Mrs. Slattery is going to have lots of chances to do this and I won't get another." Nancy Carsello hugged him, kissed him recklessly, clung to him far longer than was decent or necessary. "I think you're wonderful, just wonderful," she said with one last hot embrace.

The pirate princess was more than an armful, but not a molecule of hormone entered his bloodstream.

She let him go. "I hope you don't mind, Mrs. Slattery." She was now scared by her own recklessness.

"Be my guest," Lynnie laughed. "I know how you feel."

Washington Boulevard was insufferably humid. Lynnie was carrying her shoulder bag, the one she called her "assignation bag." She had come with love on her mind.

"Lynnie," he mumbled as they stood in the river of people crossing to the rust-colored Civic Center, "I . . . I got rid of the tension last night by disposing of a fifth of expensive whiskey. I have to sleep it off. I'm sorry, I really am. Why don't you celebrate with the kids? I'll talk to you tomorrow. We'll feast over the body of the dragon." He tried to sound wan but cheerful.

"Whatever you want, Jim," she hesitated, wet her lip as she searched for words, and extended her hand in a tentative, meek plea. "How can I ever thank you? How about that for a cliché?" The magic, mischievous grin forced its way back on her face.

He had such a terrible headache. The peach dress hurt his eyes; he must get back to bed. "Well, one way you can repay me is to wear this occasionally." He clumsily searched in his pockets and found the larger of his two purchases, took it out, and wrapped it around her wrist. "And remember the dragon we dispatched together."

With water-filled eyes and radiant face, she held up her arm and admired the diamond-studded bracelet. "Oh, Jimmy, it's too good for me. You shouldn't have."

His headache was worse. "All right, I'll take it back." He reached for the wrist.

"You'll do no such thing," she said hotly, pulling her hand away.

"If you say it's too good again, I'll spank you, even if we are on Washington Boulevard."

"That's an interesting prospect, but this is nicer." Now an embrace which made the passionate young woman from Taylor Street seem like a neophyte. "I won't have that greasy-skinned Italian woman trying to steal my man."

He knew he was asleep. He could even hear the ambulance sirens on the drive. How, then, was he back on the shore of the lake?

"Ah, poor Seamus," said the dark brown woman dressed in white who so often came to him in his dreams and always by the lake of his childhood. " 'Tis a hard time you've been having."

"At least she didn't drown," he defended himself. Sometime he would have to ask her why she affected a brogue. He knew who she was, didn't believe in her, and knew that she wasn't Irish.

"Poor dear man." Her smile was a mixture of Lynnie's and Clare's. "You misunderstand our symbolism altogether." She touched his forehead in benediction and then drifted away in the blue sky.

The next morning he did not remember his dream.

However, he never remembered his dreams about her.

He is a creep. She'd be better off if he bought his damn Air France ticket and went home. He had routed the U.S. Attorney, saved her and the family from disaster, given her a bracelet worth several thousand dollars; regardless, he is a creep.

"Marty, would you turn the TV down, please?" she asked her silent son. Did the kids know that James was weird? They didn't say. The impromptu celebration had pooped out when Cora asked, "But if James beat Mr. Masterman, why didn't he come to the party?" Her explanation fell flat. James was exhausted after the nervous tension of the fight. She couldn't say he had a gigantic hangover. It didn't make any difference; both the explanations were weird—exhaustion, hangover, whatever. You come to a party after you've saved the princess. Hell, it was his idea that she was a princess.

Only creeps sneak back into lonely hotel rooms and feel sorry because they've killed the dragon and won the princess, and only real creeps get more fun from killing the dragon than from winning the princess. He wanted to save her, all right. But he didn't want her saved. Bracelet or not.

She looked at the bracelet. Too much money. Consolation prize for the old woman. Thanks, dear, for being a princess for a while so I could get some kicks. Now I must go back to my French women. See you some other lifetime. Well, good riddance.

" 'Night Mom." Marty kissed her on the forehead. "Nice bracelet."

" 'Night, honey. Yeah, not bad for the old woman, huh?"

Marty hesitated, struggled for the right phrase, and then ended up with an abstraction. "James is a remarkable person, isn't he?"

"You can say that again, hon," she said guardedly.

He shoved his hands into his white denim slacks. "I mean, the courage and self-confidence to pull something like that off. Was he always like that? I can't imagine that I'd ever—"

She cut him off with a motherly reassuring laugh. "Kid, you are a couple of centuries ahead of where James was at your age. He had a lot of growing up to do, just like all of us. Anyhow, don't go comparing yourself with your mother's boyfriend. The son of a bitch partly just lucked out."

Marty grinned. "I *like* the son of a bitch, Mom. How can you compete with a guy as great as he is?"

"Oh, go to bed, darling." She waved him away. "Someday I'll tell you all the whole story of James. Cut him down to size."

That night as she was falling asleep she knew exactly what she should do, and she shivered with delight at the prospect.

The next morning, however, feeling every day of her four decades, she could not recall the delight. Old hag, she told her weary face in the mirror. She stumbled to the kitchen for breakfast and poured herself a cup of coffee which the kids had kept warm for her on the Mr. Coffee machine. Good kids. Lovely spring day. Must go to the lake sometime soon, not wait till July

4. What was it I thought of last night? It sure made me feel good.

 18

He carefully slipped the Air France ticket envelope into his inside jacket pocket. No reason to feel guilty. He was behind in his work. Two months in Chicago had disrupted his schedule. He had to honor his commitments.

A terrible city, he thought, as he emerged from the soothing Air France office into the late June humidity of Michigan Avenue. The ninety-degree heat had hung on for more than a week, the skies were somber and hazy, people's tempers were already drawn tight, and the summer had yet to begin. The waters of the Mediterranean would be cool, not numbing cold like the great silent lake which stirred listlessly beyond the park. He touched the ticket envelope in his inside jacket pocket. It was still there. Air France 030.

It was the beginning of the rush hour. Despite the heat, he would have to walk up Michigan Avenue to the Drake. A stop-and-go half-hour in a cab would mean trouble for his restless stomach. God, he would be happy to go home to Paris. The dismal confrontation awaiting him in the Drake was all that stood in his way. It would be grievously painful; her voice told him that she thought his phone call was an invitation to begin again their long-dormant sex life.

The magic of the city battled with him. His throat still tightened at the transformation of Michigan Avenue: tall, slender skyscrapers creating an elegant canyon through which flowed a stream of smartly dressed, if now wilted, people. The third Chicago School, they called it, its new buildings dwarfing the gleaming white Wrigley Building and the gothic Tribune Tower which had been the wonders of his youth. The river, lake, park, Michigan Avenue, the Venice-like wonderland of the brightly painted ethnic neighborhoods—he had been astonished, moved, almost reduced to tears. Chicago disarmed him. Yet he was leaving the day after tomorrow, counting the hours till he could escape from this magic city. Hog butcher of the world, player with railroads, it had been in 1950; now—A metaphor escaped him. Whatever it was, he had to leave it.

The city and Lynnie. Lynnie and the city. Elegant, outrageous, crude, energetic, unbearable, astonishing, brilliant, shallow, captivating, and finally, imprisoning. Two decades ago he did not know why he ran away; now he did. He had to be free; he could not go on being Lynnie's pet poodle, the great novelist as captured animal, paraded at the weddings and graduations which seemed to occupy every day as the horrors of the summer heat began.

He crossed the river and entered the narrowest part of the canyon. The old stone Water Tower six blocks away signaled the end, as it cowered in the shadow of the lordly Hancock Center.

She was an operator, a female wheeler-dealer, a precinct captain in style if not in substance, shaking hands, hugging, smiling, laughing. Her business required such political charm, of course, but she loved it. She was her father, only better at the game and more honest.

Some of the faces at the weddings and graduations—and the three wakes—were haggard memories out of the past, folks from the old neighborhood who were dutifully impressed by the great novelist returned to the campfire. Others were strangers, also impressed by Lynnie's catch, many of them eager to talk about his books. He retreated behind a polite, vague smile.

He stopped short, just escaping a car wheeling off Michigan onto Ohio Street. He was damp already with perspiration. He took off his jacket and folded it over his arm. He didn't like her kids either. They took up a lot of room, made a lot of noise, intruded on his life, and were too much like their mother. They took him for granted; he was already part of the environment—"James"—a bit of scenery to be tended when needed and moved around when he got in the way, a stepfather-in-waiting.

Chicago as Camelot, Lynnie as Guinevere. He looked up at the massive slab of the Hancock Center, unbelievably tall and yet so carefully proportioned as to be totally unoppressive. Nice towers in this Camelot.

He passed a Good Humor truck, remembered the times as a child when there was no money for ice cream because his father was on a binge, and paused to buy one. Thirty cents. Sixfold rate of inflation.

The lobby of the Drake, fading but dignified, was blessedly cool. It recalled a quick, sharp image of the old basement church and his confessions to the young priest on Saturday afternoon. The Drake still had the most expensive-looking elevators in the world. He got out and walked unsteadily down the corridor.

Lynnie was lying on his bed wearing a pale beige robe, her dress tossed casually on a chair, trim, pantyhosed legs inviting his eyes. His hand was wet on the doorknob; his heart beat rapidly. He had to tell her.

"I'm sorry I'm late," he mumbled apologetically.

"Shouldn't keep an old widow woman with rampaging passions waiting, James," she grinned.

He sat heavily in the chair at the end of the bed. The grin faded from her face. She swung her smooth legs off the bed and sat up anxiously, covering them with the robe. "Trouble, huh, Jimmy?" She clasped the top of the robe together at her neck.

He swallowed. "I'm going back to Paris, Lynnie," he said weakly. He passed her the Air France ticket as though it were a talisman which permitted him to leave.

She nodded. "I guess I knew it was coming—kind of, anyhow." Her voice was even, calm. She glanced at the Air France envelope and gave it back to him. A deep breath. "I still don't quite measure up, huh?" she said, her voice uncertain.

"No, that's not it at all." He tried to placate her to turn away the storm.

"Yes, it is; it's all my fault." She tightened the belt on

her robe and knotted her fists, trying to control her temper. "I knew I shouldn't have jumped into bed with you that day at the lake, but I was desperately lonely and your eyes were so damn hurt and sad. I tried to tell my conscience it was all right." Her knuckles were white. "I should have made you talk about it before. I knew something was eating at you, but big dumb Lynnie laughs it all off and hopes it goes away." Her lovely breasts were moving up and down rapidly; don't look at them. Her voice was rising as her emotions swirled around like a tornado trying to make up its mind which way to move. "I pushed too hard the last time. Now like a damn fool I don't push hard enough. Stupid, stupid."

"You haven't failed, Lynn." His voice was turning shrill. "Chicago just isn't a place where I can work. Your lifestyle," ugh, what a stupid word, "well, it's not the environment a writer needs."

She hugged her arms protectively in front of her breasts; her face was drained of color. "I could change my lifestyle."

"That's not the point, Lynn," he said irritably.

"Then what is the point?" Color back in her face, a dangerous gleam in her eye. She stood up from the bed, walked to the window and opened the drapes, revealing the glowing blue water of Lake Michigan and the swirling rush-hour traffic. "Hell, I knew something was wrong. I guess I should have asked. You don't give me many hints, though—just hide behind your solemn, pained smile. See the great writer; see how much he suffers," she trailed bitterly.

He had to strike hard to defend himself. "I couldn't stand it, Lynn," he screamed at her, leaping out of the chair. "I couldn't stand being married to a vulgar, crude woman like you. It would destroy me!" He was breathing heavily. He wanted to be cruel. She deserved it.

Hands on her hips, ice-calm now. "You know, you miserable son of bitch, if I believed that you meant that, I wouldn't much mind. It would just show that you were dumb. I don't think you're dumb. You love me and you're too goddamn much of a coward to take a chance on me. Mama's little boy is still afraid that Mama is going to come back and take away his balls again."

He hit her, rocking her head with a solid blow to the jaw. She staggered in surprise. He hit her again, knocking her to the bed. She sprawled across it, a nylon leg dangling off the edge, the belt slipping loose on her robe.

His heart pounded in exultation as though he were on an amphetamine high. He almost hit her a third time. His hands and feet turned cold; his stomach tightened; the high collapsed like a wounded animal. Shame swirled through him like angry flood waters. He reached out tentatively to touch her.

"Don't come near me," her voice was like dry ice, her eyes stone hard. No rage, no tears, just the back of her fingers against the ugly red mark on her face.

He leaned against the window frame, hearing the rumble of rush-hour traffic behind him. He rubbed the knuckles of his hand absently. Why couldn't he talk?

The dry-ice voice again. "You enjoyed it, didn't you?

Made you feel like a man? Pathetic bastard." Still no rage. She watched him for a moment more, as though he were a dying beast more to be pitied than feared. Then she rose from the bed, tossed aside the robe, turned her back to him, and began to dress. Her naked shoulderblades, drained away the last traces of anger. He wanted to touch her with gentle affection. Would a caress earn him forgiveness? He hesitated.

Hooks quickly in place, lime green dress sliding over white shoulders, zipper abruptly tugged, robe crushed into her bag; a sleek matron in a light summer dress ready to exit onto Michigan Avenue, a red mark on her face—too much sun, perhaps.

She spun on her heel just before slamming the door, her eyes no longer blazing but as cold, as despair-filled as he had ever seen them. A single venomous word: "Coward!"

Many hours later, the moon glowing dully on the lake, he still leaned against the window frame, numb with shock, unable even to name the questions he wanted to ask. He saw his haggard face in dim light reflected in the mirror. A stranger, a man he did not know.

EPILOGUE

He went through the next two days in a trance, auto-matically eating, sleeping, checking out of the hotel, taking a cab to O'Hare. Abstractly he knew the heat wave continued; but he felt cold, as though a winter chill had penetrated his bones. Mechanically he paid the cab driver, waved aside the redcap, and lugged his two bags toward the Air France counter. The air conditioning in the windowless international terminal was not working. He checked for his passport, glancing at the picture—a couple of years old. Or a couple of centuries.

How long had he been in Chicago? He took out his pocket calendar. The meeting in Los Angeles had been on Good Friday, he remembered with irony, Easter Tuesday when he got off the plane at O'Hare. His calendar said that this was Pentecost Sunday. One day less than fifty. Good Friday, Easter, Pentecost— once these names had meant something to him; probably all that was different now. Who was the Holy Ghost these days? Clare called him the Holy Spirit; he kind of liked the ghost idea. He would have to ask Lynnie what they believed about the Ghost these days. He wouldn't be seeing Lynnie. . . .

The international terminal at O'Hare was tacky, a barely disguised "temporary" building from the past smelling of kerosene and unchanged diapers, echoing with the sounds of wailing children and broken English. He was glad he would be flying first class. Maybe he could sleep on the way over. It would be good to be with the DuLacs again. Would they see the horror frozen in his eyes?

There was someone beside him, a woman in jeans, floppy white blouse tied at the waist with some kind of

265

rope belt, and huge sunglasses. She was cutting ahead of others in line.

"*Bonjour,*" she said brightly.

"You can't go to Paris, Lynnie."

"Sure can. I've got a ticket that's just as good as yours." She waved the ticket at him defiantly. "Always wanted to see if the city was as sinful as they say it is."

The sunglasses hid her eyes. Had he given her a black eye too? He took the ticket. "How did you know I was going today?"

"You showed me your ticket." The ice was gone from her voice, replaced by affection. Now she was starting to grin at him. That was no way to react. He had hit her—twice. It was not a laughing matter.

"I'll upgrade your ticket to first class," he said wearily.

"You're just doing that so you can paw me on the way over," she sniffed.

He hadn't thought about that. There was a distant stirring in the back of his brain. "The women I push around always fly first class."

"Will you listen to him?" She took off the sunglasses—no black eye. "He loses his temper once in his life and he thinks he's a jet-set caveman." Her voice was unsteady, her eyes anxious.

A curious kind of absolution. Without confession or contrition. There was only an old couple between them and the clerk at the check-in desk. "Lynnie, you can't go to Paris." A sudden thought, blessed relief. "You need a passport."

Her azure eyes shining now, she produced with a

dramatic flourish the required green booklet from her copious shoulder bag. He thumbed through it like a dull immigration bureaucrat of some Third World country. "Ready for anything," he muttered, still unable to comprehend what she was doing in the Air France check-in line. He gave the passport back.

She shrugged her wonderful shoulders. "Keep one step ahead of them, I always say."

The movement of her body sent a pang of lust through him, intense, sweet, paralyzing. "Luggage?" He was still trying to organize the trip to Paris. "Have you checked it yet?"

She patted the shoulder bag. "The toothbrush is here. I left in kind of a hurry," she tittered. "The kids threw me out of the house."

So she had hesitated. Ticket, passport, and all, it was a last-minute decision. Why did that restore some of his confidence? "What are you going to do for clothes?" He edged his bags closer to the ticket counter. The short-haired girl was having a hard time with the old couple even in her fluent provincial French.

Again the movement of her delicious shoulders. "I hear they sell things in Paris. I've got my American Express card." Her voice trailed off, the violet eyes became uncertain, the crow's feet around them deepening.

She was losing her nerve. Impulsively he put his arms around her waist. No resistance.

Would the clerk never finish with those people? "How long will I be disgraced?"

"Until you buy me a drink. Maybe even two drinks. I'm so afraid of these damn things I'll need all the affection I can get." She studiously examined her passport, avoiding his eyes.

"You're afraid of flying? Then why are you going to Paris?"

The heat was terrible. He took off his coat and carefully draped it over his arm. His head was clouding again, too foggy for thought to land.

"Figured it was time to find out what the French broads have that I don't." She waved a flippant hand, but her smile did not make its usual pilgrimage from pathos to mischief. The muscle in her neck was twitching violently. Poor woman is frightened half to death.

He felt the same gentle affection that slipped through his fingers in the hotel room. Then lust came crashing against him like a huge wave shattering a beach. He pictured her spread-eagled and cherished on his Empire couch in Paris. He wanted her as badly as the night in her office. He clenched his fists to keep his hands under control. I'll do it slowly, teasing her with love. The night in the office I didn't make her wait nearly long enough. He forced the obscene pictures out of his imagination.

The Air France clerk shook him out of his fantasy. "Next?"

"Madame will be flying first class," he said, passing Lynnie's ticket across the counter.

The girl's bright eyes sparkled. She took the two of them in with a swift glance, then looked again at

268

Lynnie. "Monsieur is to be congratulated on his excellent taste," she said smoothly, reaching for a blank ticket coupon.

"That's what I've been telling him for a long time." Lynnie grinned conspiratorially at the girl, who smiled broadly as she accepted O'Neill's credit card. Despite Lynnie's good looks, other women never seemed to resent her. The girl raised her eyebrows appreciatively when Lynnie said she had no luggage to check. He studied the number on his passport.

The girl gave Lynnie her boarding pass. "I am sure Madame will enjoy France," she said.

"Let us hope Monsieur will too," Lynnie countered. The two women laughed over their wicked little secret. He did not look at the girl. The emerald was still in his pocket. They turned away from the counter. He took her hand; it was passive, unprotesting. *I don't know what the hell I'm doing. . . .*

"Every little bit of progress helps," sighed Lynnie. "Tell me, am I as sexy as Monique? Will you think of her when you're tormenting me in Paris?" She was beginning to babble. He tightened his grip on her hand.

"No, she's not. I mean, yes, she's sexy but in a different way. And for the thousandth time," his exasperation and impatience rising, "I don't sleep with her. She's just a friend. Please, don't embarrass me."

"See, darling," she cut in, "you can get angry at me if you try. After a while it even gets easy."

So pathetically eager to forgive me. Her eyes are turning sad now because I'm not saying anything. She's discouraged, almost beaten. Now's the time to send her home.

They were at the counter of the Hole-In-The-Wall bar, which was the best the city of Chicago could do for its international travelers. There was a flight departure announcement. He felt a moment of panic; no, it was Lufthansa.

Lynnie released his hand to brush the hair away from her eyes as he ordered two gin-and-tonics. He quickly recaptured her hand.

His own drink at his lips, time stood still. He could see the years of their life together stretching out ahead of them—two badly mismatched people caught in a love they could neither end nor enjoy—missed signals, misunderstood cues, mounting frustration, conflict, hurt, pain, sorrow, a touch of tenderness, then the same cycle of torment beginning again. Growing old in anger, vicious words, discontent, hatred, the moments of tenderness more infrequent—two hardened old warriors counting up the points in their endless battle, lovingly saving the injuries and pains so that the next twist of vengeance would be more pleasurable. Again he pictured her naked on the Empire couch. He dismissed the image. Now was the time. He would tell her she could not come with him.

The bartender put the second drink in front of her. O'Neill picked it up, took her hand, and closed it around the glass. "Drink up, woman; I can't paw you over the Atlantic if you're sober enough to be scared of that big aluminum monster." His eyes smarted.

Lynnie turned toward her drink, wanting privacy with her own emotions. "I better call my kids," she

270

said huskily, "and tell them you're letting me come."

"I had a choice?" he asked, but she had fled to the phone booth outside the bar. He sipped his drink slowly. He enjoyed his own sense of irrevocable destiny for a moment and then thought of Paris. He pushed the gin away. It would mean the end of gin and Scotch in his life, and a lot less wine and brandy too. Doubtless he would be forced to take up running. He sighed.

She came back from the phone booth red-eyed, slightly uncertain in her walk, dampness spreading over the blouse from under her arms. A gin and a half on an empty stomach, probably no food for two days while she struggled to make up her mind. Prayed all the way out in the cab—he resented being the object of her prayers. Then he thought of all the pleasurable, tender things he was going to do to her and decided that the prayers were all right.

"What did the offspring say?" he asked casually.

She leaned against the bar and began to work somewhat more cautiously on the remains of her drink. "I won't tell you; you already think they're amoral," she giggled.

"Sorry for asking." He tried to sound hurt. On the plane he would apologize for hitting her. Contrition and firm purpose of amendment after absolution instead of before.

A bored male voice with the inevitable French accent announced the departure of Flight 030.

His magic princess turned pale as a sheet of typing paper and threw her arms around him, hugging the breath from his body. "You miserable bastard, if you don't hold me tight while I stagger to that awful airplane thing, I'll get right back into the cab and spend the rest of my chaste widowhood in prayer and good works."

He kept his arm firmly around her as they walked down the long corridor to the Air France boarding lounge. He looked down at her face; a touch of February despair was frosting over her eyes. As he tightened his embrace, it changed from protection to the faint beginnings of seduction. She grinned weakly. Much better than hitting her.

The sun shining mercilessly through the big windows made him squint. He could see where he was going, every inch of the way. He imagined the mistakes and the pain of the years ahead lurking on either side of the corridor, demons laughing outside the windows. That was a good line. He'd have to use it in a story. She'd want to be in it. Comic heroine, she'd said long ago. Well, no comic heroines in this story. Comic hero? Maybe.

Center Point Publishing
600 Brooks Road • PO Box 1
Thorndike ME 04986-0001 USA

(207) 568-3717

US & Canada:
1 800 929-9108